Praise for Stefan Themerson

"This man Stefan Themerson should be better known than I suspect he is. *The Mystery of the Sardine* . . . is a fascinating piece of work, written with the elegance of haute couture."

—*Times* (London)

"Stefan Themerson has an absolutely elegant sense of humor."

—*New York Times*

"Themerson's neo-surrealist style enables him felicitously to interweave incongruities, ludic exercises, shrewd observations, jokes, lightly worn learning, cris de couer and parables."

—*Times Literary Supplement*

"What an extraordinary writer Stefan Themerson is. While other novelists seem hell-bent on creating great, enormous doorstops of books with very little in them, Mr. Themerson produces *The Mystery of the Sardine*, a slim and modest volume which is absolutely jam-packed with ideas."

—*Punch*

Other Works by Stefan Themerson

Stefan Themerson

M^{The}ystery of the Sardine

Dalkey Archive Press

NORMAL · LONDON

First published in the U.K. by Faber and Faber, 1986
First American edition published by Farrar, Straus and Giroux, 1986

First Dalkey Archive edition, 2006

Library of Congress Cataloging-in-Publication Data:

Themerson, Stefan.
    The mystery of the sardine / Stefan Themerson — 1st Dalkey Archive ed.
        p. cm.
    ISBN-13: 978-1-56478-455-1 (acid-free paper)
    ISBN-10: 1-56478-455-X (acid-free paper)
    I. Title.
    PT6039.H37M92 2006
    823' .914—dc22

                                                          2006017024

Partially funded by a grant from the Illinois Arts Council, a state agency.

Dalkey Archive Press is a nonprofit organization whose mission is
to promote international cultural understanding and provide a
forum for dialogue for the literary arts.

www.dalkeyarchive.com

Printed on permanent/durable acid-free paper, bound in the
United States of America, and distributed throughout North America and Europe.

Contents

Principal Characters

Bernard St Austell
Anne, *his wife*
John *and* Piffin, *their children*
Marjorie, *Bernard's secretary*
Tim Chesterton-Brown
Veronica, *his wife*
Emma, *their daughter*
Miss Prentice, *a palmist*
Revd Paul Prentice, *her brother*
Ian, *her son*
General Pięść, *Ian's father* (*More about him in* 'General Pięść *or the case of the forgotten mission' by the same author*)
Dame Victoria, *mother of Anne St Austell*
Sir Lionel Cooper, *her half-brother*
Lady Cooper, *his wife*
Perceval W. Cooper
Joseph Kszak, *'Minister of Imponderabilia'*
Captain Casanova-Bridgewater
Mr McPherson
Sally, *his girlfriend*
Dr Goldfinger, *friend of* Princess Zuppa, *the friend of* Cardinal Pölätüo (*of whom more in* 'Cardinal Pölätüo' *by the same author*)
Also: Mrs Pięść; Dr Brzeski; Bill, *the newspaper boy;* Mr Newman *and his 'niece';* an ambassador; his butler; policemen; detectives; Mother Superior; Judge; Mrs Massgrave; Don José María López; a Spanish priest; a French lady; a German *Ärztin*; Mr Adamczyk, *a chauffeur;* Mr Mirek, *a helicopter pilot;* a Mr Krupa, *an American in Paris; and the* Mad Hatter.

Axioms are mortal,
politics is mortal,
poetry is mortal, –
good manners are immortal

PART ONE

ONE

The Colour of his Eyes

He knew that his hatred had its own existence, that it was all the time in him, in his anatomy, he knew this as one knows that one's gall bladder is there permanently, and not only when one has a bilious attack and feels its bitterness creeping up to the taste buds in one's tongue. He neither liked nor disliked his hatred. He cultivated it. He cultivated it because it so happened that precisely those pages which he wrote when the hatred was at its highest proved the greatest success, bringing him both critical praise and money. He lived in an old but modernized country house in a little village not very far from the city, but had a flatlet in London where he used to do most of his writing. His wife took it for granted that it was the great air of the metropolis that he needed for his creative work (as she called it) but he knew that it was his hatred. Because it was when in London that he felt his hatred properly. It was there that he felt free to hate. Everything. And though his hatred didn't show directly in his writings, it was this very hatred that gave him both the stimulus and energy to work.

And yet, as soon as he got out of the train and put his foot on the platform of the tiny railway station, a mile or two from the village, his hatred like a watch-dog retreating backwards to its kennel would lie down and be replaced by a feeling of friendliness to everything and everybody. As a rule, his wife would be waiting for him in their estate car and take him home. There would be flowers on the dinner table, except in winter; there would be their two children, when not at school; there would be no business telephones, except perhaps occasionally an urgent call from the publishers' lawyer, saying: 'Look here, it's serious, either you cut out the word "swindle" or you disguise the names, both Christian names and surnames.' And he would perhaps answer: 'All right, I'll change "swindle" to "transaction,"' and he would put the receiver down and forget about it, and he would go for a stroll in the village where he knew everybody and would be greeted by friendly people who had never read a word of what he wrote. On Sunday morning he would go to church and after the service have a chat with the vicar and his wife. In the evening – bridge with the local squire. On Monday he would pop into the local pub to exchange some democratic smiles over a pint of tepid ale.

Occasionally, he would go to a little circular bower in the middle of his garden, a little hut which he called Sibylla (more on account of its round shape than because of the oracles). There, there was one rustic table, one basket chair, and a small wickerwork bookshelf. In summertime the light reflected from the surrounding foliage was soft and green. Through a small round skylight he would look at the tree tops, and then would – perhaps – write a poem. First, however, he would take from the shelf his Virgil, open it at hazard and read the first passage his eye lit on. Sometimes it would be *Georgics*:

> *O fortunatos nimium, sua si bona norint,*
> *Agricolas! Quibus ipsa procul discordibus armis*
> *Fundit humo facilem victum iustissima tellus, –*

some other times, perhaps, the *Eclogues*:

> *Omnia vincit Amor, et nos cedamus Amori.*

He would scan the lines aloud, not in order to imitate – not in order to *at*tune his mind to that Latin perfection, but simply to tune it, as one tunes a musical instrument before playing. Curiously, just as his feeling of hatred didn't show directly in his 'proper' professional writings, so his lyrical bucolic emotions kept well out of sight in his poems, which – one could say, if one had to – possessed a wryness closer to Juvenal than to Virgil.

His poems he would not publish. Not today, anyway. Some years ago, when he was still 'a man from the Ministry', and his weekends in the country were very short, he did publish a few in some literary magazines, and a slim volume, which however had passed disappointingly unnoticed. Nowadays, he kept his verses hidden in the drawer; publishing them today would

4

spoil his public image, the image of a successful professional writer.

It lasted for many years, this division of the week, three days and four nights in town, throbbing with hard work fuelled by hate, and then four days and three nights in the village, where he would not allow any of those friendly people ever to think of him as anything other than a nice, prematurely retired, sort of higher-ranking official. But then, one day, after all those years, something irrational happened. Irrational, because the cause was so absurdly out of proportion to the effect. And yet, though unexpected, it could have been anticipated. When children grow up, their personalities begin to take their own shape and like a Trojan Horse insinuate themselves gradually, subtly, into the family's kingdom.

They were sitting in the drawing room, just the two of them. There was an electric guitar on top of an old pianola, there was a small Ben Nicholson among a number of nineteenth-century engravings, there were cut flowers everywhere, and hollyhocks behind the bay window.

'I want to ask you something, Dad. May I?'

'Of course you may,' he said, and wondered what it could be, something about cricket? or something about sex? Good Lord, the boy is sixteen, he must be having some sex life by now, mustn't he? or something about politics? is he interested in politics? How little one knows about one's child!

'Well, Dad, it's rather difficult to say, because I disagree with you . . .'

'We are all entitled to our own opinions,' he answered, without having any premonitions.

'Well, Dad, I read what you have written about . . .'

This was quite unexpected and definitely against the rules established in the household, nay in the whole village.

'No, son, I do *not* wish to discuss my work,' he said in a tone of voice the boy had never heard from him. 'This has nothing to do with you, son,' he added. 'I do not wish to discuss my work with anybody.'

'But why . . . ?'

'I do not wish to discuss my reasons either,' he said. And got up. And left the room. But what he saw in his son's eyes went with him. And it burnt a pin-hole through which the imprisoned

5

hate began to ooze out slowly. In all those years he had never felt it when in the country, in the village, in his own home. And that it had to start with his own son as its object – was astounding. And he didn't curb it. Either because he wouldn't know how, or because he didn't want to. And so, slowly, gradually, week after week, it grew darker and spread on the house, on the garden, on the whole village. When he would shut himself now in his Sibylline temple, he felt more as if he were in a bunker than in a summer-house. The foliage around him was green no longer, and the birds' songs screeched.

*

London, on the contrary, seemed to have become somewhat brighter, sweeter, friendlier. The very first Tuesday, on his way from the railway station, he stopped his taxi by Fortnum & Mason and bought a two-pound box of chocolates. Nothing of the sort had ever happened before.

His secretary did not live in his flatlet, but she used to spend most of her time there. She was in her early thirties, well dressed, handsome in a sort of healthy way, her face was intelligent, and her eyes showed that she knew more than she was prepared to say. And she was completely, unquestioningly devoted to him and to his work. She was not only his secretary, answering telephones and writing letters, she was also his typist and researcher. He would scribble a few guiding thoughts on bits of paper, and then, walking around the room, dictate straight to her typewriter. Such things like checking up some dates, the spelling of names, occasional quotations and their sources – he would leave to her. His dictation was not at all fluent. He would repeat himself and then ask her to cross out, he would go back pages and alter a word, he would stop in the middle of a sentence, reflecting, meditating, for an interminable time, while the tips of her fingers were suspended above the keyboard. Occasionally, he would stop behind her chair, grab her shoulders, and silently lead her, or drag her, to the bedroom. A few minutes later, she would be back at her typewriter, and he – finishing the sentence. Her body would be covered with bruises, scratches, and bites. If somebody asked her whether she derived pleasure from her own pain, she would probably

6

deny it. If somebody asked her whether *he* delighted in cruelty, she would certainly say: no. She had no doubt that she understood him. The hate that fuelled his writing had to erupt. But she knew it was not directed against her. She knew she was neither here nor there. She was of no relevance. And the things he hated were not personal though they were human. Perhaps his past had something to do with it. He had had the experience of being a small-farmer's grandson and of having been to a public school, of the high-level intricacies of the Establishment and of the lower ranks in the army. The depersonalized people whom he hated so much when, searching for words, he walked around the room of his London flatlet were politicians and civil servants, financiers and trade-unionists, Marxists and capitalists, left-wingers and right-wingers, clever foreigners and stupid natives, believers and unbelievers, and – above all – writers and readers. That was, anyway, how she saw it, and she was healthy and strong enough to take his violent temper, passions, blows, bites, and abuse as an integral part of the reality of things. In their professional capacities they were using words so much that speech had become somewhat deflated for ordinary purposes, and thus they never talked about their love-making, and this reticence suited her perfectly, she liked it to be like that.

And that was why, when he brought her the box of chocolates on that memorable Tuesday, she accepted it with rather mixed feelings. The unexpected gift disturbed the long-established pattern. It filled her with apprehension that something unnecessary was going to happen. The next Tuesday, he brought her a bottle of perfume, and when a week later he appeared with flowers, she had no doubt he was falling in love with her. Which was regrettable. Because she didn't want him to be in love with her. To be loved would put a burden on her which she didn't want to carry. She shared his work and his London bed and that was that. Any new ingredient, any deviation from the routine, would spoil the very nature of her devotion. She didn't know, and didn't ask, what was the cause of the sudden change, but she felt ill at ease. Especially as it seemed to be affecting his work. His dictation had lost its staccato harshness, his voice softened, his aggressive syntax mellowed, and – worst of all – he stopped noticing that he repeated himself. The metamorphosis, if one may call it so, developed slowly, gradually, but it began –

7

definitely – on the Tuesday he came to town and bought the box of chocolates. She didn't know that from the preceding Friday to Monday, in the country, it had grown in the opposite direction.

The village ceased to be the green harbour, free from enmity and torment. 'I would rather be good than great,' his son said one day, when the vicar asked him what he wanted to be. The vicar's wife nodded approvingly, though her little shiny snub nose twinkled at the prudishness of the avowal. But he recognized in his son's eyes the same look of defiance, and he knew that the dart was aimed at him. His Aristotelian logic was absolute. Therefore, if one disagreed with him, one was either a fool or one disagreed with his premises. If the former, he would not suffer fools. If the latter, one was worse than Enemy, one was Spiritual Foreigner. His son was not a fool. And to have a spiritual foreigner in the bosom of one's family was unbearable. He felt that he could murder him. And he hated the boy still more for having forced this feeling on him. The jaundiced taste of gall made him now cast aspersions on everybody and every-thing. The vicar was a hypocrite; the scoutmaster – homosexual; the schoolteacher – a whore; the MP – a thief; the people in the pub – vulgar; their laughter – idiotic; and the imaginary rainbow above the overclouded village was just glorifying its greyness. And so he would turn away, go into his Sibylline temple and, having soothed his anger by having recourse to the *Sortes Virgilianae*, would attempt a poem, and then polish it again and again without end. This state of things lasted for nearly two years. It was strange that as his peculiar blend of hatred and contempt, disdain and derision moved house from London to the village, his London professional writing declined (the common opinion was that his star was waning), while his poetry consolidated and grew in stature. By the end of the second year, he contributed to the cost of publishing a volume of his selected verse, and was immediately acclaimed as a major poet of the second half of the twentieth century. *Habent sua fata libelli*! Some people didn't realize that the new poet and the old, famous, but now somewhat less popular, author were one and the same person. Especially as he now used two initials in front of his surname, instead of the full Christian name as before.

That's how things stood when one spring Saturday (he was going to the country on Saturdays now, not on Fridays, as he used to), in the first-class compartment of his usual train, he asked a fellow passenger to open the window. The fellow passenger lifted up his eyes – 'Why doesn't the chappie do it himself?' – but then noticed that the chappie was undoing his tie and unbuttoning his shirt collar, so he got up and opened the window. And when the train stopped at a station, he called the station master, and they found a stretcher, and took him off the train, and put him on the floor of the waiting room. When the ambulance arrived, he was dead. His last words – according to the station master – were: 'Let me go . . .'; according to the barmaid: 'Get me God.'

*

A fortnight after the funeral (he was buried quietly and old-fashionedly in the little village cemetery) his wife (I shall call her 'his wife' though she was now his widow) went to London to see what could be done with the flatlet. His secretary (I shall go on calling her 'his secretary') showed her over the rooms. Shelves with hundreds of books (they can be sold to an anti-quarian bookshop, especially the first editions), a wardrobe full of manuscripts and files (some can be given to the British Library, some can be sold to the archives of some American university), boxes containing correspondence, etc. (these will have to be scrutinized and catalogued before deciding what to do with them). 'Will you have a drink?' his secretary asked. 'There is a bottle of Pernod. Do you like Pernod?' His wife had never seen him drinking Pernod. And yet he must have imbibed it with quite some ceremony. There was a tall glass and a gadget on top of it, with a lump of sugar, over which water trickled slowly down into the greenish liquid. They were sitting on a sofa, drinking their Pernod, at first – silently. But it tasted like medicine, like cough mixture, and it made them think about children. 'The boy, John [he was eighteen by now], is back at his university in Manchester, the girl, Piffin [she was now six-teen], is soon to begin her studies at Reading.' 'So you'll be all alone there?' 'Yes, the house feels empty already.' They listened to the ticking of the clock. The clock was hanging in the other room, and yet they were hearing it ticking. 'I have bought some food,' his secretary said, 'quiche Lorraine. I'll put it in the oven.

9

And there's a bottle of wine. I thought you might like a little supper . . .' 'How nice,' his wife said, and she helped lay the table. The quiche Lorraine was already in the oven. His secretary opened a bottle of wine and gave it to his wife to pour. 'I don't live here, you know that?' she said. 'Yes, I know,' his wife answered. 'I have my own flat not far from here,' his secretary said, taking the quiche Lorraine out of the oven. 'He never came there,' she said.

They ate their quiche Lorraine. 'It's nice. I don't think I've ever eaten it before,' his wife said. 'It's very practical,' his secretary said, 'you buy it all prepared, and just put it in the oven at 350°, till it's hot. That's all.' It was very hot and they sipped some wine with each bite, so as not to burn their tongues. The telephone rang. 'Must be some journalists,' his secretary said, went to the corner of the room, bent, and pulled the plug out of the socket. 'Will you have Turkish coffee?' she asked. '*Turkish* coffee?' his wife repeated. 'When I said "practical", I meant in town,' his secretary said. 'In the country, I imagine, you don't need that sort of ready-made dish, as you probably have some servants?' 'Well, yes, sort of . . .' his wife said and looked at her watch and, getting up, exclaimed: 'Good Lord, if I don't rush at once I shall miss my last train!' 'Oh, but must you?' his secretary said. 'You can sleep here, you'll be quite comfortable, I'll show you,' and she took her to the bedroom.

There was an atmosphere of peace and calm there, quite different from that of the other rooms. Was it due to the soft light of the bedside lamp, or to the fragrance coming out through the open door of the bathroom? The thick carpet on the floor, or the heavy curtain at the window? There was a treble mirror on the dressing-table and a framed photograph on the mantelpiece. His wife looked at the photograph and recognized herself, standing on a diving board, ready to dive into a swimming pool – some twenty years ago.

'You are as beautiful as in the photograph,' his secretary said.

'My dear, I shall be forty next month,' his wife said.

His secretary turned back the bedclothes and exclaimed: 'Oh, I forgot to change the sheets!'

'Did you sleep with him here that last night?' his wife asked. 'Yes.'

'Oh, it's all right, I don't mind,' his wife said, meaning the sheets are all right, there is no need to change them.

10

They stood facing each other. They were exactly the same height. They were the same height from the floor to the knees, to their thighs, to their breasts, to their lips, to their eyes. 'Tell me *how* he made love to you?' his wife asked. 'Oh,' his secretary started. 'The last two years he somewhat mellowed, was somewhat soft and sentimental. Before that, well . . . , he was rather brutal – ' she stopped. They both knew this was not what the question was about, but they both knew that sex and love, and the compound of the two, at whatever proportion, is made up of a number of things that languages are incapable of describing. In spite of the fact that so many talents have been attempting to do so for millennia. From King Solomon's 'Song of Songs' ' synthetic metaphor, up and down the gamut, to Erica's, Molly's, Sylvia's anatomical metonymy. Scornful of words, the two women looked into each other's eyes and were silent.

And then something strange happened to time. It was as if time were a long ribbon, extending in both directions, into the past and into the future, and as if there were two men, each with a pair of scissors, standing at each end of the ribbon, and cutting off inch after inch of it, regularly, mercilessly, inch after inch, both of the past and of the future, and the two women knew that in a while the two scissors would come close, only one inch apart, and there would remain and be only the present, and if they made the slightest movement before the moment came, the magic would vanish, and if they made it after, it would be too late. So they waited, silently, and when the moment came the younger took the other into her arms and kissed her on the lips. They were not in need of any words. Soundlessly they undressed each other, and they did it more naturally than men would do. And then, when between the unchanged sheets they were eagerly busy exploring each other's body, the sounds they produced were not the sounds of any articulate language till, some hours later, some hours of the futureless and pastless present, in the middle of the night, the younger woman said: 'How relaxing to know that one couldn't possibly have got oneself pregnant.'

*

It took them two months to arrange things. To rent the house in

11

the village (except for two rooms reserved for the children – if ever they wanted to spend some time there – and the Sybilla shrine in the garden, which they padlocked), to move things from the London flatlet to a storehouse, and to rent the secretary's flat to an American university couple. Free at last, they went to Majorca, where they bought a small villa on the not-too-crowded stretch of the north-eastern coast.

There were six thick-stemmed palm trees in the front garden. Three on each side of the path leading from the gate to the entrance door. And flower beds in the back garden. They had no newspapers, no books, no typewriters, and the batteries of a small transistor radio had run down. The only gadget they brought with them was an electric sewing machine. And the most expensive thing they ordered to be sent to them from England was a few square yards of turf, which, after removing the flower beds, they planted in the back garden; and some wooden balls, mallets and hoops for the game of croquet.

They didn't know any Spanish, except a few polite phrases, but Spanish was not the dominant language in Majorca. They did their shopping in a nearby village store, run by an Englishman retired from the army. They always went there together. They went everywhere together. Swimming together, walking together, having coffee in a little bar together. They seemed to be so inseparable that they were really noticed only when one of them happened to be seen alone. Then people would stop and ask with concern: How is the other lady? hoping she was not ill.

They had the same figure and could have worn each other's clothes, but they didn't. The older woman was always in blue or green, the younger – in red or bright yellow. (I am now calling them the older and the younger woman though the difference in age was only a few years, but calling them 'his wife' and 'his secretary' belongs to the vanished past.) On Saturday nights they used to go to the hotel on the beach where one of the itinerant dance bands would play in the ballroom. On these occasions they used to wear their own creations, heavy brocade supporting the breasts, and immediately flowing down, in straight lines, to the floor.

They danced with each other only. The moment they stepped on to the parquet, other couples would make room for them

12

and, as if by centrifugal force, be swept towards the edges, where they would stand and look and clap. Some had no doubt that they were professional dancers. Yet they were too genuine to be professional. On the other hand, they were too perfect in posture and timing to be amateurs. They had their own style. How they found that style, they themselves would not be able to say. Perhaps, to find its origin, one should go back to that 'inch of time' when they had stood facing each other, hypnotized by each other, in the London flatlet, before they kissed for the first time? Perhaps their dance was an attempt to recreate that minute. To repeat and prolong it? Because, whatever the music the dance band played, their movements were always the same. They never touched each other. But the distance from tip to tip between their breasts was always the same one inch, neither less nor more, whatever the turns or steps they were making, as if some force kept them at the same time together and separate. They had become the Saturday attraction of the hotel. The manager used to offer them drinks. Later on he used to offer them dinner. It was offered not as a payment but as homage. And as such it was gracefully accepted.

One Saturday, a year or two later, they noticed a young Englishman trying with stubborn determination to approach them. They manoeuvered themselves out of his way.

*

Next morning he knocked at the door of their villa. Reluctantly they let him in. In the room was a matching pair of old-fashioned brass bedsteads. One on the left, one on the right. And some flowers in a vase on a little table under the window in between. The older woman, in her blue swimsuit, was sitting on the bed on the left, the younger, in a red swimsuit, on the bed on the right. He was standing between the beds facing the flowers, the little table, and the window. He was awfully sorry, he said, to impose himself on them but he was leaving the island that evening and it was only last night that he had learned who the ladies were and he would never forgive himself if he missed such a Godsent opportunity of meeting them. They would understand, he trusted, if he might be allowed to intro-duce himself. He was a post-graduate student of the University

13

of East Anglia, writing his PhD thesis on the great writer, the lady's late husband. Would the lady be willing to answer a few questions? The Master was such a controversial figure. So modern, so avant-garde as a poet, and yet, as a public spirit, he didn't seem to believe in New Departures unless they were five hundred years old. So full of contradictions! Some critics say that he loved people, yet some others say that he hated them. His own view is that he (the Master) perhaps loved mankind but was impatient with its individual representatives, or, perhaps, the other way round, that he loved Men but was disillusioned with mankind. Would that be correct? Again, some critics say that his sympathies were with the left, others say with the right. Would it be possible to learn how he voted?! Now that would be, at last, something factual, something objective. And a new objective item would have enormous scholarly value in a thesis. Again, there is another objective point which could produce a decisive contribution to solving one of the most significant puzzles. It concerns the great writer's famous poem 'The Tinted Mirror'. Now, is that an autobiographical poem, or not? Some critics say yes, others say no. But all their arguments are so subjective . . . He, on the other hand, has found a clue which, if it can be followed, would provide an objective answer. And this is how: in the third stanza of the poem, there is a mention of the colour of the eyes seen in the mirror. Now, if the colour of the eyes is that of the poet's eyes, it will be almost conclusive to say that the poem is autobiographical. He has already done serious research on the subject. He has collected and scrutinized dozens and dozens of photographs of the author. Unfortunately – they are all black and white. So this, here, now, is his Godsent opportunity: will the lady be good enough to tell him what was the colour of her famous husband's eyes?

The wife of the famous husband seemed to be lost in thought. Then she woke up with a start and said: 'It's funny, but I don't remember.' And, turning to the famous writer's secretary, she asked: 'Do you?'

TWO

The True Earth

'Oh, but you don't understand. The decoding I'm talking about has nothing to do with any military secrets, or industrial secrets, or . . . Well, if you want to decode some black squiggles printed on a sheet of white paper you can't be a bookworm eating its way through it, you have got to go outside to be able to see that they make a shape, say a shape: APPLE. And to decode the shape APPLE, you must go away from your eye and into your brain to find there the word: APPLE. And to decode the word APPLE, you must again go out, into an orchard or to a green-grocer, where you will meet a real apple. But what if you want to decode the real apple now? Where must one go to be able to decode it?'

'I don't know,' he said. 'Maybe you should dissect it, analyse its chemistry, discover its physics. Eat it?'

'Oh God,' she said. 'You don't understand.'

She turned round, opened the french window, and went out. There was the sandy beach and the sea.

'The sea,' she said. 'Look at the sea. It is full of creatures, big and small, it *consists* of creatures, big and small, immense and minute, who do nothing, do nothing all the time but devour each other. Devouring and reproducing. Devouring each other and reproducing themselves. Is it because they are what they are? Or in order to become something else?'

Her bare feet stood in little pools of water.

'Don't go,' he said.

'I'm not going. It's the tide that is coming to me. To decode the sea, one mustn't dive into it. One must watch it from the dry land. And to decode the dry land one must go up, into the cosmos. And to decode the cosmos, well? Where must one go to decode cosmos?'

They were standing now at the porch of the house, watching the incoming waves, for a time in silence. Then she lifted up her eyes and said: 'Look, the Earth is rising. How beautiful!'

A pale circle detached itself from the horizon and was now coming up, slowly, into the blue sky.

'As a matter of fact, it isn't the real Earth,' he said. 'It's a mirror image of the real Earth.'

'Is it?'

'Yes, it is.'

'Well, if it's a mirror image of the real Earth, then where is the real Earth of which it is a mirror image?'

'We are the real Earth,' he said.

'How do you know?'

'I just know it. I feel it in my bones.'

'And I feel it in my bones that we are a mirror image.'

'So it's a dead end.'

'Not at all. I've got some arguments.'

'Oh, yes,' he smiled, wryly.

'You'll agree with me that on the real Earth there is the real logic, won't you?'

'I don't know whether logic can be real or not real. But, anyway, mirrors reverse the image, they don't reverse the logic.'

'The plain mirrors don't, yes,' she said. 'But we are not a plain mirror image of the real Earth. Our mirror is in a continual fever. It becomes convex in the very spot where a minute ago it was concave, or cylindrical, or bell-shaped. And the images of the real Earth dance in it, revert, deform, multiply . . . You do read the papers. You do listen to the radio . . .'

He looked at his wrist-watch.

'What's the matter with Emma?' He turned round and went in. 'Emma!' he shouted, running up the stairs. 'Are you in bed still? Do you know the time?' he asked as he opened the door.

'Oh, Daddy, don't shout, I had such a lovely dream! I saw Yoko Ono, she was floating in the air, and she had both tits showing, and she was interviewed by Mr Rees-Mogg of *The Times*, and she was telling him to ask them: Why don't they go to see each other before pressing the button? Are they going to pollute us with plutonium without even looking at each other's eyes? Why don't they go to see each other, and fuck each other,

16

and produce a generation of lovely mongrels with multinational loyalties to save the world? And then it was a Russian Greek-Orthodox church, I wasn't *in* it but I saw it from the *inside*, all white and gold, and round, and in the centre stood Margaret Thatcher and Leonid Brezhnev, and the Pope, John Paul II, was marrying them, and there were so many guests all around, there was Mr Reagan, and Mr Tony Benn, and Mr Kania, and Mrs Gandhi, and – and – well, many people, all with their wives, and they were wife-swapping.'

'What do you know about wife-swapping?'

'Everything, Daddy. It was so beautiful!'

For breakfast they had cornflakes and honey-bran, soft-boiled eggs, toast, marmalade, and coffee.

'Daddy, who was Dostoievsky?'

'A writer.'

'Nice?'

'No. Disgusting.'

'Don't bend over your bowl. Sit up straight and lift the spoon up to your mouth.'

'No newspapers this morning?'

'Must be a strike. Or else the newspaper boy is late.'

'As usual.'

'Not as usual. As sometimes.'

'All right. As sometimes.'

'Daddy, did you tell Mummy my dream?'

'No, I didn't.'

'What dream?'

'Oh, Emma's dream.'

'I know it's Emma's dream. But what was it about?'

'I don't remember. I don't remember my own dreams. Why should I remember hers? Do you still remember it, Emma?'

'No, I don't. And I want to know, what is the posh way of eating a soft-boiled egg?'

'You try not to get some of it on your chin.'

'That's not an answer.'

'Oh yes, it is *an* answer.'

'I don't like people who dip a piece of toast in the yolk.'

'Prejudice.'

'No. I find it disgusting.'

17

'Like Dostoievsky?'
'Not very funny.'
'Oh yes. It is. A little.'
'Mummy, why don't *you* take me to school today?'
'Because Daddy is going to town anyway.'
'To do what?'
'To cast pearls before swine.'
'No?!'
'Well, it's a metaphor. It means . . .'
'Don't tell me. I know what a metaphor is.'
'What is it?'
'It's like calling people swine. Is Daddy going to town to call people swine?'
'Not exactly. He's going to give a lecture.'
'How much?'
'How much what?'
'How much are they going to pay him?'
'Fifty pounds.'
'For telling them what, Mummy?'
'You'd better ask Daddy.'
'What are you going to tell them, Daddy?'
'I'm going to tell them that calculating, planning, researching is analytical, but understanding is always analogical. Meaning that dissecting things brings results, but to understand something you must be able to compare it with something you have already learned by letting what you were born with be moulded by the outside world.'
'Fifty pounds isn't enough. How do you spell analytical?'
'A–N–A–L–Y–T–I–C–A–L. Now, get ready. Be in the car in five minutes.'

*

The house had two front doors. There was golden sand between the south front door and the sea, and there was a little garden between the north front door and the country lane, leading from a far-away village to the main road. And inside the house, between the south front door and the north front door, was a long hall which served them as a breakfast room. On the west side of the hall was the kitchen, and a bathroom above it. On

18

the east side, a drawing room, his study, her study, and a staircase leading up to the bedrooms.

She was still in her bathrobe. It was his bathrobe. She liked it because she felt in it the warm smell of his body, and because it was black and her long hair looked so decisively blonde on its background. She had just put the breakfast plates in the kitchen sink and was now back in the hall, uncertain what to do next, when she heard the familiar sound of the newspaper boy's bicycle being put against the fence of the garden and then his steps approaching the front door. She looked at the door, expecting the paper to appear in the slit of the letterbox. She heard the little metal flap being lifted to uncover the slit, but the paper didn't appear in it. She was puzzled. She frowned. She didn't move. She waited. And then she smiled. The newspaper boy was peeping at her through the open slit of the letterbox. Slowly, she undid her belt and let the loose-fitting robe open. That tiny smile, spiteful, ironical, amused, and benign, all at the same time, was still on her face as she turned a chair so that it would face the door and draped the black bathrobe over it. But when she sat down, her naked spreadeagled body facing the invisible eyes, the smile disappeared, and her lungs took a deep breath, as if to swallow the universe for which no human being bears responsibility. At this moment, the folded newspaper appeared in the slit, and was catapulted with such force that it lifted the lid of the letterbox and fell on the floor in front of her.

She jumped up. The letterbox front door had a Yale lock. But she heard footsteps. She turned, rushed to the sea-front door and locked it. Though the footsteps didn't go round the house. They ran along the little garden path, back to the fence where the bicycle had been left, and in another moment she heard its bell's tinkle fading away into the distance. She put on the bathrobe and fastened the belt tightly. Everything was now exactly as it was some five minutes before. The episode had no cause, no consequence and no witnesses, it didn't exist, therefore. Even in the past. She picked up the newspaper from the floor, unfolded it, put it on the table, and read the first page headlines:

RHUBARB RHUBARB RHUBARB BOO BOO BOO
BOMB BOMB BOMB REAGAN REAGAN REAGAN

'When the real true-Earth has turned a few times round the

19

sun, who'll remember, who'll know, who'll understand what it was all about?' She left the paper on the table and went to the sea-front window. The sun was now much higher above the horizon and the true Earth was circling around it. When she closed one eye and put her thumb in front of the other, so as to eclipse the blinding brightness of the sun, she could see the Earth more clearly. The Isthmus of Panama was the easiest landmark to spot and watch for its appearance and disappearance as the Earth was turning around its axis. The thumb of her left hand still screening the brightness of the sun, she pressed the fingers of her right hand to her left wrist and started counting her pulse: seventy-four heartbeats from one appearance of the Isthmus of Panama to the next. About one minute. The day and night on the true Earth lasted about one minute. And its orbiting around the sun, its spring, summer, autumn, and winter – just about six hours. 'Indeed,' she said, 'the crooked mirror, in the image of which we live, deforms not only our Logic and our Space. It also deforms our Time.'

*

After dinner, Emma safely tucked up in bed, they put their anoraks on top of heavy pullovers and went out to sit on the wooden bench jutting out from the sea-front wall of the house. The night was cold and dark. Now and then, a few stars appeared in the sky to be quickly clouded again by the black air before they had time to build their reflection upon the rhythmical waves of the sea.

'How did it go?' she asked.

'What?'

'Your lecture.'

'All right.'

'No better than that?'

'Well, quite all right.'

'Good.' And then she giggled. 'I still think it's funny.'

'What's funny?'

'Your profession.'

'Meaning what?'

'Philosophy, of course.'

'What's so funny about it?'

'Well, you read a lot of books, and then you write a paper for a philosophical review. But the chaps who wrote the books you've read must have read other books before writing theirs. And those who wrote those other books must have read yet other, older, books, and so on till we come to some ancient chap who had nothing to read before writing his book, I mean nothing except the Book of Nature. It puzzles me – why can't you go directly to the Book of Nature, why must you read all those intermediary ones?'

'Because they tell me how; they give me the method. And they also tell me what has already been said on a particular subject by other philosophers, ancient and modern, great and not so great.'

'Yes,' she said. 'Millions and millions of pages. And when one asks you a simple question, you are stuck.'

'For instance?' he asked.

'For instance: why is there something rather than nothing?'

'Oh,' he said. 'That's Heidegger.'

'Is it? I thought it was Heisenberg,' she said.

'No,' he said. 'Heisenberg was a physicist. It was Heidegger who was a philosopher.'

'Yes,' she said. 'But I thought the question belonged to physics.'

'Yes, the question belongs to physics. But the answer belongs to philosophy,' he said.

She looked at him searchingly.

'And do you know the answer?'

'Look,' he said. 'This is not so simple. Try to understand. The question belongs to physics. The answer belongs to philosophy. But philosophy doesn't deal with questions that belong to physics. It is by its nature beyond physics.'

'Oh, I see,' she said. 'It's just the opposite to what happens to moral questions.'

'How do you mean?'

'Well, the existential question is physical but the answer to it has to be philosophical. With moral questions it's the other way round. Questions are philosophical but the answers are physical.'

'Nonsense,' he said. 'Searching for physical reasons for moral problems is precisely what's known as the "naturalistic fallacy".'

'My naturalism's not fallacious,' she said.

'How do you mean?' he asked.

'Well,' she said. 'Why don't I eat Emma, even when I'm very, very hungry?'

21

THREE

The Black Poodle

'Who is taking me to school today?'

'Mummy, as usual.'

'Not "as usual". *You* took me yesterday, Daddy.'

'I didn't say "as always". I said "as usual". "As usual" admits of exceptions. And yesterday was an exception.'

'Do finish up your breakfast. It'll only go to waste if you don't.'

'Yes, Mummy, but . . .'

'No buts, please. You may go now. See you in the car in ten minutes.'

The girl jumped up, ran to the sea-front front door, and made secret signs to him to join her outside. When he did, she said:

'I want to ask you something, Daddy.'

'Yes . . .' he said.

'But promise you'll not shout at me.'

'Do I ever shout at you?'

'No. But I've never asked you such a question.'

'Well, what is it?'

'It's about Mummy.'

'Oh, do you think we should be talking about Mummy behind her back?'

'Why not?'

'Well, one doesn't.'

'But I want to know . . .'

'Why not ask her?'

'Don't be silly, Daddy!'

'All right. Out with it!'

She looked round and then asked in a whisper:

'Is Mummy mad?'

It was he now who looked furtively around him.

'Why do you ask such strange questions?'

'Because the window was open and I heard Mummy talking to you about this world not being the real world, that the real world is there in the sky turning round the sun and why she shouldn't have eaten me when she was hungry. She must be mad, mustn't she?'

'No, darling. Your mummy is not mad. Not mad at all. You see, she is not mad, she is a poet.'

'A poet?' Emma's eyes brightened. 'Has she got a Nobel prize?'

'No, she hasn't.'

'Why not?'

'Well, not every poet is given a Nobel prize, and then, you see, she hasn't written any poetry.'

'But Daddy, if Mummy hasn't written any poetry, how can she be a poet?'

'Oh!' he sighed. 'There are soldiers who've never killed anybody and they are still soldiers. There are professors who've never taught anybody anything and are still professors. And there are little girls who have grownup thoughts and are still little girls. And now, off you go. Mummy is waiting in the car.'

He took a deep breath of morning air. The sea was calm. The sun was climbing effortlessly on to the cloudless sky. 'Is Mummy mad? Indeed . . .' he grimaced sardonically to himself as he was going to the kitchen to do the washing up after breakfast. His left hand still in the washing-up bowl, he dried the tips of his right-hand fingers and, from the pocket of his blazer, took out a picture postcard. He found it in this morning's copy of *The Times*. A bunch of pink roses tied up with a yellow ribbon and, on the other side I LOVE YOU, scribbled coarsely in pencil. He was certain the postcard was tucked in between the pages of *The Times*, so it must have been put there by the newspaper boy. Or – why not? – by the girl at the newsagent. If it was from the boy, then it was for Emma, who else? It couldn't have been for Veronica, could it? But if it was from the girl? He must pop in at the newsagent and have a look. But no, it must have been meant for Emma. Smiling, he displayed it in the centre of the mantelpiece in the hall. The copy of *The Times* was there on the table. He looked at the headlines again:

OPERAHTERBBPOGANLCHEBRNEV
THATCHER REAGAN POPE BREZHNEV

'Bloody hell!' He left the paper where it was, without touching it, and went to his study upstairs.

In his plushy armchair, a writing-desk in front of him, the sea and the sky behind the window-pane on the left, the bookcase on the right, he mused secretly (not for the first time on an occasion of such solitude), that if he had it in him, he would now be writing a poem. But he didn't have it in him. He could, of course, write a learned paper for a philosophical journal. A paper discussing what he actually meant by 'to have it in him'. But he had never felt in the mood for writing papers. No, not really. She was quite wrong in thinking that he had that sort of ambition. The ambition to improve his academic status. No. Not at all. No desire at all to complicate his life by competing. If he needed more money, then perhaps he would have to join the rat race. But he didn't need more. The house was his property, his academic salary was adequate and he didn't have to work too hard to earn it. Only the faces of his students were changing from one academic year to another, his lectures were always the same. An anecdote on Frege and Russell, an aphorism on Wittgenstein, a pinch of symbolic logic, too much of it, perhaps, for his students and not enough for the computers. And then, some interest on his deposit account and some dividends paid on the shares she had as her dowry made their life financially secure. He didn't need to compete. Competition, he thought, was the main cause of the misfortunes recurring in the Western world. Economic bankruptcies, industrial unrests, political fight-ings for power. Let them, the stupid countries, compete with one another and think that each one can be a winner. He – no, he doesn't want to win. To win, he thought, showed no virility but bad manners. Why should he add another book about books written about books about books? Well, 'Why can't you go directly to the Book of Nature?' she had asked him only yesterday. Why, indeed? Doesn't she know that the world is no longer what it was at the time of Benjamin Franklin? Doesn't she know that the Book of Nature has been torn to pieces by millions of trained scientists who are eating their way through its pages? And what? And produce physical theories which help to produce some gadgets! Why has no literary theory ever helped to produce a poem? Because a poem is not a gadget? Because it is a phenomenon? Physical theories, too, are *about*

24

phenomena. They don't *produce* them. Or do they?

He yawned. Not with boredom. With pleasure. Behind the window on his left, halfway between the seashore and the horizon, a dark shape was bobbing up and down. Was it a boat? A motor-boat? Too far to be sure . . . He stretched his legs under the writing-desk. A book lay open on the window-sill. He hesitated for a moment. And then he took it. A paperback detective story. Now everything will be so beautifully simple. Peaceful. This was the time of day when nothing was ever happening.

And then, three things happened nearly at the same time.

The sound of a motor-car, approaching and slowing down, came from the direction of his right. Intrigued, he got up, but as he was doing so he noticed through the window on his left, against the glare of the sun on the water, a silent, small boat – was it the boat he thought he'd seen, its bow just having touched the solitary rock on the sandy beach, some fifty yards to the east? There was not a single human being on the deck, but there was a dog. A big, black dog. A poodle? Yes. A big, black poodle. It jumped on shore and started running towards the house. There was something strange about the poodle, but at the same time the telephone rang in the hall and, as he rushed down the stairs to answer it, the knocker at the garden front door sounded twice.

He lifted the receiver.

'Tim?' she asked.

Of course it was he, Tim, who else?

'What's happened?' he asked, apprehensive, because she never used to phone him at this time of day. 'Is Emma all right?'

'Of course she's all right. Why shouldn't she be? I'm phoning you only to say that I'll be late. I've decided to go to the hairdresser.'

'All right,' he said. 'But hold on for a moment. Somebody is knocking at the door.'

'Who is it?' she asked.

'I don't know. Don't put it down.'

He left the receiver hanging and walked to the garden front door. A young man, whom he had never seen before, stood at the threshold.

'Do come in,' he said to the stranger. 'And shut the door

25

behind you. There is a mad dog running around. I'll be with you in a moment.'

He went back to the telephone and said, 'Hallo, are you there?' several times. There was no answer. He tapped the little nodules on which the receiver rests, and the line disconnected. He put the receiver down and turned to the french window, opening on to the sea. The boat was moving slowly stern foremost away from the shore.

'Come here and look,' he said to the strange visitor. 'Your eyes may be better than mine. Can you see anyone on the deck of that boat?'

'No, I can't.'

'Can you see a dog? A big black poodle?'

'Nope.'

'Well, so we don't know. Is it back on the boat or is it running around loose? There was something pretty odd about that dog. I bet it is hydrophobic. Rabies, you know? Did they bring it here and leave it on the shore on purpose? I wonder. Perhaps we should warn the police. What do you think?'

'I'm sorry I called on you at an inopportune time. I should have written first, or phoned . . .'

'Nonsense. Come up and have a drink. What's your poison?' he asked somewhat artificially as it was not his familiar idiom.

'My name is McPherson,' the visitor said. And, as they were entering the study upstairs, he added, 'I understand that I'm talking to Professor Chesterton-Brown?'

'Not "professor", my dear fellow. Lecturer. You were not one of my students, were you?'

'No. I'm a journalist. Freelance. But what I want to ask you about *is* a sort of academic matter. For the PhD thesis I'm writing. On the work of the late Bernard St Austell. I understand that you knew him . . .'

'Bernard! I dare say. If he hadn't married his wife I would have married her and he would have married my wife. And where would Emma have been, I ask you? Emma is my daughter.'

'. . . and I presume you know his poem "The Tinted Mirror"?'

'Do I? What about it?'

'You surely remember that in the third stanza there is a mention of the colour of the eyes seen in the mirror. Now, in my thesis I want to prove that the poem is autobiographical. Or, eventually, that it is not autobiographical. All depends on the colour of the eyes. Do you remember what the colour of his eyes was?'

'I beg your pardon?'

'What I am asking you is, do you happen to remember the colour of Bernard St Austell's eyes? You knew him well. And he died not so long ago. You must remember! This is very important. Crucial to my thesis.'

'Good gracious! No. How can I? You should ask his wife. I mean, his widow.'

'I have.'

'You have? So you have seen her? How is she? Tell me about her. Where does she live now?'

'She lives in Majorca. With the Great Man's secretary girl. The two make a formidable couple. Dancing in a hotel nearby.'

'Dancing? No! Not professionally?'

'No. They always dance only with each other. For pleasure. And neither of them remembers the colour of his eyes. *Sic transit . . .*'

His Latin was cut short by the growling of a dog. They jumped up out of their chairs and ran downstairs. There it was, behind the sea-front front door – the french window – the big black poodle, its muzzle touching the window-pane. They looked through the glass and exclaimed 'My God!', and then there was a slow-motion second of thunder and of pain and then an eternity of nothing.

FOUR

The Ambassador, the Admiral & a Third Milieu

On the same coast, some five hundred yards westwards, was a villa, called for some unknown (perhaps prosodic?) reason Villanelle. It belonged to an ambassador. It was his butler who, having heard and seen the explosion, telephoned the fire brigade, ambulance, and police. Upon which, he went to His Excellency and told him what he had done. 'The police are bound to come and ask you questions,' the ambassador said. 'When they arrive, please bring them here at once, to my study. I want them to interrogate you in my presence.'

'Very well, sir,' the butler said.

But the police didn't come till the evening of the next day. There were two of them. In civilian clothes.

'Sit down, gentlemen,' the ambassador said. And, turning to the butler, he added, 'Sit down, Jones.'

'Your name is Jones?' the older policeman asked.

'Yes, sir. That's to say, when I'm on duty. Otherwise my name is Ostrowski.'

'That's a Slav name, isn't it?'

'Yes, sir. My great-grandfather came from Poland. That's to say, from the Austro-Hungarian monarchy. Before the First World War, sir. Actually, his father's, that's to say my great-great-grandfather's, name was Ostrower. But I had eight great-great-grandfathers, sir.'

'You may smoke, gentlemen, if you wish,' His Excellency said. 'And you will appreciate Mr Jones's considerable presence of mind which made him telephone you promptly, as soon as he saw what he saw, before even telling me what had happened.'

'And what *did* you see, Mr Jones?' asked the older policeman. 'Take your time over it. Don't omit any details, please.'

'I was in my room, which is situated on the second floor and has a little balcony facing south-west. I happened to be on the balcony when it happened.'

'Did you notice the exact time?'

'It must have been just a minute or two before you received my call.'

'It was good of you to be so quick, Mr Jones. But didn't you say on the phone that it was a bomb explosion?'

'I might have. Yes, I probably did.'

'How did you know it was a bomb?'

'What else could it have been, sir?'

'Many things. Gas from the gas cooker, for instance.'

'Oh, no, sir. If the room was filled with gas, the impact would have blown the french window and the wall outwards. And I saw it collapsing inwards, as if it were sucked from the inside.' He hesitated for a moment, and then started: 'Besides . . .'

'Besides?'

'There was something unusual about the boat, sir.'

'A boat?'

'Yes, sir. There was a motor-boat there, some hundred and fifty, well more than a hundred and less than two hundred yards, so far as I can judge, from the coast, in front of the villa.'

'This villa here?'

'Oh, no, sir. Not in front of our villa. In front of the other one.'

'And you thought there was something unusual about the boat?'

'Yes, sir. I thought it was unusual that there was nobody on deck. Neither before nor after the explosion.'

'So you did notice the boat before the explosion occurred?'

'Yes, sir. And whoever was there in the cabin must have heard the noise and felt the blast, and I would expect such people to go on deck, out of sheer curiosity, to see what was happening; instead the boat turned round and ran away.'

'You may be right, Mr Jones,' the policeman said. 'It may be important. So try to concentrate your attention on the boat, and tell us what you remember.'

'Mr Jones must be commended upon his great presence of mind,' the ambassador said. 'He has taken a snapshot of the boat. Here it is.' He handed the print and a magnifying glass to the policeman. 'Unfortunately the picture isn't very clear.'

29

'When did you take that picture, Mr Jones?' the policeman asked, before even looking at it.

'At once, sir.'

'Before you went to the telephone?'

'Yes, sir.'

'Where is the telephone you used?'

'In the hall on the first floor, sir.'

'You mean you saw the explosion, you watched the boat turning round and going away, you took the picture, you went downstairs to the telephone, and all that didn't take more than two minutes?'

'I believe so. It just so happened that my camera was there, on the table, ready for use.'

'Mr Jones is an experienced photographer,' His Excellency said.

'And, of course, I was in a hurry. That's why the picture is blurred. If I had had more time, I would have used a polaroid anti-glare filter. The boat was right between me and the sun.'

'Could you give us the negative of the picture, Mr Jones, please?'

'I doubt if one can make a better print than this one, sir.'

'Oh yes. We can do some image processing by computer to clarify a blurred photograph.'

'Be good enough to go and bring the negative, Jones,' the ambassador said.

'It is a 35mm film of twenty-four exposures, sir.'

'You can cut out the relevant frame and bring it here,' the ambassador said. And when the butler shut the door behind him, His Excellency added, in an explanatory, benign tone of voice: 'Mr Jones is an excellent nude photographer. He treats it as an art form.'

The younger policeman looked at his wrist-watch.

'Now, gentlemen,' the ambassador said, 'it's I who would like to ask you some questions. Will it be all right with you to tell me what you have found so far?'

'Perfectly all right, Your Excellency. We want you to know everything. Especially as it is not excluded that we may be in need of Your Excellency's help, at some later stage, sir.'

'Indeed?'

'At present, we are just busy eliminating some false clues and red herrings. The only positive thing we know so far is that whoever did it can't have been a dog lover. From the bits that have been gathered, we deduce it was a trained dog, a black poodle, they taught to carry the bomb. Detonated electronically from a distance. Perhaps from the boat your butler saw. Perhaps not. I wonder that he didn't mention seeing the poodle.'

'Mr Jones *is* an animal lover, gentlemen.'

'Yes, of course. So, apparently, was Mr McPherson. The young man who was killed. His car was left in front of the garden. We have notified his parents. They came this morning. Brought his girlfriend with them. A girl called Sally. The girl-friend is quite positive that he came to see Mr Chesterton-Brown to discuss some purely academic matters. But we don't know if he was the same person Mrs Chesterton-Brown told us about. Mrs Chesterton-Brown is very distressed, naturally. But she told us that she telephoned her husband at about ten o'clock yesterday morning and he told her that somebody had been at the door. She tried to phone again from a coin box to find who it was, but couldn't get a connection. Now, was it Mr McPherson, or was it somebody we don't know?'

'But', the ambassador said, 'if you know that the bomb was planted by the dog and exploded from the boat, then those other considerations seem to be irrelevant.'

'We do not *know* about the boat. We only conjecture. The thing could have been exploded from anywhere in the vicinity.'

He took from his pocket a picture postcard in a transparent plastic envelope and put it on the ambassador's desk. His Excellency examined the pink roses and the yellow ribbon and the letters I LOVE YOU written in pencil on the other side. 'How charming,' he said, handing it back to the policeman.

'Quite so,' the policeman said. 'We found it standing against the wall in the middle of the mantelpiece. It is unlikely that it could have been put there after the explosion. On the other hand, it is rather strange that the postcard was the only thing that seemed not to be displaced by the blast. Besides, Mrs Chesterton-Brown is quite certain that she has never seen the postcard and that it was not on the mantelpiece when she left in the morning.'

'You are very thorough,' the ambassador said.

'We have to be, sir. We have traced the origin of the picture postcard to the newsagent's stationery. They don't remember selling it. But their newspaper boy did blush. He had two reasons for blushing. Being in love, and not having paid for the card. We pretended not to have noticed his embarrassment.'

'You are psychologists,' the ambassador said.

'Well, Your Excellency. We have to build for ourselves the overall picture of the situation before we start analysis.' He put the picture postcard back in his pocket and, from another pocket, took out a photograph which he put on the ambassador's desk. A photograph of a man, *en face*, and profile.

'Straight from Madame Tussaud's?' the ambassador asked.

'How interesting that you say that, Your Excellency. That's what he looks like. His name is Smith, of course. Yesterday morning, between ten and eleven, he tried to force his way into a factory. The guards stopped him and called us.'

'What sort of a factory?' the ambassador asked.

The policeman waited for a moment, and then said: 'This is going to be an anticlimax. A biscuit factory.'

'Well?' the ambassador asked, noncommittally.

'He told us he had seen the king and queen, the halberdiers, the wet-nurses and the civil servants, but he had never seen any ordinary workers. That's why – to see some – he tried to force his way into the factory. Otherwise he sounded quite sane. Just a bit cranky, and yet clear-headed. We kept him overnight but we had nothing on him and let him go this morning. We intended to follow him for a bit, but he just slipped away.'

The butler came in, the negative of the snapshot of the motor-boat in his hand. The ambassador took it and, without looking at it, handed it to the policeman. Then he took the photograph of Mr Smith and showed it to the butler.

'Do you know this man?' he asked.

'Unmistakably, sir. When I happened to be in our garden yesterday morning, around nine o'clock, he appeared on the road, stopped in front of the gate and started a conversation. He passed the time of day with me, and then asked, Is there a factory somewhere not far from here? What sort of factory? I asked. A sardine factory, he said. I presumed, sir, he was looking for a job, or for employment, and told him there was a biscuit factory some two miles up the road. Upon which, sir, he thanked me civilly and went in that direction.'

32

'You haven't seen him since?'

'No, sir.'

The ambassador looked at the policeman. They nodded.

'Thank you, Jones. That will be all.'

And when the butler left, he turned to them and said: 'I understand, gentlemen, that you are considering the possibility that Mr Chesterton-Brown was attacked by mistake. Putting it clearly: that the bomb was originally meant for me.'

'We are considering it as a hypothesis, yes.'

'But, surely, that is not the only hypothesis possible. Further down the coast, at a similar distance from Mr Chesterton-Brown's house, is another villa, belonging to one of your own very important personalities.'

'An Admiral of the Fleet, yes, sir.'

'Therefore, I presume, you do not exclude the possibility that it was he for whom the explosives were intended?'

'That is correct, sir.'

'In which case you need to divide your forces. You must search among groups of people who have a grudge against me, and also among those who have a grudge against him. Two distinct milieux, gentlemen.'

'There is a third milieu still, Your Excellency.'

'Yes?'

'Of those who are against both of you.'

FIVE

The Way of Not Answering Questions

On the road to Damascus a jet-black poodle snuffed his way along. His track was traced with little tongues of fire, though that might have been some optical illusion. And the little squeals of pain uttered by the little tongues of fire might have been some acoustical illusion. But the jet-black poodle dog was not an illusion.

And it was the middle of the day, and a light came from the sky, more brilliant than the sun, and a white poodle appeared on the road in front of the black poodle and said: 'Poodle, Poodle, why do you persecute me?' And the Black Poodle said: 'Why are you always asking me that? You know that I'm only doing my job.'

'That's what *you* say,' said the White Poodle.

'That's what *He* ordained,' said the Black Poodle. 'You select in, and I select out. That's His method. Continuous Creation.'

'Of what?' asked the White Poodle.

'Of men,' the Black Poodle answered . . .

Dame Victoria opened her eyes and looked at the watch on her bedside table. It was 6 a.m. Too early to get up. So she closed her eyes again and continued her dream:

. . . and the Black Poodle rose to his hind feet, stood upright, and said to the White Poodle: '. . . and I'm telling you, Don't touch her, leave the girl alone, because, whatever you say, and whatever He says, I shall not weed her out. Do you hear me, Poodle?!'

And the White Poodle answered: 'I am not a Poodle, I am a Lamb.'

And he was.

34

Dame Victoria opened her eyes again. It was 6.10. But a moment later it was already 7 a.m. Time to get up. 'The Black Poodle is a red herring,' she murmured.

Some hundred narrow family houses glued to each other on the odd side, and another odd hundred on the even side of the sunless street filled with the smell of bacon emanating at this morning hour from all the kitchen windows save one. Shuffling her heelless slippers, Dame Victoria moved from her bedroom to the bathroom, to the bedroom again, to the kitchen, to the dining room. She was tall and thin and walked slowly, stooping with age. Still in her dressing-gown but wearing a hat, a black straw hat, to hide the bald patch on her head of white hair. Now in her dining room, she had just spread the cloth and was very meticulously laying the breakfast table. Just for one person. Herself.

While the coffee was brewing, she put an old overcoat on top of her dressing-gown, and went down, on her thin legs, to the front door, to fetch a bottle of milk, a copy of the *Daily Telegraph*, and the post. There were two envelopes, one would contain a bill, the other was embossed with the crest of the House of Commons. She put them, unopened, in the pocket of her overcoat and was now examining the headlines in the paper. She didn't seem to be displeased by not having found what she was looking for.

Back in the dining room, she ate her soft-boiled egg, while glancing at the Personal column: Births, Marriages, Missing friends, Deaths. Her lips had lost some of their agility, and a crumb of honeyed toast fumbled in the corner of her mouth. She wiped it with a napkin, and got up.

Now she went again to the kitchen, put two eggs, two slices of bacon and a sausage in the frying-pan, and started cooking a proper breakfast. When it was ready, she put it on a tray – the sizzling plate, bread, butter, milk, condiments, a napkin and a huge pot of tea. Then she took a long iron poker with an ornamental handle, placed it along the edge of the tray, and tottered with it upstairs to the attic. There, she put the tray on the floor at the bottom of the door, looked through the keyhole, and said: 'Go away from the door, Piff.'

She took the poker in her left hand, with her right she took the key from her dressing-gown pocket, and opened the door.

The girl whom she called Piff was sitting in her nightshirt on the edge of a narrow bed. Dame Victoria took the poker into her right hand now, with her foot she pushed the breakfast tray into the room, and then shut the door behind her.

'You know that I need to go to the loo *before* breakfast, Grandma,' the girl said.

'You have your potty under the bed,' Dame Victoria said.

'That's not enough,' the girl said.

She took the tray from the floor and put it on the bed beside her.

'You look very very funny with that poker in your hand, Grandma.'

'I know,' Dame Victoria said.

'Like a heroine in a Gothic novel.'

'I know, you've told me that already.'

The girl got her teeth into the sausage. Dame Victoria was sitting on a chair, by the door, watching her. A pigeon landed on the ledge of the little window of the attic, just opposite the door. This was not as commonplace an occurrence as it used to be, since the last winter was very long and severe and not many pigeons had survived. The girl attacked her bacon and eggs.

'I bought you some Tampax,' Dame Victoria said. 'The chemist looked at me curiously, so I said it was to be put in a food parcel for a friend in Poland. Then he asked me about the poodle. It was the first time he saw me without Diamond. I said I left him with some friends in the country. I hate telling people lies.'

'Well, you know what you can do.'

'No, I don't.'

'Oh, all right, Grandma. I love you, you know that, but . . .'

'But what?'

'Never mind!' She poured herself some more tea.

The alarm clock on the bedside table showed nine.

'I got a letter,' Dame Victoria said. 'From your uncle.'

'Yes?'

'I haven't opened it yet. I know what he wants. He wants to know, Have I heard from you? Which means I'll have to tell more lies.'

'And you hate telling lies, I know. You've already told me.'

'Piff . . .' Dame Victoria started.

36

'Yes?'

'Why do you pretend you don't love your uncle?'

'Love him? Why should I? He just happens to be my uncle. And he is an Enemy. He and his precious wife.'

'Listen to me, Piff,' Dame Victoria said. 'You do realize that this will leave him marked for life.'

'So what? Damn him! I told you I don't care!'

'But he is my son, Piff.'

The girl jumped up and went to the little window. The pigeon, frightened, flew away. The morning sun poured in. Silhouetted against it, her body in the silk see-through nightshirt, stood there, tense, keyed up, in front of Dame Victoria. 'How young, and beautiful, and strong, her body is,' Dame Victoria admired silently. 'Poor Piff. Sooner or later, perhaps when I'm no longer here, they will catch her body, perhaps five years from now, perhaps ten, in ten years' time she'll be twenty-eight, high time to have a baby, twenty years? fifty years? Who knows what the world will be like in fifty years, everything may be the other way round, if they catch her in fifty years from now, who knows? They might put her on a pedestal, many people have their monuments, people who did things one doesn't. Poor Piff, how keyed up she is. She's going to tell me that I don't love her, that I've been keeping her incommunicado not for her sake but for her uncle's, and I'll answer that every single thing has many causes, and each cause brings many results. Well, what is done cannot be undone.' In a quiet, gentle voice, she said: 'You may go to the loo now, and do have a bath. I'll be waiting for you here, Piff.'

The alarm clock ticked away on the bedside table. The girl rushed at it and knocked it down. It showed seven minutes past nine.

'You don't understand, Grandma, you don't understand, you don't un–der–stand!' she screamed, and threw herself on the bed. 'Leave me alone, leave me alone,' she began to sob, and buried her face in the pillow.

Dame Victoria took the tray and the poker and left the room. She locked the door behind her and put the key in her overcoat pocket. She went down to the kitchen and put the tray on the table. That was when the knocking at the front door started. By the time she had managed to totter down (the kitchen, the drawing room and the bedroom were on the first floor, the ground floor was unoccupied), the knocking had changed into hammering.

'Who's there?' she asked.

'Friends,' the voice said. 'Open up! Quick! There's no time to waste!'

She opened the door and two men in Balaclava helmets burst in. A car, its engine left running, stood at the kerb.

'Where is she? The police may be here any moment.'

'Up in the attic,' Dame Victoria said.

One man, pistol in hand, remained standing at the door, the other rushed up the stairs. Dame Victoria, fumbling in her pocket for the key to the attic, followed him up the stairs. By the time she reached the landing of the first floor, he was already at the top, kicking the locked door in, and, before she arrived there, he and the girl, still in her nightshirt, hurried past her down the stairs. The very whirl of their flight seemed to have knocked her down. She was now sitting sideways on the top stair, her back against the wall, the ridiculous poker beside her. Soon she heard the sound of the car revving up and moving off. She sighed with relief.

She didn't feel anything. Was it a little, a tiny, stroke? An unimportant, little, tiny stroke would be something nice, welcome, in the circumstances . . . She tried the left foot – it moved. She tried the right foot – it moved. She tried the left hand and the right hand – they moved. She shut and opened one eye, and the other. But can she speak? Will she hear her own voice? She must try. She must say something aloud. But what? She might try to say: 'Now that Piff is gone, there is no reason why one shouldn't let the empty ground floor rooms.' But no, she can't possibly say such a heartless cynical thing aloud. Not now. Not so soon. One doesn't. It wouldn't be proper. But what else can she say? She cleared her throat and said: 'Hallo, hallo, A,B,C, one, two, three.' She said it in a soft, timid voice, but she heard it all right. All the same, an unimportant, little, tiny stroke would be useful, under the circumstances. Will I ever see you again, my dear Piff, she mused, you are young and strong and of course if you really wanted to break out you could, poker or no poker, but so long as I had it in my hand you would have had to lay your hands on me, and that

38

you wouldn't do, would you? You know it's true that you wouldn't, true though paradoxical, considering . . . considering what? considering what you've been capable of doing? You love me, you said, but, you said, I just don't understand that this is war and you are a soldier, you receive your orders, you fight your enemies, for a Cause, and I look at you as if you've murdered people! But, my dear Piff, what sort of enemy was the young man who was killed? Or that poor university lecturer who had to have his legs amputated above the knees? Oh, you said, that was a mistake, Grandma, they marked a wrong spot on the map. Things like that do happen in wartime. Well, my dear Piff, I said, and what about my poodle? He was killed deliberately, and not by some logistic mistake. Oh, no, Grandma, you said, he was not killed, he was sacrificed, for a Cause. Yes, I said, my dear Piff, but he was sacrificed for *your* Cause, and not for his Cause, whatever it could have been, my poor, poor Diamond. And you said that I don't understand. That I don't understand about Ideas. But I'm so thankful that I don't understand about Ideas. I'm thankful that when I was a young girl I wasn't educated to have Ideas. As a matter of fact, I wasn't educated at all. It was called 'privately educated', which was a posh way of calling it but no education as it is known to people. *Pauvre* Mlle de la Chaussée, *ma gouvernante suisse*, was forbidden to teach me arithmetic and the sciences, the sciences used to be called 'stinks' at the time, because something called hydrogen sulphide smelled like rotten eggs, so the sciences were out of the question, the only thing about Sir Isaac Newton I learnt was that his dog knocked down a candle and so set fire to some of his learned papers, upon which Sir Isaac exclaimed, 'O Diamond! Diamond! thou little knowest the mischief done!' That's why, when my poodle was a little puppy, I called him, thoughtlessly, Diamond, not thinking it may be *nomen omen*, and of history I was told only how to use some famous historical names without committing a *faux pas*, and geography was useful to know how to travel, and I had no religious education either. I was taught languages instead, and what-one-does-and-what-one-does-not. And then I was sent to a finishing school, where, again, I was taught what-one-does-and-what-one-does-not. Which came quite naturally to me, as if it had already been in me from birth and needed only to be externalized,

39

so to speak, and they, the governesses and the mistresses, would never say 'one should', because if they said 'one should', one could ask 'Why?' and 'Why?' and 'Why?' and they were in the possession of the Wisdom which made them know that there is no ultimate answer to such a procession of why? why? why? and so it was more honest just to say 'one does' or 'one doesn't', no questions asked, full stop, and that knowledge has remained very firm in me till today, partly because I wasn't educated by males, because male conventional education undermines that sort of Wisdom. Your grandfather was conventionally educated and he insisted that your mother too must be so educated, and so your father, my poor Piff, married an educated girl, and when you were born they both insisted that you too be so educated, and that education gave you all plenty of excuses to offer for doing what one does not, and not doing what one does, it told you that the ends justify the means, which means that your Ideas justify killing people who don't share them. Oh yes, oh yes, that's precisely what they do, and whatever age you and your friends are, I've been the same age once upon a time, and I've known them all, them and their Ideas, I've seen them all, standing on their high altars, sitting on their thrones, lying on a dirty bed in a small hotel room with the lavatory in the corridor, and getting the poor Piffs trapped between Ideas and the real world, between the world of words and the world of what one does, and when it is done unto them what they'd like to do unto others, they squeal and vengeance they ask and cry, and, I'm sorry, but so did Jesus, though *He* sacrificed Himself first, and made us all feel guilty and made us declaim after Him: Love, Love, Love; didn't He know how much hatred in the world is produced by Love? Instead of teaching Love, why didn't He teach what my governesses and the mistresses in the finishing school taught me, that there are things one does, and there are things one does not, and no questions asked, full stop. Yes, full stop.

There was a beautiful smile on her old face. It was so quiet now. But somewhat draughty. They must have left the front door open. Well . . . never mind. How long had she been sitting there on the top stair – two minutes? two hours? No, her body didn't mind, her body was quite comfortable, the legs stretched out, touching the banister, shoulders leaning against the wall, hands relaxed, no need for them to do anything, her head bent down, her eyes focused on the lower button of her overcoat, her ears waiting for the police siren to wail.

But they came silently, without any dramatics. Two policemen and one policewoman. 'The girl's gone,' they said. 'Did they hurt you?' they asked. 'Look at the poker, the old duckie was trying to defend herself,' the policewoman said. 'Do you think you can get up if we help you?' they asked.

Down in the bedroom, they took her overcoat off her and made her lie in her dressing-gown on the bed. The policewoman took off her slippers and covered her with a blanket. But when she wanted to take off her hat, Dame Victoria silently objected. 'Don't you worry, duckie, you'll be all right,' the policewoman said.

In a drawer in the bathroom they found a dog's collar. In the pocket of Dame Victoria's overcoat – a key, an electricity bill, and an unopened envelope embossed with the crest of the House of Commons. They hesitated, and then decided not to open it. With an MP, one never knows.

'Don't you worry, duckie,' the policewoman repeated. 'I'll go to your kitchen and brew up a pot of nice strong hot tea with a bit of milk and plenty of sugar for us all, duckie.'

At that moment the alarm clock lying face down on the floor of the attic started to ring shrilly. They all jumped up. Except Dame Victoria. She had found her way of not answering questions and telling no more lies.

SIX

The Wheelchair

There was more than a mile (or, perhaps, only more than a kilometre) from the hotel to the village. Slightly uphill, most of the time. Somewhere halfway, a little van carrying newspapers hooted twice and then, carefully, slowed down to walking pace. The driver's head leant out of the window: 'I've got a piece of rope, mate. Can haul you up if you want me to.'

'I'm all right. I can manage. Thank you all the same,' and when the little van had gathered speed and was out of hearing, 'I'm enjoying it.'

He did enjoy it. He enjoyed the feeling of strength and healthy tiredness in his arms, as he propelled his wheelchair up the road, and then the feeling of pride when he got, without any help, to the village. It was Sunday morning and the market place was empty. People were still in their beds, at this early hour, or in the church from which the bass booms of the organ were bursting now and again through the closed portals, which one couldn't reach without climbing tiers and tiers of steps rising high above the pedestrian gravel. On the white wall, there was a sundial:

Jo sense sol
tu sense Fe
no valem res

was inscribed on it. At the other edge of the market place, opposite the church, grew a solitary tree. He propelled his wheelchair towards it. From here, he could see the far-away horizon above the roofs of little houses climbing down the slope towards the blue sea. Somebody's motorcycle was parked on the other side of the tree. A stray bitch came and circled around, sniffing. At the back of the wheelchair, at the tree, at the motorcycle. Then she sniffed at what looked like a leopard skin, covering the front of the wheelchair, and she growled and barked. His body stiffened. A dog's barking was the last sound he heard before the explosion, the pain, and the black nothingness that followed.

'Go away!' he said. '*Va-t'en!*' He wasn't sure how to say it in Spanish.

She kept barking.

Suddenly, some male steps approached the wheelchair from behind and the bitch vanished. A young priest was standing by the tree. He lifted his soutane to mount the motorcycle, but then changed his mind. He fished a packet of cigarettes from under the soutane and lit one. Then, turning to the wheelchair but looking at the top of the tree, he said: '*Cigarrillo?*'

Tim Chesterton-Brown smiled a kind of senior lecturer tutorial smile: 'That's exceedingly kind of you, but I've stopped smoking, so please don't tempt me.'

'You were not here when I came first. Otherwise I would have wheeled you into the church. There are no steps if one goes through the cemetery to the sacristy.'

'But that was not my intention.'

'You are not a Catholic?'

'I'm afraid I'm not.'

'And what is your religion?'

He was going to say 'Church of England', but no! He had had enough of that interrogation. Silly ass. Thinks everybody must have a religion. And with a sardonic smile, unnoticed by the young priest, he said something so old-fashioned he would never have dared to put it in that form in front of his university colleagues or students.

'I'm a logical positivist,' he said.

'Is it a Christian religion?' the priest asked.

'No, it isn't. Not really.'

Now that he was asked that question, he wondered. After all, it all started with August Comte, not within the cultural sphere of Hinduism, Shintoism, Judaism, Zoroastrianism, Confucianism or Islam, but in the midst of Christendom. Logical positivism! Religion of Humanity! Catholicism without God! The *logical* unbelievers of the 'Vienna Circle' came later. Yes, the unbelievers! But, if you look at it without prejudice, isn't the internal content

43

of Christianity embedded in the hearts of unbelievers much more purely than in those where it is overgrown by so much worship, faith, and idolatry of that Virgin and her circumcised Son? No, his wandering thoughts were too sophisticated for the ears of the young priest. Thus, he said simply: 'No, it isn't. Not really.'

The priest looked pleased – if Logical Positivism was not a Christian religion then, thank God, it was ignorant of the Truth and its value, and therefore there was no room for heresy in it.

'But, all the same, you do believe in the immortality of the soul, don't you?' he asked, as one asks a rhetorical question.

The philosopher in the wheelchair sighed. He knew something about the mortality of his legs. But what did he know about the immortality of his soul? What a funny chap that priest is! He must have been in a hurry this morning because he hasn't shaved. On Sunday! Perhaps he is too young to shave every morning? He hasn't yet had his breakfast and he doesn't mind talking about the immortality of the soul on an empty stomach. Ha ha. What a subject to discuss in that little village in Majorca, of all places. Nothing of the kind could have happened by the seaside of Brighton, or Bournemouth, or St Mawes, or St Ives, or Blackpool – nor at his university seminar. He came to like the priest. To his own surprise, he came to be pleased with this chance encounter. He felt as if he were bodily translated into the time when doing Aphoristic Philosophy was OK, the time when one could divagate freely, without verifying, falsifying, testing, identifying the meaning, and making things consistent on paper by pruning away the nuances of life. All this amused him. He felt relaxed. 'Well,' he said, 'infinity and soul are two different concepts. For a mathematician infinities may be large and small; in Space infinity may be closed but edgeless; in Time infinity may be starting with the Big Bang of Creation and ending with entropy or whatever else the natural philosophers may invent.'

The priest knitted his thick black brows and, taking the heavy Spanish cigarette out of his mouth, said: 'Now, now, my son. That's a despicable way of manoeuvering off the coast. What I asked was: Do you have any doubts that your soul will survive your death?'

'Goodness me, Father. You may probably say that my soul has survived the death of my legs. Will it survive the death of

44

the rest of my body? How can I know? We have dissected ourselves into so many parts: Body, Mind, I, Soul. Do we need them all? Are we not breaking the Law of Parsimony? *Entia non sunt multiplicanda praeter necessitatem*? Is it all right looking for Descartes in Rimbaud? Rimbaud said, ". . . *vous ne comprendrez pas du tout, et je ne saurais presque vous expliquer* . . . Je *est un autre.*" What did he mean? What was *un autre*? A sort of inner state which some philosophers might call a buzz of bioelectricity, and you, with your woolly terminology, will call a soul?'

The priest squashed between his fingers the burning end of the cigarette he was smoking. 'My terminology?' he asked jeeringly. '*My* terminology is woolly?' he repeated. 'And what about yours? Is it not a hundred times more woolly? When you give me that buzz of bioelectricity, how do I know what you are referring to? Perhaps to something in the body of a shark? Or that of a dung beetle? But when I say soul, you know perfectly well what I am talking about. Even when you deny its existence you know what you are denying.'

'Touché.'

'This is not a duel.'

'Touché again. Sorry. Of course this is not a duel.'

'Now,' the priest said, 'I agree that your scientists can describe other people without using the word "I". But, when they are talking about themselves, they cannot, they have to use the word "I", and, when they are honest, they have to use the word "soul" as well. For them, your body and your mind may be two aspects of the same thing. But they are not one and the same thing. And your I and your soul are not one and the same thing either. Because God gave your I its free will which your I ought to use to change your soul for the better.'

'There is no final argument why one *ought* to do things one way or another.'

'Never mind the arguments,' the priest said contemptuously. 'I'm not advocating arguments, I'm advocating Truth. I'm appealing to your I's heart to use its free will to get rid of the evil that dwells in your soul.' He spat to remove the bit of tobacco from his lower lip, and added: 'Unless you want me to say that I'm appealing to your I's fibrous sticky pump to use its surge of hormones to get rid of the evil noise that perverts your buzz of bioelectricity.'

The positivist in the wheelchair laughed goodhumouredly. 'I like it,' he said. 'All the same, you talk about evil as if it were a bit of an insect embedded in a lump of solid amber, or in a silicon chip. I don't think it is *in* what you call "soul". I think it is around it, in the very fabric of the living world.' He paused for a moment, and then, a far-away secret melancholy in his eyes, he avowed: 'My wife believes that this earth is all false, but that there is a true Earth cruising invisibly around the sun. That's a sort of poetic vision she's created. But I know what she means.'

'So do I,' the young priest said. 'And as for you, my son, you think you are very far from the faith. In fact, you are very near it.'

'No, Father. You are making a mistake. I am not. There is a wall between us. You believe that we possess our moral code because it was given to us by an Outside Power. I think that we have found ourselves in possession of it because dead bodies stink.'

'They do,' the priest said.

'And men don't like the stink of dead bodies.'

'True,' the priest replied. And added reflectively: 'A slight whiff of the smell they may like, especially if mixed with the smell of incense. But there is a limit to it, I agree.'

'So there you are. Beyond the limit you mention, man's nose happens to be negatively chemotropic to the stimulus of that kind of smell. But the world around man's nose, the world around man's hungry stomach, is such that he finds it necessary to kill and produce dead bodies. I don't say that he minds killing. I say that he doesn't like smelling. This is the essence of the conflict. He wonders – what is that extra-terrestrial force that makes him hold his nose against the offensive smell of putre-faction that spoils his pleasure of killing, and in answer to this fundamental question he invents his religions, his ethical codes, and allows the upper part of his nervous system to create the beginning of civilization, at the end of which he invents not only refrigerators, to retard the decomposition of the flesh, but also hermetically sealed gas chambers, flame throwers oxidiz-ing proteins *in vivo*, and smell-less, clean, atomic bombs. Thus civilization has invented the means of suppressing what once upon a time gave it its birth. No, it is not by atheism, it is by

46

deodorizing death that our civilization is in the process of committing suicide.'

'What you say is horrid,' the priest said.

'I know it is.'

'How can you carry the burden of such a philosophy without being comforted by the thought of there being . . .'

The philosopher in the wheelchair finished the sentence for him: 'The thought of there being one *more* Jew who died for me would only add weight to the burden.'

'But He *did* die for you.'

They both kept silent.

And then the priest said: 'Whenever you want to come' – he pointed to the door of the church – 'I will be there, to wheel you in.'

He jumped on to his motorcycle, gave it a kick, made a sign of the cross, and went off.

So, after all, it was a duel. Sort of. But whose folly was mixed with whose wisdom? He shrugged his shoulders and it made him think of Emma. She had got into the habit of solving her teenage problems by shrugging her shoulders. What is she doing at this early hour? Bicycling? Swimming? Playing with that little boy, what's his name? Ian? And Veronica? Still in bed? He moved his wheelchair. The way back will be easy. Downhill most of the time. The road was in the shape of the letter Y. The village market place was at the end of the left arm. The right arm continued to far-away Palma, from which the little van was bringing the newspapers. And the stem, right in front of Captain Casanova's shop, was running down southwards to the hotel, the beach, and the sea.

When passing the shop, he slowed down. Thought of buying a newspaper. But the door was closed. And altogether why should he bother? It was Sunday. Sunday morning.

Further down the stem of the letter Y, hidden behind some bushes, stood the Dancing Ladies' villa. He would rather they didn't show up. He didn't want to see them. Not now, anyway. The road was empty. It reached the hotel, stopped, and imperceptibly, mingled its gravel with the sand of the beach. A little to the right, between the hotel and the sea, there was a patch of green lawn, on the edge of the sea. His favourite place. That's where he parked the wheelchair.

47

SEVEN

The Philosopher & the Mathematician

He was amazed at himself. Why was he so serene? It couldn't possibly be the result of all those general anaesthetics. That was months ago. And felt like ages. How bizarre! Odd! Grotesque! Everything seemed to be so calm. Tranquil. The Mediterranean sea. The blue sky. Beautiful. Even his artificial legs were beautiful. A work of art. Equal to a Praxiteles. The legs of Hermes. Winged with electronic devices. So marvellous to look at. Though he still needed his crutches to walk. And even just to stand. And he felt much better in his wheelchair. His wonderful legs he would lock in the wardrobe. Not to frighten the maid who was doing his room. His wife, Veronica, had booked two rooms. He slept in one, she with Emma in the other. There was a door between the rooms, but each had its own bathroom, which spared him a lot of embarrassment.

There was no traffic at all between the hotel and the sea, and their rooms were level with the ground with no steps to negotiate in his wheelchair. That was precisely why Veronica had chosen that particular hotel. The fact that the late Great Man's widow and the late Great Man's secretary girl lived in the same village, and danced on Saturday nights in the same hotel, was a pure coincidence.

His daughter, Emma, worried him. Or, maybe, not worried but just puzzled. When he was still in the hospital, and then, when they moved back to their home full of builders still busy repairing the damage, she was full of life, bright, loving, not to say proud of the drama that put them all, so to speak, on the stage. Here, in Majorca, all that had suddenly changed. He had the feeling that she was avoiding him. In the hotel restaurant, where they were given a separate table for three, by the window, with plenty of room for his wheelchair, Emma was always late,

48

and fidgeting, as if she wanted to dissociate herself from him. Nor would she ever approach him when he was sitting in his wheelchair in his favourite place, in front of the hotel, at the very edge of the lawn, looking for hours and hours at the open sea. Was she embarrassed by a father who cannot go swimming with her? Was she ashamed? Had somebody said something to her? Perhaps that small boy, what was his name? Ian? who seemed to be so often somewhere near her? Maybe the boy expected her father to be a war hero and was disappointed to learn that he was a victim of an accident. Though it was a bomb, after all, wasn't it? Strange that the police still don't know who did it. Or, perhaps they did know but wouldn't tell for some reason or other? Well, it didn't matter, did it? Didn't it? Well, did it or didn't it? He wasn't sure. Anyway, they won't bring him his legs back. Funny, would he recognize them if they did bring them? Did he remember what they were like exactly? He must have looked at them thousands of times in his bath, he must have looked at them when paring his toenails, but what were they like? Actually? They were not too hairy, yes, but what else? Funny, he remembered his socks better than he remembered his legs.

'How do you do, Mister Professor Timothy Chesterton-Brown? How are you today, sir?' That was how Don José María López, Don José for short, would greet him every morning, as soon as he saw him stopping his wheelchair on his favourite place at the edge of the lawn, facing the sea.

'Fine, and you?'

And Don José, standing behind the counter of his cocktail bar, in a sort of loggia of the tiny ornamental pavilion, open to the lawn and the beach, would invariably say: 'What I need is a swim and a girl, and what I have is the full bottles behind me and empty clients in front of me.' He would say it as if it had some special meaning. And then, sometimes he would add in a different tone of voice: 'Your Madame *esposa* went to see the Dancing Ladies, sir.'

Now, why should he say that? From where he stood, behind the bar, he could see the road leading to the villa where the 'Dancing Ladies', namely the late Great Man's widow and the late Great Man's secretary, lived, but he couldn't possibly see the villa itself. And the road went still further up. And further up was a shop, which he had just passed by on his way from the village. That was the shop where a few days after their arrival Veronica met the two women. 'Why, it's Veronica,' the widow had said. 'Surely it's Veronica. Why on earth are you here?' 'On holiday,' Veronica had said, 'and you?' 'Oh, we live here. This is my friend Marjorie. Is Tim with you? You must come and see us.' And then, introducing the man behind the counter, she said, 'And this is our famous womanizer, Captain Casanova.' The man clicked his heels and said, 'You flatter me, madam. Actually the name is Bridgewater. Captain Bridgewater.'

There was something incongruous about Captain Bridgewater. He seemed to be out of place in his own shop. Had he really been in the army? Discharged? In disgrace? Or TB? Or was he an actor affecting military manners? Even the shop was not unlike a Nissen hut, except for a flight of steps leading up, and the goods displayed pell-mell – aqualungs and Worcester sauce, paperbacks and Oxford marmalade, toothpaste and tights, English newspapers and a garden hose and two prams, looking as if transferred lock, stock and barrel from a high-street department store in Kent or Sussex.

'If you need anything from the old country, do tell me and I'll have it sent in a jiffy.'

That's what he said: 'In a jiffy.'

*

'Barbara Celarent Darii Ferio
Cesare Camestres Festino Baroco . . .'

That's how he used, year after year, to start his first lecture, at the beginning of the first term. Some uninformed freshmen thought it was a Concrete Poetry piece, and weren't sure whether to applaud or boo, till they were told that what they had just heard was the work of a thirteenth-century chap called Petrus Hispanus of Lisboa, representing some of the 256 kinds of syllogisms (ha!) of which only 19 were valid (ha! ha!) which proportion suggested that the procedure was surely extravagantly wasteful (ha! ha! ha!), upon which he would take them some sixteen centuries back, to Aristotelian formal logic, viz the theory of syllogisms, and then, swiftly, some twenty-two centuries forward again, to Frege, Russell, Carnap, Tarski etc, thus presenting them with a general sur-

50

vey, a bird's-eye view, a snapshot of the framework within which they would have to learn how to translate their vernacular common sense into typographical squiggles.

He pushed the right wheel of his wheelchair an inch forward, which made the wheelchair turn a timid degree to the left, away from the bar, and Don José understood that the conversation is now over, and the Mister Professor wishes to be left alone with his thoughts till the time half an hour before luncheon when he'll be asking to be served a drink.

'Darapti Disamis Datisi
Felapton Bocardo Feriso
Bamalip Calemes Dimatis
Fesapo Fresison!'

He recited it now to himself, just for the pleasure of hearing its sound, without bothering what sort of calculus it represented, the calculus that anyway hasn't yet helped anybody to find a conclusion about the black poodles that explode in front of your knees. He dismissed the thought. He was very keen on dismissing his own thoughts nowadays.

The sky was blue, and the sea was blue, and the waves were moving incessantly towards him, never to arrive. So much nicer to watch the waves than to watch his students' heads, which he tried to stuff with that bloody nonsense about *verité de fait* and *verité de raison*. Our truths about the facts of this world are not absolutely necessary because God could have made a different kind of world. But even God cannot make a truth contradict itself, therefore the truths of reason are completely certain and necessary. What rubbish! How do they know that He could have made a different kind of world? It is the *verité de fait*, the truth of the blue waves and black poodles and blown-off legs, that is undeniable, and it is the *verité de raison* that consists of nothing except tautologies and paradoxes and cannot cope with this best of all worlds. 'No, no, it doesn't really matter whether she's visiting the Dancing Ladies or the military shopkeeper,' he told himself, dismissed all thoughts, and fell asleep.

*

His was a quiet slumber. He woke up at noon, to the sound of

51

church bells mixed with the whistle of a ship's siren. The first thing he noticed, with some trepidation, as soon as he opened his eyes, was a book. A paperback. He at once recognized its cover. It was the book he had stopped reading when the three events occurred at the same time: a dog's barking, Veronica's telephone ringing, and that poor Mr McPherson's knocking on the door. Now he saw a copy of the same book in the hands of a small boy, Emma's age, sitting on an ornamental iron bench, reading.

He wheeled his chair nearer to the boy.

'Excuse me. Your name is Ian, isn't it?'

'Yes, sir.'

'My name is Timothy. But you may call me Tim. Do you think you could lend me the book you are reading, when you have finished with it, of course.'

'It's a thriller, sir. A detective story.'

'Yes, I know. I have already read some of it. But then it so happened that I couldn't finish it.'

'Because of the bomb, sir?'

'So you know about the bomb . . .'

'Yes, sir. I know all about you, sir.'

'You do?'

'Yes, sir. And if you want to read the rest of the book, I can sell it to you now.'

'You can what?'

'I can sell it to you now, sir.'

'Did you say "sell it"?'

'Yes, sir. How many pages have you read already?'

'I don't know. About half the book.'

'But you must remember what you were reading when you stopped, mustn't you, sir?'

'Yes, I think I do remember. I remember that the detective said, *Good God, it's him!"*

'Oh, now I know.' The boy wetted his finger and turned a few pages. 'Here it is: *Look out! Oh, my God, it's he!*, page 124.'

'Does it matter?'

'Oh yes, sir. I'm not going to charge you for the pages you have already read.' The boy consulted the back of the cover, and the last page of the book, and said: 'The price of the book printed on the cover is £1.95, and the book has 272 pages, which means that it costs 0.717 of a penny per page. As you have already read 124 pages, sir, you need to pay only for 272 minus 124, or 148 pages, which, at 0.717 of a penny per page, makes £1.06116, which, at the average rate 184.50 pesetas to a pound, makes 195.78402, or, let's say, 196 pesetas in round figures.'

'My dear boy . . .' The man in the wheelchair looked at the boy on the iron bench with a mixture of admiration and disbelief. And fear. He was going to say something, but he didn't. He took the book, counted 196 pesetas, and gave them to the boy.

The boy stood up and said with the utmost courtesy: 'You will allow me to buy you a drink, sir.'

The man in the wheelchair smiled.

'What a good idea. May I have an orange juice, please?'

'Oh no,' the boy said. 'Orange juice will be for me. For you, sir, I recommend either an iced vodka – I was told that my father used to drink iced vodka – or else pink gin – my uncle drinks pink gin – and if Don José doesn't know how to make it, I shall be able to instruct him.'

'Pink gin sounds all right, thank you.'

It was already time for his usual whisky and soda, but he agreed to have pink gin.

The boy went across the lawn to the bar and said: 'One orange juice with ice and two straws, please, Don José, and one pink gin . . .' He lowered his voice and whispered, 'for the old buffer who is going to be my father-in-law.' A while later, he corrected Don José loudly, 'Not in that sort of glass, man! Take the other one. Yes. That's better. No! Don't pour the gin yet. Put two drops of angostura in first. That's right. Now turn the glass round and round, horizontally, to stain it pink, good, now turn it upside down to let the surplus angostura drop out, that's it, now you can pour a generous portion of gin into it. Thank you.'

He put his 196 pesetas on the counter, said loudly: 'Keep the change!' and took the drinks to the man in the wheelchair.

'Cheers, sir.'

'Cheers.'

'Before we go any further, I think I ought to tell you, sir, that I'm in love with your daughter.'

'With Emma . . . ?'

'Yes, sir.'

53

'Was it she who told you about the bomb?'

'Yes, sir.' His eyes brightened. 'Do you think I could have a look at your legs? I mean those you lock in the wardrobe?'

'So she told you about that as well?'

'Yes, sir.'

'And what did you tell her? Would you mind telling me that?'

'I told her there is always an alternative.'

'An alternative to what?'

'Well, sir, you see, she thinks that the bomb couldn't have been put there by a Palestinian because you are not a Jew, nor by an Irishman because you are not an Orangeman or an IRA-man, so it must have been put by a fascist and that would mean that you are a communist, or by a communist – which would mean that you are a fascist, and she thinks that she is against both.'

'And that's why she's been avoiding me?'

'I don't know, sir. But I told her there is an alternative.'

'An alternative?'

'Well, yes, sir. The bomb could have been sent to you by God, sir.'

'By God! Why should God want to do such a thing?'

'That I don't know, sir. But it's logical to think that everything that isn't done by man's will is done by God's will, that's to say if there is a God; my uncle, the one who drinks pink gin and is a Church of England chaplain, doesn't believe there is a God, and he says that I have a small heart, on the right side, by biological mistake or by chance, and it is our friend Dr Brzeski who says it is God who made me like that, and it is because of my small heart on the right side that I cannot ride a bicycle with Emma and am not allowed to swim, and she says I am not a genuine article.'

'She doesn't seem to be very kind to you, dear boy. Are you quite sure that you like her?'

'Oh no, sir, I haven't said I like her. I've said that I love her. That's not the same. The person I like is not Emma but your wife, sir. I told your wife everything, every single thing that makes me not a "genuine article". Not only about my small heart on the right side but also about other things, about my mother – Oh! look, sir, you can see her now, she is the lady in the green bikini water-skiing behind that boat there further to the left, do you like her, sir? She and I, we are a one-parent family because, you see, my father who drank the iced vodka was a Polish general, he was three times older than my mother, and he fired a pistol and died of a heart attack before I was born, and he left her a white Mercedes car which we still have, it is now twelve years old, and you know, sir, my mother is a palmist, she is a graduate palmist, she reads from the lines on your hand, she graduated from the Sisterhood of the Sacred Heart in Wales, and I have a half-brother who is half black and pretends to be wholly black because he is an awfully cruel dictator in Africa, and I have a half-sister who is an Italian princess, and she is a friend of a cardinal who is nearly two hundred years old, and Emma doesn't believe in the cardinal because she says nobody is two hundred years old, and of course I know nobody is, that's precisely why the cardinal is so extraordinary, and your wife says that Emma doesn't understand that I have a great poetic imagination, that this one is not the true Earth, that the true Earth is somewhere else, cruising around the sun, invisible to astronomers, and that perhaps I come from this true Earth because I am a poet, and I like your wife very much but I think she is mistaken, because I know that I am not a poet, I am a mathematician, I know because I thought up the differential calculus myself before Mr Leibniz and Sir Isaac Newton did, I mean before I learned that they did so three hundred years ago, and I'm admitted to Oxford to read maths when I'm twelve years old, next autumn, they have no minimum entry age, you know, sir? But just now I should like you to tell me, sir, what I actually mean when I say "I thought up" the calculus – do I mean that I invented it as one invents a story, or that I discovered it as one discovers what has really happened?'

'My dear boy, it depends on whether you are an axiomatic formalist who thinks that his mathematics is entirely in his head, or else a Platonist who thinks it is as real as a table though you cannot touch it with your hand.'

The boy shook his head disapprovingly.

'But sir, things like that should depend not on what I am but on what the world is. It is wrong to decide just by thinking whether at the moment when Achilles catches the tortoise the distance between his toe and its tail is zero or an infinitesimal smaller than any imaginably small distance but not zero, or that

55

at the point he catches the tortoise the length of time is zero or not zero. Perhaps the world is so made that there is a distance so small that anything smaller would have no properties of space, and perhaps there is a length of time so short that anything shorter would have no properties of time? And it is wrong to decide such things by meditation. You need a physicist to find out if there really is the tiniest indivisible dot of space and the tiniest indivisible bit of time, and if he says yes, there is, then the whole of Euclidean geometry has to be rewritten. Because Euclid's point has position but no size, but our dot has size but no shape, because it has no parts, and it has no position because it lasts for only one tiniest bit of time each time, so it is Constant Vibration, and the whole world is Constant Oscillation, and Euclid's line has no thickness and can always be divided in two halves, but our line is one dot thick and you can divide it in two halves, only if it is made of the even number of dots, and if our space and time is really made of such dots and bits, then a perfect square either cannot exist or cannot have a diagonal because no number of dots will fit it exactly, so at one bit of time the square will be a little crooked in one direction, and at the next bit of time it will be crooked in another direction, and it will vibrate and the whole universe will oscillate, and, for Euclid, what happens to his figures does not depend on their size, a small circle is for him as ideal as a big circle, but for us even the value of π will be changing because when the circle is very small and its circumference is made of only six dots, the circle becomes a hexagon and the π for such a tiny hexagonal circle will be exactly 2, but I don't know if it will still be vibrating or if it will stop vibrating, things like that cannot be found by thinking, they must be found by finding, and so perhaps I should become a physicist and not a mathematician. You know, sir, some people think that a twelve-year-old boy is too young to go to university, but there are so many things one has to find out about the universe and life is so short; if I become a physicist, perhaps I'll find out that one dot of space per one bit of time is the only velocity that exists in the cosmos, and all the slower speeds are made by moving two dots forward and one dot backward or ten dots forward and nine dots backward or sideways so that the whole universe is made of such vibrations, of which one dot forward and one dot backward would be what we call "perfect stability", and, you see, sir, maybe I'll find that my half-sister's – Princess Zuppa's – friend's, the cardinal's, calculation is all right? He assumed, sir, that a human ovum must be naturally somewhere in the centre of the universe, halfway between the two infinities: the greatest and the smallest, and, as the radius of the human ovum is 10^{30} times smaller than the radius of the universe, then the smallest distance in the universe must be 10^{30} times smaller than the human ovum, or 10^{-32} cm, which is very nearly what is called Planck Distance, which is 10^{-33} cm, and if my dot of space is the same as Planck Distance, then perhaps my bit of time is the same as Planck Time, which is 10^{-44} second, and perhaps we should measure everything now in bits and dots and say there are 10^{33} dots of space in one centimetre and 10^{44} bits of time in one second but, you know, sir, things like that cannot be given *ex cathedra* by a philosopher from his wheelchair, they must be found by a physicist, and even that is not enough so long as we don't know what there is in the physicist who finds them, so perhaps I should become a biologist who would study the physicist who studies the universe, but that I couldn't do, sir, no! I could not, because biology is so bloody, so messy, so ugly, all living things are so ugly . . .' He raised his voice and repeated, 'So ugly!'

'But why, my dear boy? Look at that bird there, soaring in the sky, look at the people sunbathing, swimming . . . they are all lovely to look at, are they not?'

'Yes, sir. They are lovely to look at. But they are ugly under the skin. All that blood and guts and glands and cells killing fighting devouring growing dying. They are ugly. Ethically ugly. You do see what I mean, sir.'

'I do, yes, I do indeed, dear boy, and do call me Tim, please, we are friends, and it is my turn to order drinks. Another orange juice? Or what about an ice-cream?'

But the boy didn't seem to have heard the question.

'Tim?' he asked.

'Yes, Ian?'

'If you are going to tell Emma that I love her, you don't need to add that I don't like her, do you?'

'Of course not.'

The boy kicked his sandals off.

'I'm going to have a swim,' he said.

'Should you? Didn't you say that you are not allowed to swim?'

'I'm only going to paddle.'

But he was already pulling his T-shirt off. His skin was pale and smooth as if it had never seen the light of this sunny island.

'Ian?'

'Yes?'

'Wouldn't you rather finish the book you were reading?'

'I'll borrow it from you when you've finished with it.'

'Ian?'

'Yes?'

'Don't go swimming, please. If you want to, we can go to my room and I'll show you my legs. They are technically beautiful and ethically harmless.'

But the boy was already walking with slow steps in the water. He didn't paddle along the edge of the lawn. He went straight on, till the water reached his shoulders. Then he stopped and lifted his arms. 'So he is going to swim nevertheless,' Timothy thought. But the boy's movements were unnaturally awkward and Timothy got frightened. His body jerked up in its wheelchair as if it wanted to run forward, but his legs were phantom legs. So he turned to the right and shouted: 'Don José! Look! The boy! Help!' Don José had already jumped over the counter and was now splashing his way to where the boy had disappeared under the water. All this took just a few seconds. And here he is, Don José, carrying the boy in his arms, and laying him gently on the lawn by the wheelchair. 'Kiss of life, quick!' Timothy said. But Don José stood there helplessly, his eyes filled with tears. 'Put me down!' Timothy commanded. Don José lifted him from the wheelchair and put him down on the lawn. Timothy opened the boy's mouth, took a deep breath, sealed his lips round the boy's lips, pinched his nostrils together and blew his own air into the boy's lungs. Again and again. Every four seconds.

And then Don José found a doctor. She was a German lady, *die Ärztin*, a big athletic blonde, still in her bathing robe over the bathing costume. She knelt and gave the boy a smart slap on the chest. Then she waved Timothy off, put her own lips to the boy's mouth, at the same time pressing and depressing the

58

lower half of his breastbone. Six pressings on the lower ribs to one exhaled-air inflation of the lungs.

'The boy's heart is very small and it is on his right side,' Timothy said, not sure whether it was of some importance, or not.

The *Ärztin* didn't take any notice of it. Perhaps she didn't understand? He tried to recollect his long-forgotten German, and said: '*Des Knabes Herz ist klein aber es ist an seine rechte Seite.*'

He didn't know why he said *aber* instead of saying *und*. He wouldn't have made that sort of mistake in English.

EIGHT
The Dancing Ladies

The Dancing Ladies had their five o'clock tea at precisely half-past four in the afternoon. Every day, except on Saturdays, when the ritual was changed. On Saturdays they slept in the afternoon, to be fresh and rested for their evening dance in the hotel ballroom. The tea was Darjeeling, bought from Captain Casanova's Casa Nueva village shop, served from an old silver teapot, and with assorted biscuits in a big round tin box, bought there also. 'Do come, Veronica. You must come. They can't possibly know how to make tea in the hotel. You must, whenever you feel like it. This is a standing invitation.'

She had tea with them three times. The first time it was sad and pleasant. The second time it was indifferent. The third time it was awful.

When she visited them the first time, they asked her about the bomb; they hadn't heard about it before at all so it was sad because it *was* sad but it was pleasant because it was good to be able to put things in words and make them sound so impersonal, like the news in a newspaper.

'And have they caught the bastards?'

'No, they haven't.'

'But do they know who they are?'

'Perhaps they do, but they don't say.'

'And what about that young man who was killed? Who was he?'

'But you must know. You've met him.'

'No! How come?'

'Well, he was here, wasn't he? Tim told me, and the police, that the poor boy was writing a thesis on your husband and was seeing you here.'

'Good Lord! So it was him. And he was killed. Do you remember him, Marjorie?'

'Of course I do. He wanted to know what was the colour of the Great Man's eyes. And we didn't remember.'

'Didn't you?'

'No.'

'He should have asked me. I do.'

'Do you?'

'Yes.'

'And did you tell him?'

'How could I? I've never seen him. I mean, I've never seen him alive.'

'You haven't?'

'No. I took Emma to school that morning, and then I went to my hairdresser, and it was there, as I was having my hair done, that I heard the ambulance, and the police, and the fire brigade passing by, and I didn't know they were rushing to my house.'

'How awful!'

'Quite. And his poor parents. Mr and Mrs McPherson. Such a dear old couple. They were short, both exactly the same size, and masses of white hair and the same pink faces, looked more like brother and sister, more like twins, than like husband and wife. They came all the way from Carlisle to fetch the body. Brought the boy's girlfriend with them. Called her his fiancée. And Mrs McPherson thought that the girl was pregnant and she begged her on her knees to have the child and to give it to her when it was born.'

'How was she so sure that it would be her son's child?'

'Oh, Marjorie, how can you?' Veronica said.

*

When she went to have tea with them on the next occasion, the Great Man's widow turned to the Great Man's secretary, and said: 'You know, Marjorie, had I married Tim, as at the time I thought of doing, Veronica would have married the Great Man, and it is she who would now be the Great Man's widow.' She sighed, mockingly. And added, 'And poor Mr McPherson wouldn't have died without knowing the colour of the Great Man's eyes.'

'Not very funny,' Veronica said.

'It wasn't meant to be funny at all, my dear Veronica. It was my deep philosophical reflection on the ways of this world. Had the Great Man put it in the right kind of words, it would now be quoted in the best literary journals of the old country.'

'Don't you two long for the old country sometimes?' Veronica asked.

'No,' Marjorie said curtly.

'All we need from the old country we can get from Captain Casanova,' the widow said.

'But . . .'

'Have some more tea,' Marjorie said, and it sounded like: mind your own business.

'But . . .' Veronica turned to the widow, 'but your children are still there, are they not?'

She said 'your children' because she didn't remember their names.

'The umbilical cord is cut, my dear Veronica.' She said 'my dear Veronica', but she was looking at Marjorie. It was somewhat funny that both women were looking all the time at each other, even when talking to Veronica. Slightly funny but also a trifle disconcerting. 'My children have their own, independent life, my dear Veronica. The girl bought herself five pairs of orange tights, orange knickers, orange *soutiens-gorge*, and went to India. She has enough money of her own to be of some interest to her guru. And the boy . . . When he was very young he used to be disapproving of his father. Then, when his father died, he disapproved of me. He disapproves of my remarriage.'

'Have you remarried?' Veronica asked.

'Well, I am married to Marjorie, am I not?'

*

When she called on them for the third time, she knew, as soon as they opened the door, that it would be awful. She forgot that it was Saturday, Saturday afternoon, the time they rested in preparation for the evening dance. She wanted to retreat at once, but they said, 'No, do come in, we are having our tea anyway,' and they enveloped her lavishly with the sweet fragrance of lavender, the welcoming warmth, and the mature nakedness exuding through the lightness of their peignoirs, one roseate, the other lapis lazuli. This time they didn't have

62

their tea in the loggia open to the garden. This time they arranged it in the small drawing room which they called 'our cosy *petit salon*'. It had a curious shape. It was pentagonal.

They made her sit on a Sheraton chair under the wall, after which they pushed a round table towards her so that the edge of the top touched her stomach, and when they too sat, one on her left, the other on her right, she felt trapped. She wouldn't be able to budge now without moving the table, disturbing her peignoired hostesses, or breaking down the wall behind her. She saw her own face reflected jeeringly in the silver teapot and hastily looked up. There, hanging between two narrow windows, full of green sunshine coming from the garden, was a picture. She knew it. *'Les dames à la baignoire.' La baignoire* meant, of course, a bathtub. But with all those curtains draped in folds above it, she thought it was more exciting to see it as a box in the theatre, a royal box with two topless ladies of great beauty, the one on the left (was it Gabrielle d'Estrée?) touching with such exquisite elegance the nipple of the right breast of the other lady (was it la Duchesse de Villas?) – actually, not only touching, holding it between her thumb and her finger. Now, Veronica blushed: Is this what Marjorie and the Great Man's widow do in their bathroom? She blushed at the thought of it and then, to her surprise, she recollected what she herself had done when she had noticed the newspaper boy peeping at her through the letterbox – and she blushed again.

'You must be telepathic, Veronica,' the Great Man's widow said.

'Why?'

'Well, I'm going to ask you something, and you blush before I open my mouth.'

'I know what she is going to ask you,' Marjorie said.

'Shut up, Marjorie,' the widow said.

'She's going to ask you if Captain Casanova has already made a pass at you too?' Marjorie said.

'Why do you say that? Why should he?'

'My dear Veronica,' the widow said, 'Captain Casanova makes advances to each and every pretty tourist girl who comes here. Whenever you find the door to his shop locked, it means there is a lady in his bedroom upstairs. As Marjorie here can tell you.'

'Ha, ha,' Marjorie said.

'But I must warn you that he never makes love twice to the same person.'

'He thinks it's safer not to,' Marjorie said.

'No,' the widow said. 'He thinks that if it is just once, it doesn't count. Repeating it with the same female would make him feel that he's being unfaithful to his wife.'

'Is he married?' Veronica asked.

'Yes and no.'

'How do you mean?'

'His wife died some twelve years ago. But it doesn't seem to make much difference to his marital qualms about sex.'

'He killed her,' Marjorie said.

'Nonsense. It was an accident. And anyway, I've warned you.'

'I don't think I needed to be warned.'

'Of course not. Nothing was further from my mind.'

'It's Tim she has on her mind, not you,' Marjorie said.

'I don't know what you two are talking about,' Veronica said.

'Of course not,' Marjorie said.

'Have some more tea,' the widow said.

'Thank you.'

'It's a good hotel where you are staying. I hope you are comfortable.'

'Oh yes, quite.'

'You must be. You have those two beautiful rooms on the ground floor, don't you? Tim sleeps in one, and you with Emma in the other.'

'You seem to be quite well informed,' Veronica said.

'Emma is a very intelligent little girl,' the widow said.

'You haven't been questioning Emma?'

'Questioning?! My dear Veronica, of course not! Here, one doesn't need to question anybody. In a little place like this, one just knows. One knows when people do things they shouldn't, or don't do things they should.'

'For instance?' Veronica asked, though there was something in her that warned her not to.

'Well, it's no use beating about the bush, Veronica. Don't you see that a man in Tim's condition needs sex more than any other man? That he must reassert himself?'

'It's no use to talk to her,' Marjorie said. 'I know the type. For her it's either the missionary position or not at all.'

64

'What are you talking about?' Veronica looked at them in confusion. 'Tim never wanted to be a missionary.'

'Good Lord!' Marjorie exclaimed.

'"Ignorance, madam, pure ignorance",' the widow quoted.

'Do you really think she doesn't know?' asked Marjorie.

'My dear Veronica,' the Great Man's widow said. 'For your edification: "the missionary position" is the Christian way of making love, man on top of the woman, face to face. Poor Tim obviously must have it done to him differently.'

'It's no use talking to her. She wouldn't hear of such a thing,' Marjorie said.

'You shut up, Marjorie,' the widow said.

'She wouldn't let *us* do it to him either.'

'Stop it, Marjorie,' the widow said.

'She would rather let him sit there, on the beach, among all those gorgeous bodies, and masturbate in his wheelchair.'

She wanted to vanish. To disappear from the face of the earth. But the secret of how to become invisible she did not possess. So she wanted to *do* something spontaneous. But when she pushed the table in front of her, she did it carefully, not to upset the tea things. And when she stood up and walked to the door, she wanted to *say* something spontaneously. But nothing spontaneous came to her mind. 'I'm afraid I really ought to be pushing along now,' she said. 'And thank you for my tea,' she added. That's what she was told to say when taking leave, once upon a time, when she was a little girl.

65

NINE
Captain Casanova

The little van came all the way from Palma. It moved gaily like a light cavalry horse, and the driver could have been taken for a hussar, as he reined in, dismounted, and ran with a bundle of newspapers towards the front door of Captain Casanova's shop.

'Hi!' he said; the form of greeting he must have learned from American films watched on television.

'Hi,' Captain Casanova answered.

The hussar slammed the bundle down on the counter. THE DAILY TELEGRAPH, THE TIMES, THE GUARDIAN, LE MONDE, LE FIGARO, JOURNAL DE GENEVE, ALLGEMEINE ZEITUNG. All two days old.

'Any returns?'

'No.'

From the drawer below the counter, Captain Casanova took a packet of condoms and handed it to the hussar. It was his customary weekly tip.

'Much obliged,' the hussar said. 'Ta ta!'

It was Sunday. And Sundays were difficult. Especially Sunday mornings. Because on Sunday morning nobody bothered to come and the shop was empty. And he liked to have people around him. Because then, when he had people around him, he was indeed what they thought he was. That's to say, he was naturally, effortlessly, what they thought he was. Which was not always the case when he was alone. Though it's true that if one were to look at him through the chinks in the shutters of the shop, or through the keyhole of his bathroom upstairs, one would see the same bright crisp fellow in his early forties, clad in a T-shirt with bright horizontal stripes, informal slacks and sandals, and yet unmistakably a soldier, whose military posture and air of authority, aura of command, in combination with his kindly face and the hands ready to open the door for you, pick up a lady's handkerchief, or pour a glass of wine, made one feel: here is a man, a gentleman, who can be relied on in a crisis. But if one tried to listen, one would be likely to hear him muttering away to himself. Some such words as 'Bloody politicians . . .' 'Bloody press . . .' For the last twelve years, since his own name (his real name) had appeared in black ink on the front pages, he would mutter some such words as 'bloody politicians', or 'bloody press' every Sunday morning when the new pile of newspapers appeared on the counter. He had to switch to an electric shaver because as he muttered 'Bloody politicians', his hand would jerk uncontrollably, and even his safety razor wasn't safe enough. Nature had filled him with a joy of living, made him expansive, open, vigorous – that's how he was at school, that's how he was in the army, and that's how he was even now, effortlessly and naturally when he had other people around him, but with difficulty when he was alone. Because when he was alone, especially on Sunday mornings, he was invaded by his own thoughts which tried to remodel his character into something that he disliked, despised, when he saw its traces in other people. Thus, in order to be what he really was, straightforward and uncomplaining, he had to defend himself against his own mind which, when he was alone, forced upon him some unwelcome snapshots and noises and isolated words from the past, making him feel as if he had a bad conscience, which he had not, as if he were guilty, which he was not. Of course not. There was a physical impossibility of it being anything else than an accident. A physical impossibility . . . ? No, a physical possibility there was, but there was a non-physical impossibility, of that he had no doubt, because he loved her, and that would have made it impossible. That was the non-physical thing he knew. But the only physical thing he knew on that fateful day, twelve years ago, when he stood there in the telephone box by a country lane – was what he saw; and what he saw was the telephone box, and ambulances, and police cars, and the man standing at the door of the telephone box asking, *Does he remember that he phoned to report the accident?* No, he doesn't. *Does he remember that there was an accident?* No. What accident? *Can he tell why there is not a scratch on him?* No. Why

67

should there be? *Who was driving the car, he or his wife? Wife? Can they tell him please what it is all about? Was he at the wheel when the car hit the tree, went down the slope into the bushes and overturned, or did he jump out before it all happened?* The tree? Tree? What tree? He had never seen any trees! *How did he walk to the telephone box he is in now, up the slope or along the road? Could he show the soles of his shoes, please? Did he notice that Lady Constance, his wife, was wounded? Does he know that she is dead?* Oh God. No! They called it amnesia. Some of them believed him. Some didn't. Her brother, who was a bloody politician, didn't. Still, they had no proof. Either way. So they started looking for a motive. A motive. He was lucky (what a tragic word, lucky! Ha ha) that she had left all her money to her brother. So money wasn't a motive. Motive. But they went on hounding him, because she was a titled lady and her brother was a bloody politician, so the thing made good headlines, as it was not yet *sub judice,* and they were hunting high and low, and they unearthed the fact that she had a lover, and the lover was a bloody exile, from a bloody enemy country, and they weren't sure whether he was a bloody dissident, or a bloody spy, or nothing at all, but all the same they tally-ho! So ho! Yoicks! on the radio and in the press, but they couldn't prove he knew she had a lover, though the experts said he must have know sub-consciously because he loved her, which he did, and still does, Good God, whom else does he have to love if not her, though she is dead, dead, dead, lover or no lover, and though they couldn't prove anything, there were too many innuendoes, the message was loud and clear, and he, Captain Bridgewater, now better known as Captain Casanova, had to resign his commission, get out of the army, and of the country, and himself become an exile, like the bloody lover, though no, he's a British exile, which makes a great deal of difference because, exile or not, he is British and proud of it, he doesn't go round, cap in hand, begging, playing the martyr, and doing his best to spit at and spite his own country, no, *his* country right or wrong, that's the spirit, because for him, for the exiled Captain Casanova, his country isn't the bloody government and the bloody politicians, not the House of Lords and the House of Commons, not Big Business and the Press and the Trade Union Barons, for him, his country is the Queen, and the Army, and the Ordinary

People, that's what *his* country is for him, for better for worse, even if he *is* a bloody exile and will never go back home to the old country to pay taxes and have his legs blown off like that poor devil who came here in a wheelchair with a kid and a pretty wife, now, Good Lord! talk of the devil and here she comes . . .

As the water in the electric kettle started to boil, he switched the kettle off and, lifting his eyes to the shop window on the right of the door, he looked through the space between the packets of cereals and bits of diving gear, and saw Veronica coming up the road. The kettle in his hand, he watched – will she pass by the door and go further up the hill, or will she stop? She stopped, opened the door, and came in.

He could not be sure – did she say, 'Good morning' or not? Maybe that's why he said it twice, 'Good morning, good morning,' echoing his own voice. He knew her Christian name was Veronica, but he had forgotten her surname. She was wearing a T-shirt, white slacks, and blue plimsolls. It was the T-shirt that he noticed first, because it was the twin sister of the one he was wearing, though its horizontal stripes curved differently round her full bust. She walked straight to the counter and sat down on one of two wooden chairs in front of it. A fat ginger cat was curled up on the other chair. Without a word, she stroked the cat's furry neck with the tip of her finger. But her thoughts were somewhere else. So were the thoughts of the cat, who didn't move. She glanced at the pile of newspapers but she didn't see the words. Her eyes moved along the shelves but she didn't seem to see what was on them. She had no shopping bag. She didn't look like a customer who had come to buy something.

He was going to ask, 'What can I do for you,' but, instead, he said: 'I'm just making coffee. Will you have a cup?'

'Yes, please.'

'Black?'

'Yes.'

'Sugar?'

'Yes.'

He hesitated for a moment. And then he said: 'Shall I lace it with a little brandy?'

'Yes, please.'

They sipped their coffee silently, she on her side of the counter, he on his.

69

And then she said: 'I've just met a madman. I'm sure I've already seen his face sometime somewhere but I can't place it. Do you know who he is?'

'Should I?'

'Well, he said he bought a tin of sardines from you. Yesterday.'

Captain Casanova took a glance at one of the shelves. 'There was a chap, yes . . . Nondescript sort of chap. Good English. 'V'never seen him before. Or since. Was he a nuisance?'

'No. Quite polite. Asked did I know where he could find a sardine factory, meaning a place where they pack sardines. I said there was nothing of the sort here. Was I wrong. Is there?' she asked.

'No. You were right. There isn't,' the Captain reassured her.

'I'm glad I didn't mislead him. He looked very disappointed. Took a tin of sardines from his pocket and made me read what was printed on the label: *Packed at factories at Portimao Peniche Sines and Matosinhos*, and asked, *What about those places? How do I get there?* So I said, "But those places are in Portugal." To which he said, *But we are in Portugal, aren't we?* I said, "No." And he said, *What were you pleased to say?* So I repeated, "No. Portugal is far away in the west. On the other side of Spain. On the Atlantic." He looked at me suspiciously for a moment, and then said *I believe you,* but he said it in such a tone of voice as if I were the only person in the whole world whom he would consent to believe. And then he said that when he came down from the north to a place called Valencia, that was how he put it: *a place called Valencia*, his instructions were to turn right and go on walking, but he must have turned left, and that's why he finds himself in the wrong point with regard to the coordinates, which doesn't surprise him, after all, because it is very difficult for him to distinguish between our left and our right, *very difficult indeed*, he said. It took me a minute, or two, or three, to notice that he had said something strange. He said that in Valencia he turned left and went on walking till he arrived here. Walking on the sea? A hundred and fifty miles? I turned round to ask him, but he was no longer there.'

'Well, yes,' Captain Casanova said, 'we do have some eccentrics coming here every season. Mad Hatters. Harmless, mostly,' he added, 'mad in patches.'

There was a faint sound of bells coming from a chapel in the neighbouring village, or from a wireless set perched somewhere on a window-sill of one of the villas up the hill, or from a church submerged by the sea? The ginger cat jumped from the chair on to the counter and pricked up its ears.

'Do you go to church on Sunday mornings?' she asked.

'No. Not really.'

'Neither do I.'

Her blue eyes looked at him as if he were a page of a book opened at random – a novel, a railway timetable, a dictionary? It was he who averted his eyes first.

'Do you read poetry?' she asked.

'No.'

'Neither do I. It's silly to read poetry. Poetry is not for reading. Poetry is for writing.'

'Do you write poetry?' Captain Casanova asked.

'No. I don't. This earth is phony enough without any poetry.'

'This earth?'

'Yes.'

'You mean it is not real?'

'Oh no. It is real enough. Fakes are always real. They have to be. They are the proof that the true thing exists. When you see a faked Picasso you know there must be a true Picasso somewhere. You can't have a false Picasso without having a true Picasso first, can you?'

Captain Casanova preferred not to pronounce on the subject of Picasso.

'The same with this earth,' she went on. 'This earth is all false, isn't it? That means the true Earth must be somewhere, mustn't it? I used to think it is there, in the sky, a little globe turning round the sun, very quickly. Invisible. I even thought that I spotted it once or twice, with my naked eye, a long time ago, well, not so long ago, a few months, before all that happened, you know what, the bomb . . .'

'It must have been terrible . . .'

'It was.'

Then she added: 'And is.'

And then, without a pause, in the same tone of voice she went on: 'I heard that if one finds the door to your shop locked, it means there is a lady in your bedroom upstairs.'

'You shouldn't listen to what people say.'

71

'But it's true, isn't it?'

'Well, occasionally.'

'Then be good enough to lock the door, Captain.'

He looked at her. No, she wasn't joking. She got up, walked to the end of the counter, turned round it as if she knew the topography of the place by heart, found a tiny kitchen and, beside it, the bottom of the flight of stairs. Without hesitation, she started to climb up.

For him, to speculate upon her thoughts and feelings would be most ungentlemanly. To examine his own – would be un-soldierly, unBritish, unhealthy. He put a pile of newspapers on one of the chairs, took it outside, and left it there in front of the shop door. He put a stone on top, as a paperweight, and a wooden bowl for customers to put their money in. Then he came back, closed the door behind him, turned the key and shot the bolt. He washed his hands in the little kitchen and went up the stairs.

Did Captain Casanova choose for his shop this most unsuit-able, enormously long and gloomy building, because it reminded him of the barracks, which it might actually have been before he took it over? Was it he who added to it the flight of stairs and the room to which it led, built in a somewhat architecturally curious way, neither attic nor entresol nor mezzanine, the floor of the room being below and the ceiling above the level of the roof of the 'barracks', so that when you bent down and looked from the room through a little window-pane fixed in the lower part of the door, you saw the interior of the shop, and when you straightened yourself up and looked through a similar window-pane in the upper part of the door, you saw the 'barracks' roof and the sky, you saw it through a complicated geometry of many sheets of perspex, suspended above the landing and joining the roof of the 'barracks' with the roof above the room.

The room itself was austere but not at all gloomy. Its only window, open to the green slopes of the hills, was facing north, but the room was filled with the morning brightness reflected by the whitewashed walls. Under the window stood a narrow single bed covered with a tartan bedspread. By the bed, on a bedside table, an electric gadget combining a teamaker with a bedside light, an alarm clock, and a two-band radio. (His TV box was in the shop downstairs.) Facing you, as you entered the

72

room, there was a big writing-desk, a drinks cabinet, a few shelves filled with books, and, among some snapshots pinned to the wall above the desk, a Victoria Cross posthumously awarded to his father. On the left, against the south wall, a wardrobe, a chest of drawers and, between them, the door to the bathroom. A square of red carpet in front of it. That's where she was standing now, stark naked. Her T-shirt and slacks neatly folded on the chair by the writing-desk. Her plimsolls in a V position under the chair.

'No, please don't touch me,' she said, before he had time to move his hand. And before he had time to open his mouth, she said, 'Please don't say anything, Captain, and please, please, lie down on the bed and don't be afraid, I shall not hurt you.' It was the first time in his life (anyway, the first time since as a little boy he was taken to the dentist) that a man – or a woman! – had told him, 'Don't be afraid, I shall not hurt you.' Amused, he tried to hide his smile, and obediently lay down. She did not smile. Bending over him, she pulled his T-shirt up to his chin. He helped her by lifting himself an inch on his elbows. Then she unzipped his slacks and pulled them down to just above his knees. 'No,' she said when he tried to lift his legs to make it easier for her, 'don't move. It's all right now. I don't want them lower than this.' And she pulled the zip up to tighten the belt of the slacks around his legs, just above the knees.

'Now,' he thought, 'let's see which way the cat jumps. Is it going to be funny? Or mad?'

It was neither.

Her blue unwinking eyes looked at him steadily as she said, 'Now, Captain, please show me how to make love to my poor husband.'

*

The first person who came to buy a newspaper was Judge Ghrandt (divorce court). Seeing the door closed, he fingered through the pile of papers deposited on the chair in search of the pink pages of the *Financial Times*. Having found none, he looked through the window of the shop and spotted a copy left there on the counter. He knocked on the door and waited. As there was no answer, he resigned himself to the second best, which was *The Times*. He put 150 pesetas in the bowl (which was a lot of money for a two-day-old newspaper) and started on his way back to the hotel.

EVERY SECOND A CHILD DIES OF HUNGER
SOMEWHERE IN THE WORLD

Did his eye catch that sentence when his fingers were going through the papers, or was it his ear that picked it up when listening to the BBC World Service in the morning? He couldn't be certain.

Pacing unhurryingly down the road, he started to count his steps, one, two, three, four, five . . . At ninety-six he stopped. Ninety-six seconds. Ninety-six children have just died. No, it was very childish of him to allow himself to go for such kinds of truth. That was the sort of feeling he occasionally had in court when the procedure seemed to be correct and yet he *knew* that there was something wrong somewhere. And he had to suppress that feeling because he knew that he was powerless, that it was hopeless even to analyse what it was. Because that something wrong was not man-made. Or was it? Well, anyway . . . What does He actually want one to do? Does He want one not to eat one's lunch? Does He want one to call the waiter and tell him: *Camarero*, make a parcel of my luncheon please and have it sent to a child in Africa or Asia?

Sitting on the Bench had taught him the art of producing a ventral guffaw, coarse and loud within his corpulence yet inaudible from without. Laughter, he thought, was a part of being serious. Seriousness without a bit of laughter cannot be truly true. When his father was born, the population of the world was 1,500 million. When he, the Judge, was born, it was 2,000 million. Now it is 5,000 million. When his father was born, to have children was an asset. Today, it was a grief. He chuckled. To himself. He was the only son. And he had only one child, a daughter. So *he* didn't feel personally responsible for contributing to that surplus of 3,000 million souls who cannot feed their own bodies. Not that he accepts that it is a man-made problem. No. The only thing man can do about it is to geld or to cull the surplus. He grinned. That's the logic of it. Bizarre, bizarre, bizarre! Take such human beings as, for instance, biophysicists. They torture their animals in their refined laboratories, but

74

when you ask them to manufacture a species of mosquito, louse, flea, or bedbug whose bite would produce sterility among the superfluous 3,000 million human underdogs, they feel squeamish. On the other hand, take such chaps as nuclear scientists who wouldn't hurt a fly and who ask their wives to go to the butcher because they themselves cannot look at the sight of raw meat, no, they don't have any qualms about taking money for building gadgets that would liquidate the bloody 3,000 million at one go. Well, yes, that's the logic of it.

He bent down and took off his left shoe to shake sand out of it. He was wearing black patent leather shoes, black silk socks, lightweight black striped trousers, a black alpaca jacket, and a black bow tie. A bright canary waistcoat was the only indication of holiday. He laced up his shoe again and had some difficulty in straightening up. From his watch pocket he took out a little bottle labelled GLYCERYL TRINITRATE, unscrewed it, and placed a tiny white tablet under his tongue. Prophylactically. 'Well, that's the logic of it,' he repeated. When on the Bench, conducting a case, he celebrated Logic. She was his Muse, and his Traffic Light.

Actually, he would distinguish two kinds of logic. He called one Perfect Logic, and the other Good Logic. They were not always in agreement with each other. Sometimes they were like cog wheels, Plato's Heaven and Dante's Earth, rotating each other in opposite directions. His Perfect Logic would start from some firm convictions and march remorselessly forward, goose step by goose step, *coûte que coûte*, to some final solution. His Good Logic was different. It had safeguards built into it in case the axioms were wrong. His axioms were spelt out in the Statute book. They could be changed only by an Act of Parliament. Thus, when he saw that the perfect logical conclusion was going to be unjust to the man, the woman, or the child, he, the judge, unable to change the Act of Parliament, would cheat by mincing the steps of his logic, and that's why he called it 'good'. Because (and here he would quote Queen Victoria?) *'Goodness is the only thing that never loses its value.'* That's what he was musing upon at the moment but what he was actually dreaming of at the same time was to find himself in his room, in the hotel, as soon as possible, of lying down, and asking his wife to help him take off his patent leather shoes. And he would have

75

quickened his pace but for a female voice which tore him out of his double reverie: 'Good morning, Judge.'

From the ticket pocket of his canary waistcoat he took out a monocle and clapped it to his myopic eye.

'Good morning, Mrs Massgrave.'

That's how he imagined the Mancunian lady's name should be spelt. 'Mightn't her maiden name be De'Ath?' he asked himself, and panicked, and stepped back, and then nearly giggled as she thrust her pink parasol at the copy of *The Times* he had in his pocket.

'So you've got your paper, Judge. So the Captain's shop is open, is it?'

'Well, not really. The shop is closed, actually. But he kindly left some papers outside for us. A sort of self service.'

'Any German papers? Did you notice, Judge?'

'German papers? Do you read German papers, Mrs Massgrave?'

'Certainly not. It's that pretty Frau Doktor. She said she would like a *Zeitung*. So I'm going to buy one for her.'

'That's very civil of you, Mrs Massgrave,' he said, and here he gave one of his wicked little laughs.

'You call it civil, Judge? I call it Christian.'

'Christian?'

'Christian forgiveness. It's high time, isn't it? It's already nearly forty years, isn't it?'

'Forty years?'

'Forty since we were fighting them. Isn't it odd, Judge? And so true. I mean that we've had nearly forty years of peace, and that because we've got those devilish bombs, well, it is odd and true at the same time, isn't it, Judge?'

'My dear Mrs Massgrave. You can't possibly mean that we owe our peace with the Germans to our nuclear arsenal. Surely, we owe it to the French and the Germans themselves, who made themselves into the European Community, based not on the rhetoric of the League of Nations, and not on the arms race, but on the matter-of-fact Common Market.'

Mrs Massgrave's pink parasol burst open with a vengeance.

'Don't twist my words, Judge. I wasn't talking about the Germans, was I? I was talking about the Russians, wasn't I? You don't mean to say that we shan't have a war with the Russians if we give up our bombs and let them build that gas pipe all the way from Asia down to those French communists. You don't think that, do you?'

'Dear Mrs Massgrave. You know very well that what I think doesn't make the slightest difference. Does it?'

'Well, it's time I took myself off,' she said. 'See you later.'

'Alligator,' the Judge said when she was out of hearing. He said it with a superior smirk, of which he was immediately ashamed.

The church bells were ringing again, but now their tintinnabulation was torn by the whistle of a ship's siren.

Poor Mrs Massgrave was sorely distressed by her quarrel with the Judge. It was so utterly disagreeable. It gnawed at her heart that it was she herself who had broached the subject, thus breaking her own sacred sociability rule never to discuss Money, Religion and Politics with friends. But, really! the Judge *was* such a strange character, wasn't he? She had never seen anybody like him, had she? Wasn't he really more like one of those TV personalities than like a real judge. Which, after all, he wasn't, was he? He didn't send thieves and spies and sex maniacs and murderers to prison, as real judges do, did he? He was a divorce judge, wasn't he? Good Lord! How many dirty stories he must have heard when sitting on the Bench?! Mrs Massgrave knew something about it. Because Mrs Massgrave too was divorced. But the judge who divorced *her* was a real gentleman. Actually it was a decree nisi and was never made absolute because her poor husband had died in the meantime, hadn't he? And what it was all about, Mrs Massgrave wasn't sure she remembered. She put her pink parasol into her right hand and looked curiously at her left palm. She didn't know which palm was more important, the left or the right. That nice Miss Prentice had promised to examine the lines on Mrs Massgrave's palm and tell her her past and her future. She, nice Miss Prentice, was going to do it socially, without payment, though she used to be a professional palmist, no, not now, when she was younger, before she lost her powers when she was pregnant with Ian, she had told Mrs Massgrave all about it, all except who Ian's father was, and Mrs Massgrave was left wondering who Ian's father might have been, because Miss Prentice was so beautiful and strong, athletic, in her green bikini water-skiing behind a motor-boat, while her little son

77

Ian was so thin and pale, and Mrs Massgrave had absolutely nothing against one-parent families, but all the same it wouldn't cost Miss Prentice anything if she took into consideration other people's feelings and called herself not Miss but Mrs Prentice, would it? And then, not knowing why or what for, Mrs Massgrave started counting her steps: left right, left right, one, two, three, four, five . . .

For millions of years no creature, human or not human, had counted its steps on that particular stretch of the road, and then, suddenly, it happened twice the same morning. First the Judge, and now Mrs Massgrave. The only difference was that he counted his steps when going down the road, and she counted hers when going up. It may well be that such a coincidence can occur only once in a million years. But if something *can* occur once in a million years, then it is as likely to occur this year as in the year a million years hence. This, however, is a digression. Mrs Massgrave was not aware of all that. She counted her steps from one to twenty and then stopped and continued her walk without counting.

It was as the Judge told her. The shop was closed. But there were some newspapers displayed on the chair outside. She took her *Daily Telegraph* from the top of the pile and fished out a copy of a German *Zeitung* (any German *Zeitung* would do, wouldn't it?) for the Frau Doktor. She wasn't sure how much money to put into the bowl for the German paper and she decided that the price shouldn't be more than that of the *Telegraph*, should it? and if it was then let the Frau Doktor sort it out with the Captain tomorrow. She again tried the handle of the door, though she knew that the door was locked. Then she walked round the building and had a look. The door to the garage was left ajar and she saw that the Captain's car was there, which meant that the Captain couldn't be very far away. But that, of course, was none of her business, she told herself not without some pride. The pink parasol in one hand, the two newspapers in the other, she started down the road. The road was empty, except for one solitary bicycle pedalling towards her. 'What a silly girl,' Mrs Massgrave said, and when the bicycle came nearer, she shouted: 'You're not in England! Here you ride on the right, Emma!'

The girl shrugged her thin shoulders, and the bicycle zigzagged. That was the time, the period, the epoch in her life when she would shrug her shoulders at anything, at least ten times a day. So she shrugged her shoulders, straightened the bicycle and went on on the left side of the road up to the shop. She wasn't going there to buy a newspaper. She wanted to buy a comb. So she rattled the door handle and knocked at the window and rang the bell of her bicycle, and then shrugged her shoulders. She didn't know why she wanted to buy a comb. She knew for whom she wanted to buy it but she didn't know why. She wanted to buy it for Ian. It was yesterday, just before dinnertime, she was sitting on her bed in her room, and Ian was sitting beside her, and the silly boy was kissing her on the lips, and she thought, she didn't know why, that she would buy the silly boy a comb. And at that moment Veronica came into the room and stood there in front of them, and it was so hot, and she stood there motionless, like a statue made of cold marble. And the silly boy jumped up, clicked his heels and said, 'I assure you, Veronica, that my intentions are honourable. To-morrow morning I'll ask Emma's father permission to talk to him man to man.' And the silly boy did an about-turn! and left, and Veronica was standing there as before without saying a word, and Emma said, 'Don't be silly, Mummy, the silly boy just put his silly little tongue into my mouth and wiggled it, and that can't possibly make me pregnant, Mummy,' but Veronica still looked as if she hadn't seen anything and hadn't heard anything, and now she bent over Emma and asked in a strange voice, 'What have you been telling those two bitches?!' and Emma knew she meant the Dancing Ladies, but she asked, 'Which bitches?', but then Veronica straightened herself up, sighed, and said, 'Never mind,' and Emma shrugged her shoulders, and now she didn't believe there was nobody in the shop, so she started battering at the door again because she wanted to buy a comb for that silly boy Ian, but as there was still no answer, she put her hands behind her back and looked into the wooden bowl and counted the money without touching it, and then she shrugged her shoulders and turned left to the shop window and made faces at the ginger cat who was napping there in a patch of sunlight between some boxes, but the cat didn't take any notice of her, nor did he more than half lift his paw at the fly that was cruising round his nose, so she shrugged her shoulders again, jumped on her bicycle and, as there was still some time till lunch, pedalled further up the road.

There had been no more customers that Sunday morning, either for combs or for newspapers, except for the porter from the boarding house up the hill who served himself to *Le Monde*, *Le Figaro*, and *Corriere della Sera*. The sun was already past its highest point in the sky when Captain Casanova came down and unlocked the door. He looked out, the roads were empty. Not a soul. The cat must have had a bad dream. It jumped up, ran to the corner of the shop window, knocked some boxes over with a clatter, and hissed.

'It's all right. It's only the cat,' the Captain called.

When she came down and they were both standing in the open doorway, she looked straight into his eyes and said, 'Thank you.'

And he said, 'I'm so clumsy with words, but I want to tell you something.'

She said, 'Please don't.'

'Let me, for my sake,' he said.

'All right,' she said.

'You see,' he said, 'in all those twelve years since my wife died, this is the first time I have felt unfaithful to her.'

'I'm sorry,' she said.

'Don't be sorry,' he said. 'We haven't invented this world as it is. No. Not we.'

He locked the door after her, and went upstairs. He took an empty wine glass and hurled it on the floor. It didn't break. He went to the bathroom and pulled the chain, with no purpose and no reason. There was a small window there, in the bathroom, in the south wall, but it was high up above the bathtub and to reach it one would have to stand in the bathtub. That's what Captain Casanova did. In his sandals, he stepped into the bathtub and peered through the window. She was not far away, walking down the road. He turned round, jumped out of the bathtub and hurried down to the shop. A step-ladder stood there, behind the counter, but he pushed it aside, stretched out his arm, jumped up, and snatched from the upper shelf a long-forgotten black leather case with a pair of Zeiss binoculars which in all those years nobody had wanted to buy. Back at his post in the bathtub under the window, he trained the binoculars upon the road. She was still not very far away. He saw her so clearly now that he could count the stripes on her T-shirt. At a point less than halfway between his window and the sea, where the road swerved for a moment to the left, she disappeared behind the bushes which surrounded the Dancing Ladies' villa. Will she go to see them? he asked himself, but he didn't believe she would. And in less than a minute the road straightened and she appeared again, a little smaller, but still nearly filling the binoculars' field of vision.

He had mixed feelings about what he was doing. There was no evil in his military chest, he was capable only of good, he approved of his own sentiment; but he disapproved of what – if he saw it done by other people – he would call 'spying'. Fleet Street reporters, for instance, spying on royalty. On the other hand, they, the reporters, were not gentlemen, they took tele-photo shots and sold them in the name of the freedom of the press. He, of course, was doing nothing of the kind. Nor was Veronica a royal princess. And yet he felt as if he were commit-ting some sort of *lèse-majesté*, as he watched her going down the road, while the big toe of his right foot bobbed up and down, and the sandal scratched the enamel of the bathtub with each of her steps. Four hundred and fifty-two, four hundred and fifty-three, four hundred and fifty-four – she stopped.

She stopped where the road widened in front of the hotel and then imperceptibly changed into the sand of the beach. There were some twelve yards, across the road, between her and the entrance to the hotel, on her right, but she didn't turn to the right. He watched the back of her head, her loose hair coming down almost to her waist, as she stood there, motion-less. She must have been looking at something. To see what it was, he lifted his binoculars a little and saw further up, above her head, other people in swimsuits, swimming trunks, bikinis, sun hats, as motionless as she was. And there was, on that beach, an overwhelming silence, a *visible* silence. He moved the binoculars a trifle to the right, and he saw. It was Miss Prentice.

There she stood, on the sand of the beach, facing him, her strong arms stretched forward, and on them, horizontally, like on the lap of the Virgin, the little limp body of her son Ian. It was as if the Other One, the one from Michelangelo's *Pietà*, had stood up and started to move and grow bigger and bigger in Captain Casanova's binoculars. But her dress was not white marble drapery, her dress was a green bikini. And her face was not that of Her in the *Pietà*. Neither was it like the tragic contorted mask of *Laocoön*. There was the calm dignity of *Niobe* in it, but it was a modern face of a strong young woman who an hour ago was water-skiing behind a motor-boat. And as she walked, slowly, forward, the hanging-down arm of the boy was swinging like a pendulum with each of her steps.

Captain Casanova closed his eyes. When he looked again, she was already standing halfway between Veronica and the entrance to the hotel. Now she turned to her left. 'Somebody open the door! Come on – jump to it!' Captain Casanova commanded under his breath. And the door opened from the inside.

He moved his binoculars to the left, but Veronica was no longer there. So he zigzagged them all over the place, and there, on the lawn, he saw the wheelchair. The wheelchair was empty. Nearby, between the two Dancing Ladies, sitting on the grass, was Veronica's husband, Tim, the legless professor of logic. Now the Dancing Ladies were bending over him, lifting him, putting him into his wheelchair, and covering the front of the wheelchair with what looked like a leopard skin. And then, all at once, the Dancing Ladies disappeared. Perhaps they had just moved to where his view was cut off by the walls of the hotel. And now Veronica appeared in front of the wheelchair. It was only now, for the first time, that he saw her through his binoculars *en face*. Not for long. Because she had already knelt in front of the wheelchair and buried her face in the leopard skin.

Above her stood Don José María López, the barman, wiping his eyes with a chequered napkin.

Captain Casanova left his binoculars on the cover of the lavatory seat and went down to the shop. He remembered that Miss Prentice had once come and bought a Spanish phrasebook from him. Which meant that she didn't know any Spanish. Which meant that she needed a lot of help in her present predicament. Such phrases as *Busque a la policía, una ambulancia, un médico* will not help her much. The only people who could help her now were Marjorie, the late Great Man's secretary, and, perhaps, the Judge. And, of course, he, the Captain. He emptied the till and put the money in his pocket. He left the shop by the back door, took the car from the garage, revved it up and moved off. He went round to the front of the shop, stopped at the door, took what there was in the wooden bowl on top of the pile of newspapers, and started off again. Two minutes later, he arrived at the hotel. He knew everybody there and they knew him. First, he must see the manager and ask ¿Qué ha pasado? to go to his private rooms he had to pass through the restaurant. It was lunchtime. One small table was unoccupied. Miss Prentice's. There was another table there, under the window, placed so that a wheelchair could be pushed towards it. Emma was sitting at it alone; she was turning her head to the waiter and ordering an hors d'oeuvre.

PART TWO

TEN

The Cedarwood Casket

Every morning a car takes some sunburnt people to the airport, and a few hours later brings the pale faces of the new arrivals, impatiently looking forward to their seven days or a fortnight of sea and sunshine. Thus, at least half the population of the hotel changes every week, just as at least half the population of the globe changes every thirty-three years or so.

The Revd Paul Prentice arrived on Monday. With the help of Captain Casanova, he had arranged for poor Ian's body to be sent to England. He himself and his sister left on Wednesday. The German lady doctor had already gone on Tuesday. The Judge and Mrs Massgrave left on Thursday. On Friday, Tim, Veronica and Emma flew back to England. On Saturday, only a few whiffs of the memory of the death remained in the hotel lore, and the evening dance in the ballroom took place as on any other Saturday. And when the two Dancing Ladies made their appearance, all the other couples made room for them in the middle of the floor, as usual. And their dance was the same as usual. Whatever twists and turns their bodies were executing, they wouldn't touch each other, the distance dividing them was exactly the same all the time, and it looked as if the real bewitching dance was being performed not by them but by the shape of the narrow space between them.

There had been only a few survivals – people who had been staying in the hotel for more than a fortnight and had already seen the dance twice or three times. One of them was a French lady, Madame B., who had a bookshop in one of the narrow streets of the Rive Gauche in Paris. She was versed in classical literature, Aristotelian physics, Cartesian rationalism; she believed in Gallic superiority in perfecting the links with which

God provides us to make occasional connections between the Mind and the Body, and in Thatcherian Monetarism.

'*Ecoutez*,' she said. 'Do you not think, Madame, that these snaky sisters [she was referring to the Dancing Ladies] are the *Filles de la Terre*, the Furies, the Erinyes who after the trial of Orestes stopped tormenting sinners, and now, as Eumenides, are trying to expunge from their memory all recollections of the *crimes terribles* they were sent to punish?'

There was haughtiness in her voice, and haughtiness in her posture, but it was haughtiness without contempt. The same haughtiness with contempt would have been unbearable.

'Look, Madame,' she went on, 'see how those poor people around them are mesmerized by those two Snake goddesses. Look at the older Serpentess [she meant the Great Man's widow]. You are not a very good observer, Madame. You are too discreet. You don't want to see the mystery. And this place is full of mysteries, Madame. One would need a Simenon to unravel all the coincidences ... *Pardon?* Sherlock Holmes? Oh, no, Madame. Your Sherlock Holmes is a puppet made of *papier mâché*, Madame. One could rewrite his stories to show that he always points out the wrong suspect and lets the real criminal go scot-free. No, no. Your Sherlock Holmes doesn't understand a thing. Especially women. And if you don't like Simenon, Madame, then perhaps Zola? Maupassant? Mauriac? Or, *pourquoi pas?* Racine? Corneille? Unless you prefer your Father Brown, Chesterton I mean, or do you find the comparison outrageous? Yet, wouldn't he – Simenon, I mean – wouldn't he be the best man to explain why she didn't cry? That poor Miss Prentice? *Elle n'a pas pleuré du tout.* She showed great dignity, like General de Gaulle, or Monsieur Giscard d'Estaing, *oui*, yes, Madame, *si, et pourtant*, and yet, *elle est folle*, Madame, she sends the body of her poor boy to England but she doesn't want to bury it there, Madame, no, she wants to bury it in Poland, Madame, because the boy's father was a Pole! *Mais quelle folie, Madame!* Doesn't she know that they would have eaten him alive there, if he weren't dead already? Would your Sherlock Holmes understand *une femme* like that? Would you, Madame, even if you had known her well?'

Lady Cooper looked into Madame B.'s eyes and she couldn't see whether they were full of mischief or of innocence.

88

'In spite of her perspicacity, did she not notice that Miss Prentice wasn't a stranger to me?' Lady Cooper said to herself.

*

The sky, not so high above, was cloudless and blue. The forest, below, was bright green.

'Will that do?' the pilot asked.

They looked at Miss Prentice. She didn't answer. There had to be the right height. And it had to be the right moment. When they were too high up, what they saw below was not real enough. A map. An abstract picture. On the other hand, when they were hovering too low over the forest, the reality of what they saw was too precise, too trivial, for the purpose. One could as well be walking there, among the trees. And then, it had to be the right moment. The right moment depended not only on the height of the helicopter. First of all, it depended on Miss Prentice. On what was taking place *in* her. And her face was inscrutable.

She was sitting on Lady Cooper's left. Mr Mirek, the pilot, in front of them. And Dr Kszak, whom some people called the Minister of Imponderabilia, on Lady Cooper's right. He wasn't *really* called that. The very word 'imponderabilia' would have had some undesirable associations, as it could remind some old people that it was once used – once upon a time – by Marshal Piłsudski, just before (or was it just after?) the coup d'état of 1926.

'Will that do?' the pilot asked again.

Each time he turned round to ask the question, his wide eyes stared at Miss Prentice as if she were an apparition from a different, incomprehensible world. Dr Kszak looked at her *all* the time in exactly the same kind of wonderment. Was it because they expected to witness grief, and were now bewitched by the simplicity of her calm?

'Will that do?'

'Yes, please,' she said. Just these two words: yes, please.

Mr Mirek, the pilot, crossed himself.

Lady Cooper was holding the cedarwood casket on her lap. She took the lid off.

'Would you like me to do it for you?' she asked Miss Prentice.

89

'Oh, no,' she said. But she didn't take the casket. She put her hand into it, scooped up a handful of ashes and threw them through the window into the air. Before they dispersed, they looked as if they were about to flare up in the brightness of the sun. And then a gust of wind blew a tiny puff of dust back into the cabin, and a sharp, painful speck fell into Lady Cooper's eye. Before reaching for the next handful of ashes, Miss Prentice took a handkerchief, lifted up the lid of Lady Cooper's eye, and removed the speck.

*

Lady Cooper had met Miss Prentice a long time before, when Miss Prentice was a little schoolgirl. Even then, people used to call her Miss Prentice, or – very occasionally – Prudence. It was only her brother who called her Pru. He was two or three years older. At the time, nobody would have guessed that she would become a professional palmist, or that he would take holy orders. Though, indeed, her palmistry and his priesthood were not of an ordinary kind.

There are religions with God, there are religions without God, and there is also a religion without beliefs. That was the religion of the Revd Paul Prentice, Miss Prentice's brother. His religion was something specific, not to be confused with the 'religion of humanity', or with atheism, or agnosticism. People who really believe in God believe also in their belief in God. The Revd Paul Prentice believed in God but he didn't believe in his own belief. He knew that other people do very often believe in things that are not true, or in things that do not exist. If something like that can happen to other people, then who is he to be sure that it isn't so also in his case? That was why he didn't dare to believe in his beliefs.

Taken by itself, the fact that Lady Cooper had known Miss Prentice for such a long time was in no way extraordinary. No more extraordinary was the fact that Miss Prentice had met the General. But the two facts taken together made Lady Cooper feel as if, lurking in the shadows of what we call coincidence, there was Destiny playing her tricks on her.

At the time when Lady Cooper stayed in her country house (she always referred to it as her husband's country house), she used to call on Miss Prentice and her brother whenever she went shopping in the nearby seaside resort where they lived. Thus, it so happened that she saw Miss Prentice on all those very special occasions: when Miss Prentice came back from the Sisterhood of the Sacred Heart in Wales with a diploma in palmistry, and on the very day Miss Prentice had her first dinner with General Pięść, and a few months later when Miss Prentice came back home after the General's death, and then a week later when Miss Prentice put the WHITE PALM sign back on the pane of the front window and tried to start her palmistry business again.

Her first customer was the local family butcher's wife.

'I heard you were back, love,' the woman said. 'I've brought you two big porterhouse steaks, for you and your brother, love,' and she sat down opposite Miss Prentice and put two steaks and her own two hands, palms up, on the little table in front of her. Their knees touched lightly. 'Well, then?' the butcher's wife was all smiles, all there, ready to hang upon Miss Prentice's lips, but as some minutes passed and no words came out, 'What is it, love?' she asked. 'What did you see in my hands? Something horrid, was it?'

'No,' Miss Prentice said. 'It's nothing to do with you. I'm sorry . . . It's only . . . well . . . I don't know. I look at your hands, I see the lines, but I can't feel them. Sorry, I just can't. I think I've lost my gift.'

The butcher's wife stood up.

'It's all right, love. Don't you worry. T'was honest of you to say what you did.' And then, bending over her, she whispered with a conspiratorial air: 'Keep those two steaks all the same. You're in the family way, love, aren't you?'

'What?' It simply hadn't occurred to her that she might be pregnant. She blamed her distress at the General's death for whatever discomfort she might have felt lately.

General Pięść was not her first lover. Her first lover was her brother, the Revd Paul Prentice. The event was happily forgotten by both, it had taken place a long time ago, when they were teenagers. At the time, it seemed to have been the most natural thing in the world, and it had no consequence of any sort, because nobody saw it or knew about it. Except God. But it would be preposterous to conjecture that the fact of having

91

been seen by the Divine Voyeur was the reason why Paul Prentice entered a theological college and his sister spent two years at the Sacred Heart in Wales, where she was trained in palmistry.

Eight months after the General's death, Ian was born. After that, Lady Cooper used to go to see Miss Prentice more regularly. Twice, she saw her when Miss Prentice was with Dr Brzeski, the special friend of the widow who had inherited that enormous sum of money won by the General on the pools and who now lived in one of the Channel Islands to avoid paying taxes on the dividends. Lady Cooper noticed at once that Dr Brzeski liked Miss Prentice in a sort of way which was probably not free from a touch of guilt, as none of the inheritance went to Ian, who (whatever the widow might have been insinuating) was (Dr Brzeski had no doubt) the General's son. It was he, Dr Brzeski, who had the unenviable task of telling Miss Prentice that her little boy had been born with his heart on the wrong side of his body and with the arteries transposed.

Some time later, when Lady Cooper went to Rome to visit the incredibly old Cardinal Pölätüo, she met there His Eminence's good friend, Princess Zuppa, and Princess Zuppa's good friend, Dr Goldfinger. Having kissed the Cardinal's ring to say good-bye, they left and went to Princess Zuppa's *palazzo*, which was just across the *via*, and had tea. Lemon tea. Served in glass tumblers.

'It is to indulge Dr Goldfinger's nostalgia,' Princess Zuppa explained. 'He insists that was how one used to drink tea in his beloved Poland.'

The hot afternoon sun was cleverly diffused by a number of screens and curtains flapping in the open windows, and it was pleasant to sit at the feet of a marble sculpture representing the Muse of History, Clio, and indulge in a lighthearted conversation – small talk actually – when, suddenly, it so happened that Lady Cooper, without any special reason, mentioned the name of Dr Brzeski.

'Jesus,' Dr Goldfinger exclaimed, 'not Jerzy Brzeski, I mean George Brzeski? With curly blond hair and enormous ears?'

'Yes, Jerzy or George, very big ears, but no hair at all. He's bald.'

'Well, of course. He's exactly my age. We used to be good

friends. Studying medicine when the war broke out . . . Do tell me how he is, how he's going on.'

She told him.

And Dr Goldfinger became reminiscent: 'How absurd it all was! In those days. The last days of peace. You see, the benches in our auditoria were divided into the left-wing benches for the Jews and the right-wing benches for the Slavs, but the Jews refused to sit on their benches and they listened to the lectures standing up, and our poor George Brzeski didn't know what to do, he refused to sit with the right-wing bastards, but he didn't want to stand with the Jews either, and to sit alone in the empty left-wing benches was too silly, so he stopped coming to the lectures altogether, which was rather nice of him, but absurd. And it was still more funny in . . .'

'Did you say "funny"?' Princess Zuppa asked.

'Yes, I did. Why not?' he said curtly. And he repeated: 'It was still more funny in the prosectorium where we had to dissect corpses. People objected that all the corpses were always Christian corpses because the Old Testament Jews had a kind of The Last Service Society that used to snatch all unclaimed Jewish corpses to give them a decent burial, and so isn't it really funny that a short time later we had a surplus of millions and millions of cadavers, enough for all the students in the world . . . ?'

'Funny? I still don't see the joke,' Princess Zuppa said.

'The joke is that I wasn't among them,' Dr Goldfinger said.

'Among the students?'

'No,' he said. 'You don't understand a thing, my dear. Among the cadavers. And that was, you see, because it just so happened, one day, just before the war started, that I climbed up a step-ladder to look at a leaking gas pipe under the ceiling, and, as it was dark, I struck a match to see better, and the explosion blew into my face, in consequence of which, when they discharged me from the hospital, my nose was twelve millimetres shorter, a perfect, pure Aryan, Slav, *retroussé* nose, which helped me to survive the war, by the end of which I found myself in Rome, where the Americans took me under their wing and helped me to finish my medical studies in a sitting position. Well, this is the candid account of my peregrinations which I should like you, Lady Cooper, to convey to Dr Brzeski, if you happen to see him again.'

He was holding a golden fruit knife and peeling an apple. Fascinated, Lady Cooper was looking at his long, thin fingers, the fingers which some years ago so wonderfully extracted a fishbone from the throat of the cardinal.

'Ha, ha,' he said.

They didn't ask him why. And he didn't explain.

A while later, when Lady Cooper was taking her leave, Princess Zuppa asked her if she would take a parcel which she could post from London or, better still, give it, if possible, personally to Miss Prentice. 'It's some toys for her little boy, Ian, my half-brother.'

She darted a glance at Lady Cooper, and added: 'I still have one more half-brother, a half-black tyrannous chief of a tribe in Africa.'

That was how Lady Cooper learned that Princess Zuppa was also General Pięść's daughter.

*

It didn't happen by chance that they were staying at the same hotel in Majorca that fateful summer when the boy died. On the other hand, their finding themselves a year later aboard the same plane, flying from London (Heathrow) to Warsaw (Okęcie), was purely coincidental. It just so happened that Lady Cooper was late at Heathrow airport and boarded the Warsaw plane at the very last moment. That was why she noticed Miss Prentice only much later, when they were already high above in the sky and far away from London. At once she half-jumped up from her seat to go to the front of the plane to greet her, but she had forgotten to release her seat belt, and was pulled down again. And then she changed her mind. She just sat in her place, observing from afar the back of the head support, at the side of which the right profile of Miss Prentice would show from time to time, and for most of their two-hour flight she was musingly thinking about her. What was she doing here, on this plane going to Warsaw, she, the extraordinary Miss Prentice? Extraordinary? Why extraordinary? Lady Cooper was sipping her gin and tonic slowly, leisurely, and she was smiling at her own thoughts. Of course she knew why Miss Prentice was so extraordinary. She was so extraordinary because she was so extra-

94

ordinarily sane. She was such a puzzle because there was absolutely no mystery about her. She was what she was. And nothing else.

Gracious me! Wasn't she a bit like old Dame Victoria, Sir Lionel's (Lady Cooper's late husband's) sister? Even if it was not easy to imagine her with a poker in her hand, carrying a breakfast tray to a rebellious granddaughter, as Dame Victoria had done . . . but – who can tell? Both Dame Victoria and Miss Prentice, one very old, the other less than half her age, possessed the art of knowing what one does and what one does not in every situation. They knew it without rationalizing. Their knowledge wasn't based on any dogma, principle, axiom, commandment. Inherited, historically prejudged, or deduced backwards, *post hoc, à rebours*, from acquired experience. And yet, there was also a difference between them: Dame Victoria noticed things. Very sharply. Miss Prentice didn't. Indeed, what a woman she was for not noticing!

Her studying palmistry at the Sisterhood of the Sacred Heart might have had something to do with it. Not directly but through the influence exercised upon her by the Mother Superior who, in her own youth, at St Hilda's College, Oxford, read not Russell and/or Wittgenstein but the phenomenologists. The very sound of the word 'phenomenology' was exciting. And what it was about, especially in the Mother Superior's interpretation, was convincingly palatable. It's rather likely that the great men, Brentano, Husserl, Sartre, would shrug off her teaching; namely, that appearances are like screens hiding the essence of things that exist behind them, the essence that (thanks to our intuition) our consciousness can see directly, whether it is the essence of the Elephant (whose shape is determined by the message on a strand of DNA), or the essence of the Unicorn or the Devil (whose shapes are determined by something in the mind), and – as palmistry (unlike physics) deals with essences – then it follows clearly – doesn't it? – that for the purposes of palmistry it is necessary to remove the screens of all appearances. 'But why, Mother Superior?' 'You silly girl! Because people see themselves as they are seen by others. Which fact perplexes them. Because, say, they see themselves as fathers but they are fathers to their sons and daughters, not to themselves. They see themselves as dentists, directors, miners, fishermen, solicitors, air hostesses, good men, bad men, etc, etc, but they are all those things to other people, not to themselves. They look into a looking-glass and see a multitude of labels which the world has stuck on to their faces, and they feel perplexed. And so, occasionally, they stop and ask themselves, And what if the World were to disappear and take all these labels with It, what else is there in us that would remain? Something would remain, wouldn't it? What is that something? It is to hear an answer to such a question that they go to the palmist. That's why [the Mother Superior said] if you want to be a *good* palmist, you must *not* notice things. Because everything you notice with your senses is a mask that hides the essence your client wants to hear about. So you just sit opposite your client and concentrate on the geometry of the lines on the palms of his or her hands. Not that there is any definite information in the lines themselves. They are like a map of an unknown country. It doesn't very much matter which country. They all have rivers, and lakes, and mountains, towns, villages and roads. Your task is to fill those lines and marks and mounts with life. To make the trees grow and the rivers flow and the church bells ring. And beware of being too clever. Don't calculate. Don't think. You are not a computer. Let your intuition guide your imagination. Which does not mean that what your imagination shows you will always be true. Oh, no. But when it *is* true, you'll know it at once. Because, as Brentano said, the criterion of truth is its self-evidence. And when this self-evident truth reveals itself, you will have an unmistakable tingling in your knees, and you will have it because there will be electricity in that quarter of an inch between your knees and your client's knees, whatever the client's sex is, and the very quality of Space and Time between your respective knees will be different, just for a few seconds, it will be something else, something more like that little space between the tip of God's outstretched finger and the tip of Adam's awakening finger, that little space that sings the hymn of Creation in Michelangelo's painting in the Sistine Chapel.'

When asked, the Mother Superior wasn't quite clear whether the physical tingling in the knees precedes or follows the moment when the self-evidence is grasped directly by consciousness. But she stuck to her own interpretation of what she had learnt in her youth, at St Hilda's College, Oxford, and she insisted that phenomena are phenomena only so long as they are *not* registered. As soon as they become registered, they become scientific data, hiding the reality that is screened behind them. And, therefore, especially for the purpose of palmistry, they must not be noticed.

The art of not noticing things came naturally to Miss Prentice. And her stay with the sisters of the Sacred Heart enhanced it by giving it a philosophical basis supplied by the Mother Superior as a worthwhile rational and moral support for the practice of palmistry. Miss Prentice was a talented palmist. Whether her talent was still in her when she stopped practising during her friendship with the General, or whether it disappeared only after the General's death, when she discovered that she was pregnant and the lines on the palms of the hands of the butcher's wife failed to inspire her – Lady Cooper did not know. The fact was that Miss Prentice abandoned her palmistry altogether and consecrated the next twelve years of her life entirely to her son, Ian. And now, suddenly, Lady Cooper remembered an unkind thought that had forced itself on her mind that fateful day in Majorca, the day of Ian's death. *How long will it take her to return to her silly palmistry again*? It was awful to have such a thought. At such a time. But Lady Cooper dismissed it at once. Provided that we can dismiss such thoughts as soon as they come – she said to herself now – we are no more responsible for them than we are responsible for our dreams. Bloody Freudians do not know how much harm they do by not allowing people to dismiss such impromptu thoughts from their minds. Still, there was something there that made her feel uncomfortable. But what was it? Was it something outside? Or was it something in herself? She could not guess what it was. But it played a part in her reflections.

She got up and walked along the narrow passageway between the seats.

'Pru,' she said. 'What are you doing here? What an extra-ordinary coincidence! You're the last person I'd expected to see!'

Miss Prentice didn't seem to be surprised. She looked at Lady Cooper and said just three words. She said: 'Hallo, Lady Cooper!'

Was she pleased to see her? Of course she was. In her own calm way. But there was nothing in her expression to show it.

She seemed to have passed beyond paying attention to the here and now, and yet it was perfectly clear that her all-seeing gaze didn't miss much. Which is not a contradiction. Though it's difficult to explain. It was as if she had two kinds of knowledge, a shallow knowledge and a deep knowledge. The shallow knowledge was practical, behavioural, pragmatic, indispensable to ordinary, everyday life. Her deep knowledge was different. Her deep knowledge was something of the *tout comprendre c'est tout pardonner* kind. But to forgive whom? All, except God, who wouldn't even bother to explain why He had taken Ian away from her? Or: *tout comprendre c'est jamais rire et jamais pleurer* – which, again, is saying the same thing in different words.

'It's high time you called me Jadwiga,' Lady Cooper said.

'Oh . . .' Miss Prentice said, 'it's never occurred to me that you have a Christian name, Lady Cooper, I mean, Yadviga . . .'

The air hostess rushed at Lady Cooper: 'Please go back to your seat and fasten your seat belt.' But they were not landing yet. They were climbing and then dropping into air pockets. The bright clouds below them looked massive and full of electricity. From the earth (Berlin? East Germany?) they surely looked black and menacing.

*

At Okęcie airport, Warsaw, the sun was shining. They walked down the landing stairs together – and across the tarmac, to the passport control.

'*Ta pani to pani wnuczka?*' the man asked.

'*Nie.*'

He meditated for a few seconds and then stamped their passports.

'What did he say?' Miss Prentice asked.

'He asked if you were my granddaughter.'

She said nothing.

The middle-aged man at customs was wearing an old-fashioned *pince-nez* and a polite smile. He addressed Miss Prentice in Polish, got angry with himself for not recognizing a foreigner (he might have thought that no foreign lady had a right to be blonde, blue-eyed and pretty) and asked her to open her suitcase. Slowly, he started to take out her underwear,

98

displaying one item after another by holding them by the edge between the thumb and forefinger of each hand, at the level of his *pince-nez*, with no haste, until he discovered, under the dressing-gown, a cedarwood casket.

'Please, don't touch it,' Miss Prentice said.

Her voice was loud but quiet. Its strength was muted. It expressed neither a command nor a plea. It was an other-worldly, synthetic voice and it ominously hushed the hubbub of the customs hall. The man's long fingers drew back from the casket, as if it were a keg of gunpowder.

'Why not?' he asked.

'Because it is my son.'

Naturally, he thought that his knowledge of the English language had proved to be inadequate, and it annoyed him.

'It is what?'

'The casket contains the ashes of my son,' Miss Prentice said in a clear, informative voice.

A man in uniform appeared noiselessly beside them. His heavy, thick, red hands dipped slowly, cautiously, into the suitcase and, very gently, lifted the cedarwood casket.

'Don't open it, please,' said Miss Prentice.

His head nodded politely.

'Don't worry, madam. We'll X ray it . . .' – it wasn't quite clear, whether he said: *We'll just X ray it*, or: *We'll X ray it first* . . . After which they asked Miss Prentice to follow them (or, rather, to precede them) to the office where they could discuss the matter. Lady Cooper offered to go with them as an interpreter but they said they didn't need an interpreter.

'I'll be staying at the Hotel Europejski,' Lady Cooper said.

'So will I,' said Miss Prentice.

ELEVEN
The Minister of Imponderabilia

. . . The following day Napoleon drove on ahead of the army, reached the Niemen and, changing into Polish uniform, went to the river bank in order to select a place for the crossing . . .

'. . . Now we shall get on! Things warm up when he himself takes a hand! . . . By Jove! . . . There he is! *Vive l'Empereur!'*

'Long live the Emperor!' shouted the Poles no less enthusiastically, breaking their ranks and pushing against one another to get a sight of him. Napoleon looked up and down the river, got off his horse and sat down on a log that lay on the bank. At a mute sign from him he was handed a telescope which he rested on the back of a page, who ran up delighted. He gazed at the opposite bank and then, with absorbed attention, studied a map spread out between logs. Without lifting his head he said something, and two of his aides-de-camp galloped off to the Polish Uhlans.

'What? What did he say?' was heard in the ranks of the Polish Uhlans as one of the adjutants rode up with them.

The order was that they should look for a ford and cross the river. The colonel of the Polish Uhlans, a handsome old man, flushing and stammering in his excitement, asked the aide-de-camp whether he might be permitted to swim the river with his men instead of seeking a ford. In obvious dread of a refusal, like a boy asking permission to get on a horse, he begged to be allowed to swim across the river before the Emperor's eyes. The aide-de-camp replied that in all probability the Emperor would not be displeased at this excess of zeal.

No sooner had the aide-de-camp said this than the old whiskered officer, with beaming face and sparkling eyes, brandished his sabre in the air, shouted '*Vivat*' and, calling on his men to follow him, spurred his horse and then dashed down to the river. He gave a vicious thrust to his charger, which had grown restive under him, and plunged into the water, heading for the deepest part where the current was swift. Hundreds of Uhlans galloped in after him. It was cold and forbidding in the middle of the rapid current. The Uhlans clung to one another as they fell from their horses. Some of the animals were drowned, some, too, of the men; the rest struggled to swim on and reach the opposite bank; and though there was a ford only about a quarter of a mile away, they were proud to be swimming and drowning in the river under the eyes of the man who sat on the log and was not even looking at what they were doing.

... Some forty Uhlans were drowned in the river though boats were sent to their assistance. The majority scrambled back to the bank from which they had started. The colonel with several of his men got across and with difficulty clambered out on the other bank. But as soon as they were out of the water, their clothes streaming wet and flapping against their bodies, they shouted 'Vivat!' and looked ecstatically at the spot where Napoleon had stood, though he was there no longer, and at that moment considered themselves happy.

In the evening, between issuing two orders – one for hastening the arrival of the counterfeit paper money prepared for circulation in Russia, and the other that a Saxon who had been caught with a letter containing information concerning the dispositions of the French army should be shot – Napoleon also gave instructions for the Polish colonel who had quite unnecessarily flung himself into the river to be enrolled in the Légion d'Honneur, of which Napoleon was the head. *Quos vult perdere – dementat.*

These passages were marked by two vertical red pencil lines in the margin of Tolstoy's *War and Peace*, vol. 2, which Dr Kszak, 'the Minister of Imponderabilia', was reading when Lady Cooper came to visit him.

She went to see him because of Miss Prentice, of course. The cedarwood casket hadn't yet been returned to her, and she didn't even know where it was at present, with customs, or the militia, or some forensic laboratory; nobody she applied to would enlighten her.

'You know these people, Yadviga. Tell me, what must I do?' she asked, sitting down on the unmade bed in Lady Cooper's room, early in the morning.

Lady Cooper hesitated.

'Well, yes, but . . . it's that I haven't seen him for some fifty years . . . I don't know if I can . . .' She struggled with herself against something in her that was warning her, 'Oh, no, don't.' She got up, stood in front of the wardrobe mirror for a while, and then she said: 'All right, old friendships don't die, I suppose. And he might be able to help . . .'

He was the right man to turn to. Not that he exercised power. He didn't. Though some people called him *l'éminence grise*. He was close both to power and to various anti-powers. Not because he needed them but because they needed him. They needed him whenever some human factors got inhumanly entangled within the wheels of their so perfectly planned (or anti-planned) machinery. As for himself, people who knew him

101

agreed that he was not possessed by that comically powerful desire to seek power, and if they called him *l'éminence grise*, it was rather because so few knew about his existence. The name of Dr Joseph Kszak had never appeared in the newspapers, nor could you have seen his face on the television screen. Those who knew him insisted that he was no less than seven feet tall, twenty stone, no fat, all bone and flesh, his resounding voice effortlessly filling any volume of space with a whisper or with a bellow. They must have been exaggerating of course. When Lady Cooper knew him, some half century ago, he was a boy and then a young man, tall and slightly stooping; he spoke softly, not without an occasional stammer. But then their ways had parted and she didn't think such a long way back. All she knew was that in November 1937 he took Holy Orders, in November 1938 he was unfrocked after he had fallen desperately in love with a pretty girl who was as tall as he, and who – in November 1939 – was killed. About what was happening to him at the time of the war, nobody knew anything precise. The Arctic Circle was mentioned. The tundra. Something far away, not polluted by the war, industry, and literature.

It took her some time to find his telephone number (it was not listed in the Warsaw telephone book). As she dialled, her hesitation vanished. She knew with a sort of absolute certainty that she would hear a friendly, welcoming voice. And that's how it was.

'Jezus, Maria, Józefie Święty!' he exclaimed. 'Jadwiga! How marvellous! I want to see you.' She said that she wanted to see him, too. 'Where are you staying?' She told him. 'Well, I hope you are free tonight, are you?' He didn't wait for her answer. 'You must come, I'll send my car to fetch you, be in the lobby at 6 p.m.' She said she could walk if he told her where he lived. 'No, no, no! My chauffeur will bring you!'

At six o'clock precisely the chauffeur appeared in the lobby. He was wearing a grey tie, grey shirt, grey jacket, grey trousers, grey socks, and grey suede shoes. His eyes were black, his moustache à la Wałęsa was black, but his hair was grey; he was wearing no cap. Silently, he conducted her to a big black saloon car. Inside, it was all shades of grey. He fitted the car perfectly. Both the chauffeur and his car were grey and black, authoritative and silent. She admired that magnificent symbiosis, as they moved smoothly forward.

102

Warsaw had changed so much that she wasn't quite sure where they were when the car slowed down, turned right into the *porte-cochère* of an old nineteenth-century mansion house, and into the inner yard. The caretaker lady's face looked at them through the little window of her lodge. 'When I am needed, I can be found in the caretaker's lodge,' the chauffeur said. The sentence was correct but clumsily unnatural. She thought he didn't know how to address her, *per* Madam, or *Pani*, or Comrade. Unless – who can say? – perhaps it was his style.

He showed her into the lift and pressed a button. She didn't notice on which floor they stopped. In front of them stood a sculpted Shepherdess with a crook (or was it a young Bishop with a pastoral staff?) in a niche on the landing. He pressed the bell on the door to their left. After a moment, they heard a buzz and the door opened automatically. The chauffeur turned round and vanished.

'Come in, come in, please!'

Lady Cooper stepped into the long darkish corridor and walked slowly between its two (Duchy-of-Warsaw-style) tapestried walls.

'Hullo, Joseph,' she said.

'My dear Jadwiga! Ages! What ages!'

He was standing in the doorway, welcoming her with open arms. As she came nearer, he stooped and kissed her on both cheeks. She couldn't reciprocate because she would have had to jump up to do so.

There was a desk in the corner of the study, on the right, a radiogram by the door near the corner on the left, a small chessboard table between two Viennese chairs in the middle, and a settee and two armchairs opposite. Not a single picture on the whitewashed walls. All the pictures, as she learned later, were hanging in the other room, his bedroom, where all his books were lying on the floor around a big iron bed with copper knobs standing in the middle.

'Would we recognize each other, if we met in the street?' he asked.

'Well, your silhouette is legendary,' she said.

They seated themselves and regarded each other in silence, thinking about the passage of time. Then her eyes were drawn to the empty desk, precisely because it was so vast and there

103

was nothing on it except a solitary open book, its pages down-ward on the desk.

'I've interrupted your reading,' she said.

He got up, walked with slow steps to the desk, took the book and, without closing it, put it in her hands. The open pages were marked with a red pencil. It was Tolstoy's *War and Peace* in the original Russian.

'You may remember, dear Jadwiga, that I, too, was, well . . . still am, a romantic . . . but . . . I must confess that today, when-ever some young hotheads do something brave but irrational, something that lifts my heart but saddens my thoughts by its useless stupidity, I open the book, read these pages again, and tell myself, "Wake up, *Napoleon is not even looking at what they are doing!*"'

'But who is their Napoleon?' Lady Cooper asked.

'There are too many of them. One is in the west, the other in the east, one more in the south-south-west, and still another one high up in the zenith,' he pointed his finger at the ceiling.

Lady Cooper wasn't sure – was he pointing at somebody who lived in the flat above him, or did he mean God in heaven?

'What puzzles me . . .' he went on, 'is this: the old hotheads, those in the Emperor's army, the Uhlans, were all the sons of some landowners, squires, the leisured classes, the gentry, while the present-day hotheads are the sons of peasants who have come to the town to work in factories, offices, or to study at the universities, and yet their adrenalin produces the same senseless excess of zeal. Why? Why should it?'

He didn't wait for an answer. He took *War and Peace* from her hands, closed it, and put it back where it was before in the centre of the empty desk. Then he sat again in the armchair, facing her, and said: 'Dear Jadwiga, I'm going to ask you a question. You needn't answer if you don't want to. But if you do, I want you to say *yes* or *no*.'

'You sound rather severe,' she said. 'And mysterious.'

He nodded, meaning yes yes, and then no no, and then yes yes again. And then he looked straight into her eyes and said:

'The question is: are you a foreign agent, yes or no?'

'No,' she said, curtly.

He sighed.

'That's what I thought,' he said. 'But what a pity.'

'Good gracious!' she exclaimed. 'Why on earth do you say that?'

He looked as if he couldn't grasp, and was trying to understand, why she was so surprised.

'It's quite simple,' he said. 'Don't you see? We so badly need some intelligent, honest agents to come and see us as we are. We are such a misunderstood people, such a misunderstood country. And all those agents they send us are such blinking idiots, mean, nit-picking; all they do is to look for what their masters want them to find, and all they report is what their masters want to hear. Our greatest enemy is their ignorance. Because their ignorance is so small. They just don't know how big the unknown is: the starry heaven above us and the moral law within us.'

He stopped. He sat there without moving, waiting for his aphorism to sink in. And then, unexpectedly, he roared with laughter. He blew his nose into a big green handkerchief he took from his trouser pocket, looked at Lady Cooper, and burst into laughter again. 'Dear old Immanuel Kant regurgitating into such a context. What an *outré* thing to do!' he jeered at himself. Then he coughed as if he wanted to cough down what he had just said and so to help himself to recover from his laughing fit he took a deep breath and, after a while, bent forward and asked with a little smile: 'Now, tell me, what is your problem? How can I serve you?'

His question was a complete surprise. She was so fascinated by his performance that the purpose of her visit had receded from her mind. For a fraction of a second she was tempted to pretend; she was tempted to say, 'My dear Joseph, I have no problem, I just came to say hallo,' but he obviously had no illusion that anyone would come to see him just for the pleasure of saying hallo. 'I'm afraid, yes, I have a problem,' she said finally, after what seemed to her a very long time, 'and I hope you can help.'

She told him about Miss Prentice ('How do you spell the name?' he asked). She told him about the death of Miss Prentice's little son, Ian, who was thought to be a mathematical genius, a future Tarski, Łukasiewicz, Sierpiński. She told him how Miss Prentice ('*Miss* Prentice?' he asked) wanted to bury her little boy's body in Poland because his father was a Pole, but she

105

couldn't cope with all those technicalities – you can't just take the body with you and there are so many formalities, so she had it cremated and brought the ashes. In a cedarwood casket. Which the customs and excise men took from her on arrival. And she's now sitting in her hotel room and waiting. And can't get any definite answer.

'What was the father's name?' he asked.

'General Pięść. He died before the child was born. Didn't even know that she was pregnant,' Lady Cooper said.

While she spoke, he was playing with a piece of string he had taken out of his pocket. He now put it back and started tapping out a tune on his knee.

'Do you like music?' he asked, getting up; it was clear that no answer was needed or expected. He bent over the radiogram. 'Brandenburg Concerto,' he announced, pressing some buttons. 'I must leave you alone for a while,' he said. Then he opened the door to the other room and switched on the light. It was at that moment that she saw through the half-open door the pictures on the walls, books on the floor, the iron bed in the middle, and the telephone in the very centre of the bed. As he was closing the door behind him –

'May I go to the loo?' Lady Cooper asked.

'The other door,' he said.

*

The loo was in the bathroom. The bath was an ordinary bath, just over four feet in length at the bottom, and he would have to sit in it or else stick his legs out of it, in which case the bulk of his body would not leave much room for water. The lavatory seat was also made to the size of ordinary mortals. It would be difficult to visualize his mighty buttocks pressing upon this miniature toy. We understand the daily difficulties which pester the lives of midgets but we underestimate those encountered by giants. Because giants are so impressive. Yet they also are a minority in our medial world. Yes, there are many minorities in our Father's house, and He made them of many colours. The previous night, in the lobby of her hotel, she had overheard a couple talking in the corner. He: *What's wrong with our country is that we are so uniform. Everybody is like everybody else. We have*

106

no minorities, no Lutherans, no Jews, no Negroes, no Martians to blame for our misfortunes. So we are bound to blame each other. To which the woman: *Yes, I agree with you, but for a different reason.* She was wearing a round black hat, with a little veil and a pompom made of feathers, and white gloves, and she was smoking a brown cigarette in a long cigarette holder. *We need minorities,* she, in her actressy voice: *but we need them because it is they who inject the majority with great men, artists, writers, scientists, and some great statesmen, occasionally.* He: *Nonsense.* But she: *No, it is not nonsense.* So he: *Well, what minorities?* She: *Aristocrats who have lost their titles; bankrupt plutocrats; baptized Jews; lapsed clergy; lumpenproletariat; redheads; stammerers; invalids* . . . He: *I don't call them minorities.* She: *Why not? What is your definition of a minority?* – and they had engaged in the fruitless task of trying to produce some of those definitions which would only open up a lot more questions, all unanswerable, and Lady Cooper had stopped listening. And now she had forgotten what it was, there in the bathroom, that reminded her of that conversation. She turned the tap on and washed her hands. There was a clean, bright yellow towel hanging on the towel rail on the side of the wash-basin. She was reluctant to use it. She looked round for some tissue paper. There wasn't any. There was only a roll of toilet paper. Each little rectangle was stamped with the words: PROPERTY OF HER MAJESTY'S GOVERNMENT. How curious. Very odd. Where did he get it? A birthday (name-day?) present from the British ambassador? Or what? On the shelf above the wash-basin she noticed his old-fashioned cut-throat razor and a leather strop for sharpening it. She looked at it with some nostalgia because it was the type of a razor her father used to use a long time ago. Her father? Well, at the time she didn't know that he was not her father. Not really. And yet . . . well, anyway . . . She remembered that he used to call it his William of Occam razor.

> Satire should, like a polished razor keen,
> Wound with a touch that's scarcely felt or seen.

This rhyme was, of course, not by William of Occam. Nor was the principle that 'entities are not to be multiplied beyond necessity' by Lady Mary Wortley Montagu (1689–1762). But, if one thinks of them, the two maxims are not contradictory.

Lady Cooper left the bathroom, went across the study to her armchair, and sat down. The long-playing record was still turning. Slowly. Now, true or not, she had read somewhere that Napoleon could dictate ten letters simultaneously to his ten secretaries. And that Russell could dictate an article and carry on a conversation on the telephone. She, Lady Cooper, could not even do two things at one and the same time, even such two things as listening to music and waiting. And, though it was a Brandenburg Concerto, the waiting, at the time, was her primary occupation. She stretched herself out, so far as it was possible in the armchair, and looked up at the ceiling, watching a fly that was walking there upside down. Her watching the fly did not interfere with her waiting. Music did. It had taken her a long time, some months, to realize and then accept the fact that she could no longer hear some very high notes, and as high notes are, as overtones, constituents of lower notes, she used to blame the performers, or the loudspeakers – or both – for the distortions produced by her own ears. Ears or brain? Brain or mind? The fly dropped off the ceiling, produced some impossible-to-watch-closely aerobatics, and – hey presto! there it was, walking on the ceiling again. The gramophone disc gave its sonorous last, and stopped. Now, through the closed door, she heard his muffled voice saying something on the telephone, but she couldn't understand a word. She shut her eyes to hear better, but then the automatic record player let the next disc drop on to the turntable, and waves of sound filled the room again and made, for a moment, something strange happen to Time. She couldn't make out whether the ceiling she saw was the ceiling she had seen a while ago, or the ceiling she was going to see in a while. It was as if experience and expectation had become the mirror images of one another – as if memory and premonition had become indistinguishable. It frightened her. How long was the moment during which such a strange thing was happening to Time? What a curious question. She looked at her watch. No! She put it to her ear but couldn't hear anything with that blasted music. She wound it up, shook it, when, suddenly, the fly left the ceiling, the bedroom door opened, the giant burst in, switched the record player off, marched across the room to his writing-desk and sat down behind it. In his big hands he carried some bits of paper. He opened the desk drawer, put them in, shut the drawer and beckoned to her to come nearer and sit on the chair on the other side of the desk. Which she did.

'Well,' he said, 'there is some good news, but there is also something that needs to be clarified . . .'

'Let's hear the good news first,' Lady Cooper said.

'All right,' he said. 'The good news is that they have analysed the stuff in the cedarwood casket and found that it consists of human ashes.'

She laughed: 'And what else did they expect, feathers?'

He didn't laugh.

'No, not necessarily feathers,' he said. 'Small arms, explosives, colorado beetles, stink bombs; marijuana, heroin, cocaine, poison gas; rabies viruses, bees' excrement with yellow pollen and mycotoxins; gold, silver, diamonds; bugging devices, identity cards, dollars; leaflets, tapes, poems – you name it . . .'

Her shoulders shrugged, involuntarily, which made her think of that poor little Emma, who shrugged her little shoulders several times a day, whenever the reality of the world impinged on her.

'Did you say "poems"?' Lady Cooper asked.

'Yes,' he said, 'I did. Poems can be as poisonous as prose.' A wave of his big hand signed to her not to interrupt him, and, at the same time, in a different tone of voice, a tone of voice that puzzled her, he asked: 'And what would you say if I suddenly conjured up a black poodle?'

'I would say: *Apage Satanas!*'

'Not bad,' he nodded. And then he said casually, 'You know a girl called Piff, don't you?' He opened his desk drawer, looked into it, shut it, and added: 'Piff, or perhaps Piffin. Unusual name.'

'Yes,' Lady Cooper said. 'She's a grandniece of my late husband. I have only seen her once, when I was visiting her father, the famous Bernard St Austell, the Great Man of Letters and a TV personality. She was a little girl at the time.'

'She is now hiding in some sort of sanctuary in India, isn't she?'

'Her mother told me that she was in India. But she didn't use the word "hiding".'

'Her mother lives with another woman in Majorca?'

109

'Yes.'

'And her brother?'

'Whose brother?'

'The girl's brother.'

'I don't know anything about her brother.'

'Well, then I can tell you. Her brother has joined the police force.'

'You seem to be very well informed,' Lady Cooper said.

'*They* are very well informed,' he corrected her.

'It must cost a lot of money to gather all that useless information.'

'Quite so,' he agreed. 'But . . . well, things are as they are. Now, tell me, what think you, how is it that such a couple, the famous Great Man of Letters and his lesbian wife, can produce two so different kids – one all for capitalist law and order, and the other a rebel?'

'I don't know. I think that any couple of parents can have any couple of children. It all depends on whether the children conform or revolt or are indifferent. In this case, it seems that both revolted but in two different ways.'

'Do you think that the brother helped his sister to be . . . spirited away?'

'How can I know?'

'All right,' he said, and looked again into the drawer. 'You did know a man called McPherson, didn't you?'

'I met him, yes . . . poor man. Killed for no reason at all.'

'No reason?'

'Yes.'

'Are you sure?'

'Of course.'

'So what was the purpose of his going there?'

'Going where?'

'Well, going to see that lecturer in philosophy, or logic, whatever his name is.'

'Tim Chesterton-Brown.'

He peeped into the drawer again.

'That's it. The man in the wheelchair.'

'He wasn't in the wheelchair at the time. He had both his legs when McPherson went to visit him.'

'Of course. But why?'

110

'Why what?'

'Why did McPherson go to visit him? For what purpose?'

'That's simple. He wanted to ask him what was the colour of the Great Man's eyes.'

'Are you kidding?'

'No.'

'Was it a sort of code? A password?'

'Not at all. It was a genuine question. McPherson was writing his doctoral thesis on the subject of the Great Man, and to solve some literary argument he needed to know the colour of the Great Man's eyes.'

'And all that happened in the villa . . . whatever its name, never mind, in the villa standing right on the coast, facing the sea, didn't it? And there were two other villas in the neighbourhood: the ambassador's villa on the left and the admiral's villa on the right. Correct?'

'I think so. That's to say, if you look southwards.'

'Now,' he said, 'there was some talk, a theory, that the black poodle was misguided, or perhaps distracted by some smell, and its original target was one of the other two villas. Correct?'

'There was some talk on those lines, yes.'

'Now, the question is: which one?'

'Which one what?'

'Which villa, the one on the left or the one on the right?'

'My dear Joseph, how can *I* know?'

'Of course, *you* can't,' he agreed. 'But it's already over a year since it happened and the British police still keep mum. Why?'

'Search me. Perhaps they don't know either.'

He smiled. He realized that she was growing impatient of this 'conversation', which she had found quite amusing to submit to at the beginning but . . . Hell, enough is enough. And yet, she was doing it for Miss Prentice, wasn't she? Miss Prentice who wouldn't understand a word of it. Miss Prentice who lived in a different world. Her own. Lady Cooper sighed. And he noticed it. He leaned forward and said pleasantly, with good humour: 'When you were in Rome, you visited a cardinal with an unpronounceable name . . .'

'Pölätüo,' she articulated each *umlaut*ed vowel.

'That's it. And you met His Eminence's friend there, a Princess Zuppa, and her friend, a Dr Goldfinger.'

111

'I did,' she said. 'What of it?'

'You knew, of course, that Princess Zuppa was General Pięść's illegitimate daughter.

'No,' she said. 'Not when I met her.'

'But now you do know.'

'Yes, of course.'

'And that she has a half-black half-brother, a little tyrant somewhere in Africa, also sired by the General?'

'Yes.'

'All right,' he said. 'Now let's go back to that poor Mr McPherson who was killed so suddenly. You have met his girlfriend, haven't you?'

'Yes.'

'You know that she was pregnant?'

'Yes.'

'And when the poor man was killed, she wanted to have an abortion?'

'I heard some rumour.'

'But his mother, Mrs McPherson, begged her not to and promised to take the child. Which she did. It's a . . .' He looked into the drawer and said, '. . . girl. The trouble is that Mr McPherson senior doesn't believe his son was the child's father. Now, what's your opinion?'

'Look, Joseph,' she said, 'I admire the efficiency of the Gossip Branch of the secret service. But what has all that to do with Miss Prentice and the cedarwood box of a few handfuls of ashes? What is the purpose of piling up and up all those isolated irrelevancies, all those unconnected facts and people near or far if you can't link them together, hiddenly or not.'

'But I can,' he said.

'No,' she said.

'Yes,' he said.

'You really mean that all those various things can be linked with something? Something definite?'

'Yes.'

'Well, what is it? What is that mysterious something?'

'It isn't a "something", it's "somebody".'

'A person?'

'Yes.'

'Can you tell me who?'

112

'I can.'

'Well, who?'

'You,' he said.

Lady Cooper laughed. She laughed and laughed and couldn't stop laughing. We tend to laugh when confronted with something that forces us to rearrange what had been settled for good in our mind. Unless that something is dangerous. In which case our laughter is stopped by fear, which garrottes it. But Lady Cooper didn't see anything dangerous in what he said. So she laughed.

'You must be joking,' she said.

'No, I'm not,' he said.

'Well then, explain. What is it that makes you think I'm a sort of linkwoman, a mysterious common denominator, or what . . . ?'

'The fact that you know all those people.'

That was an anticlimax. She sighed. And this time her sigh was not unlike a yawn. 'Look, Joseph,' she said. 'I know hundreds of people. My friends. My husband's friends. All kinds of people. That doesn't make them linked with each other. They may never even have heard about each other. Well, I know you *too*. That doesn't mean that *you* are involved.'

'How do you know that I'm not?' he asked. He put it so pleasantly that she just stared at him – there was absolutely nothing she could say. 'Well, you see,' he went on, 'you can't be sure about me, and *they* can't be sure about you.'

The fingers of her right hand were squeezed so tightly that its nails were hurting her palm. She straightened her hand and sat on it.

'I see,' she said. 'Well . . . let me put two and two together. I told you about Miss Prentice and her predicament. You, very kindly, tried to help. And you phoned where necessary. Obviously *they* looked into their files and found some disjointed bits of gossip which puzzled them. Perhaps they wanted to invite me to come and be grilled by them. And you wanted to spare me the experience. So you offered to do it yourself. Which you've just done in the nicest possible way. For which I'm thankful. But now, whatever else you might be interested in, you must already have realized that so far as Miss Prentice is concerned, there is absolutely nothing sinister about her, politically or otherwise, and, no doubt, her little box of ashes will be returned to her presently, for which we shall be infinitely grateful to you.' She looked at his impassive, expressionless face and became very angry, no, not with him, she was just filled with anger, anger in itself, by itself. 'Dear Joseph,' she went on, trying not to lose her temper, 'I have just said that we shall be infinitely grateful. This is not quite correct. I should have said: "I shall be." Because I'm not quite sure Miss Prentice will. You see, she may be finding it very difficult to understand why she should. She's a very straightforward person. She has no doubt that what she had decided to do is OK, therefore the fuss made around it is not of her doing and there is nothing she ought to be grateful for.' His face was still as before – impenetrable. 'Actually,' Lady Cooper went on, 'as a matter of fact, she herself – would you believe it? – she herself doesn't care a damn about those handfuls of ashes, you know? In England, you know, one isn't too ceremonious, you know, about dead bodies, cremated or not. Unless they've been sexually assaulted. Or dug out to please the newspapers who love to dig up a murder. Otherwise, you load the corpse into a black Rolls-Royce and go at the speed-limit speed. So, you see, she's not doing all that for her own morbid pleasure. She is doing it for his sake. The General's. Because she thinks that is what he would have liked her to do. Have his son's ashes returned to the earth of his motherland. And that it's you, the General's compatriot, who should be grateful to her, not the other way round.' Now she felt that she had gone too far and perhaps antagonized him. Without looking at him, she added: 'But Miss Prentice is a nice person, she's very polite and her good manners will not fail to charm you. So, of course, she'll say, "Thank you ever so much," and "It was so awfully nice of you to take all that trouble." That's all she'll say. Because she lives in a different world and she doesn't know. But I know, and I shall remain infinitely grateful.'

He stood up. Again she saw how tall and big he was.

'Let's go back to our armchairs,' he said. 'We'll be more comfortable.'

Lady Cooper wondered whether she had an especially suspicious mind when it occurred to her that perhaps he had a tape recorder hidden in the desk, or perhaps on the contrary, perhaps a microphone in the armchair, anyway, what did she care?

They moved away from the desk and seated themselves, he on that settee or sofa which he called *kanapa* and which proved to be not too big for him alone, she – in the armchair.

'I'm afraid,' he started in his soft, deep, giant-teddy-bear voice, 'I'm afraid,' he repeated, 'you still don't know what it is all about, my dear Jadwiga.' He looked around, pensively, as if searching for something that would remind him of what he ought to do, and, as she was rather thirsty and hungry by now, she hoped that in sudden enlightenment he'd exclaim: 'What about a drink?' That was not to be. From a little box which he took out of his pocket he extracted a pink pill. That was the first indication that his big strong body needed some medical help. Which made him look more human. He swallowed the pill without drinking, after which he said: 'Does the name Mściszciszewski tell you anything?'

'Nothing at all,' Lady Cooper said. 'Who is he?'

'A very patriotic gentleman. But tell me first: once Miss Prentice has her ashes returned to her, what is she going to do with them?'

'I don't know. She didn't tell me. Perhaps she'll ask the priest to immure the casket in the walls of a church?'

'Had the boy been baptized a Roman Catholic?'

'Maybe, but I doubt it. Her brother is a C of E clergyman. Not a very great friend of Rome, and not a great believer either.'

'Well, so that's out. She can't expect the Church to be enthusiastic about people dumping some cremated unbaptized dust on it. Even if your friend were a millionairess, which she isn't, or is she?'

'My dear Joseph, there must die in the People's Republic at least a few people who are both atheists and mortal. What do you do with them?'

'We have cemeteries,' he said.

'Well, cannot Miss Prentice buy a plot? Just one square foot?'

'Formalities, formalities . . .'

'Or just sprinkle the ashes over the graves?'

'No, to sprinkle your ashes over other people's graves, you have to have their permission. Besides, you can't go to the cemetery in the middle of the night to do it.'

'But why must it be in the middle of the night? Why can't we go there in the middle of the day?'

'Good question.' Again, from his trouser pocket he took out the same piece of string and started to play with it as if it were a rosary. 'You know, of course, the General's widow,' he said at length, meditatively.

'Yes and no,' Lady Cooper said. 'I met her once or twice when the General was alive. I haven't seen her since his death.'

'But you know that she inherited all his money, lots of money he won on – what was it? – football pools?'

'Yes,' she said. 'Everything, except the white Mercedes which she graciously consented to leave with Miss Prentice.' As she said that, it occurred to her that he was driving at something that was completely untrue. 'Look, Joseph,' she said, 'the General's widow's *amant*, Dr Brzeski, was helping Miss Prentice financially with the education of the General's son. Whether the General's widow knew about it or not is irrelevant. Perhaps she wasn't too bad. Perhaps she knew but thought it wiser to pretend she didn't. But one thing is certain, namely, that Miss Prentice never tried to establish the General's paternity, and if you suggest that she's trying to do now, when Ian is dead, what she wasn't even thinking of when he was alive, you are barking up the wrong lamppost.'

He gave a final twist to the piece of string and put it back in his trouser pocket. 'I told you that you don't know what it is all about,' he said. 'You don't know that Mrs Pięść, the widow, sent a big sum of money, dollars, pounds, Swiss francs, to Mr Mściszcziszewski, the patriotic gentleman I mentioned before. Why? What for? Do you want to guess or shall I tell you?'

'Tell me,' Lady Cooper said.

'OK, Jadwiga, I'll tell you. Ostensibly, it is to build a monument. Now, can you guess to whom?'

'No.'

'Really . . .' he said, disapproving of her being so slow in guessing. 'All right. I'll tell you what it is going to be. It's going to be an equestrian statue in bronze representing your General Pięść on a white horse. It is expressly stipulated: on a white horse. How they intend to make a white horse in bronze – search me. Well, anyway, it doesn't really matter, because they can't do it in any case, as there is no sculptor today who could sculpt a horse. A general – yes. But a horse – no. A general may be social realism, that's OK. But his horse must be neoclassic or

116

nothing. And nobody can do a neoclassic horse nowadays. A cubist one – yes. But neoclassic – no. The last sculptor who could was Thorwaldsen, who did Prince Poniatowski in the semi-nude on a neoclassic horse. But Thorwaldsen died more than a hundred years ago, and was a Dane.'

Lady Cooper could no longer stay silent. 'Good gracious me,' she exclaimed. 'General Pięść on a white horse?! I just don't believe you. You're making it up. You're writing a film script for Charlie Chaplin.'

'Charlie Chaplin is dead.'

'Yes, but . . .'

'I haven't finished yet . . .'

'Yes, but . . .'

'I know all your buts, Jadwiga, but you don't know any of mine and you'd better listen. As I said, the patriotic Mr Mściszciszewski is going to erect the monument. Very nice. Why not? . . . *But* Mr Mściszciszewski is not the only patriotic gentleman we are blessed with. There are some others, gentlemen or not. And they do *not* think it will be very nice to let him do it. General Pięść? Who is he? Never heard of him! So they do some research and find out that the General's parents were neither working class nor peasants; on the contrary, they were well born, country, you know, gentry, not exactly nobility, not true aristocrats, because only true aristocrats are *natural* aristocrats and they come from the working classes, which General Pięść's ancestors did not come from, which is bad enough, isn't it? but what was discovered next, namely that one of the General's two grandmothers was born a Frankist, and Frankists were nothing more nor less than baptized Jews, well, you can imagine, that is not only bad enough, it is going to be much worse than bad enough, it is going to be embarrassing to Mr Mściszciszewski himself. Well then, that's how things are. You see it, don't you? So now try to imagine what's going to happen if, rushing into the very centre of this exquisite hornet's nest, comes out of the blue your absurd Miss Prentice with the ashes of the General's bastard . . .'

'Miss Prentice is not Jewish,' Lady Cooper interrupted him.

'Oh Lord! You still don't see the point . . .'

'All right, Joseph. So I don't. The first and foremost point I do *not* see is, why do they want to erect that monument at all? He

117

wasn't even buried here. He is not a Shakespeare to be a monument without a tomb. I knew him. And I know more about him than you think. He was a nice gentleman. But it wasn't my impression that he'd been a victorious hero; on the contrary, one had a very strong feeling that some tragic defeat had left him marked for life.'

'But that's precisely it, my dear. All our monuments are erected to commemorate Tragic Defeats and Heroic Martyrdoms. That's precisely what we like. We don't celebrate joyous victories – possibly because we haven't had any real ones since Jan Sobieski saved European Christendom and ruined the country by driving the vanquished Ottomans from Vienna three hundred years ago exactly.'

'You are exaggerating, aren't you?' she said.

'No, I'm not,' he said.

'Well, and what about Piłsudski, on his chestnut mare, as far eastwards as Kiev, in 1920?'

'And quickly back again, to the very borders of the Vistula.'

'But then he pushed them eastward once more, to what was to become the Curzon line.'

'Yes,' he said. 'But we don't call it a victory. We call it a miracle. *The miracle on the Vistula!* The same as when we repelled the Swedes, we didn't call it our victory, we called it the victory of the Holy Virgin, our Black Madonna of Częstochowa. Yes! Miracles. We can't live without miracles. Patriotic miracles.'

There was bitterness in his voice. Lady Cooper wondered how difficult it was to understand, to pin down this strange 'Minister of Imponderabilia'. 'Isn't it funny,' she said after a while, 'well, very curious, that the same patriotic people who, as you say, will feel embarrassed when they discover that one of the General's grandmothers was born Jewish do at the same time so ardently venerate that other Jewess?'

He looked at her, not comprehending.

'Which other Jewess?' he asked.

'The Blessed Mary, Holy Mother of God, the Queen of the Polish Crown.'

His fist clenched. As of its own volition. Nothing to do with him.

'You know,' he said, 'you just try and say something like that in a public place, and you'll be lynched.'

'Well,' said Lady Cooper, 'I don't want to be lynched, not really. I want Miss Prentice to be given back her handfuls of dust, that's all I want.'

'Then tell her to keep quiet.'

'All right.'

'Not a word to anybody.'

'All right. But I don't see why such secrecy.'

'You don't, don't you? I've put you in the picture. I've put all the pieces on the chessboard for you, and you don't see. Can't you use your imagination? Just try to put yourself in Mr Mściszciszewski's shoes. If you were him, wouldn't you like to save some of the money received from the General's widow? Not for himself. For the Cause. Wouldn't you be tempted to persuade the widow that the monument should be built not in bronze or marble in the neoclassic or social-realism style, but in the constructivist style, in cement? Reinforced concrete. Much more modern and cheaper. Now, try to imagine that at this stage our Mr Mściszciszewski learns about Miss Prentice and the ashes. Will it not be a great idea to immure the back-to-the-womb cedarbox in the monument, or, better still, to mix the poor boy's sacred ashes with the cement? Glory, glory hallelujah! Here comes American Television to film the Holy Mixing, and here is the BBC crew to scoop the unveiling of the monument to the Great Exile. What marvellous publicity for the patriotic Messrs Mściszciszewskis and what silly-season news value for the Western papers! Hey ho! Here they are! Packs of journalists unleashed by their editors to sniff around and dig up some long-forgotten freedom-of-the-press *delicatessen*, preferably morbid. Come on, tell us, what was the General doing in the middle of the night in that lonely place on the river Thames some fourteen years ago when he fired a pistol loaded with one single bullet and died of a heart attack, and who were those hoodlums – were they really just hooligans? Shouldn't the police reopen their files? Fourteen years is not such a long time, his little illegitimate boy would have been thirteen now if he hadn't died a year or so ago . . . Why so young? What was it? Who was his doctor? Dr Brzeski, the General's widow's lover? No! Really?! What a coincidence! A very bright young boy, wasn't he? A mathematical genius. Offered – at his age!!! – a place at Oxford. Well, well. And then he steps into some shallow waters in Majorca and is no more. And who told you all that? Oh! And who was the last person who saw him alive? The man in the wheelchair? Why in a wheelchair? Lost his legs? How come? Because the wavering black poodle stopped half-way between an ambassador's villa and an admiral's villa? What ambassador? What admiral? How very interesting! Now, Miss, or Mrs, or Mr So-and-so, can you tell us, was it the same poodle that Lady Victoria's (or was it Dame Victoria's) green-grocer (or was it her chemist?) reported as lost, the same Lady Victoria (or Dame Victoria) whose granddaughter was whisked off to a guru in India, the one (the granddaughter, not the guru) whose lesbian mother lived with the late-Great-Man-of-Letters' secretary in the same village in Majorca where the little genius-boy died and where – heyho! what a coincidence! – the chap was staying who wrote a biography of the cardinal whose great friend, a Princess Zuppa, was our General Pięść's daughter, now – sniff sniff – wasn't her other friend a Dr Goldfinger who had an account with the bankrupt Banco Ambrosiano? What? A paltry sum of half a million lire? You can always write half a million dollars! And insert the Vatican IOR Bank, P2 Lodge, and Mafia in the headlines. Emphasis is in the heart of art, isn't it? And hark, Ladies and Gentlemen, hasn't that Princess Zuppa got yet another half-brother, a half-black half-brother, the General's African bastard son, a little Napoleon who buys arms from both sides, has gold-capped teeth in his mouth and golden ashtrays in his Rolls-Royce? Now, halloo for a script writer who knows how to mix facts with imagination as well as Mr Mściszciszewski's cement mixes with the little dead boy's ashes and, for heaven's sake, don't forget the chap who wanted to know the colour of the Great Man's eyes and was killed and left a girlfriend who had got herself pregnant by a Mad Hatter who went to Portugal to look at the proletariat packing sardines into sardine tins, and nobody knows, was he a KGB agent, or CIA agent, or just a visitor hailed from another planet.'

'Bravo! What a scenario!' said Lady Cooper.

'You think it's funny?' he asked.

'Utterly, don't you?'

'No, I don't.'

'You think it's serious?'

'Of course it's serious.'

'You think that if Miss Prentice doesn't keep quiet something like that may really happen?'

'Yes.'

'And that's why your government insists on secrecy?'

'Now, look here,' he said, 'it isn't *my* government, I'm not a cabinet minister. It is not my government, it is the government of my country. And notice how our syntax is here displaying its great wisdom. It doesn't commit itself to either of the two great philosophies of our times by deciding whether *my* country means the country to which I belong or the country that belongs to me.' He had paused for breath, and when he started again his voice was soft and small. If one heard it without seeing him one would not guess that it came from such a gigantic body. 'The government . . .' he said. 'The government,' he repeated, and Lady Cooper wasn't quite certain what his tone of voice intended to convey when he started with the same words once again: 'The government can't be bothered with such imponderabilia as your Miss Prentice's little ephemeral fancy. They have more massive things to bother their heads about. Yesterday it was how to manoeuvre so that the great militaries would choose some other country for a battle field on which to try their new-laid weapons and newfangled tactics. Today it is how to pay back the debt of twenty-eight thousand million dollars we owe the Western banks. That is something real, my dear friend. The patriotic Messrs Mściszciszewskis wouldn't stoop to consider such mundane bother. They would leave it to God and His miracles. In which they'd be disappointed. Because, oh, yes, military miracles He can make, the miracle on the Vistula in 1920, the miracle of Jasna Góra in 1655, but, alas, omnipotent as He is, He cannot produce one single green "IN GOD WE TRUST" banknote to the value of one dollar. No, He can't. He can't produce such a miracle. Why not? Because USA dollar bank-notes must carry a serial number. And He can't overprint them with numbers. *Impossibile.* Because to overprint them with numbers already issued by the USA Treasury would be forgery, and to overprint them with some fictitious numbers would be fraud, and a counterfeiter or a swindler God is not, after all, is He? So He finds Himself trapped. He is in despair. The Holy Mother of God is pleading with Him, Jesus is begging Him to help our Roman Catholic communists to pay their national debt

121

to those Lutheran Western bankers, and He cannot do it. He could produce the Big Bang, He could create Adam. And Eve. He can do everything concerning the Physical world. But he can't make miracles with Arithmetic. He could, of course, make some metal dollar coins. Easily! Coins are not numbered. Coins He can make. Fresh-from-the-mint. But . . . "Goodness Me!" – exclaims He among some forked lightnings – "28,000,000,000 silver dollar coins, 26.730 grams each, makes 748,440,000,000 grams, or 748,440,000 kilograms, or seventy-four Eiffel Towers of silver, dropping from My blue sky on the Treasury in Warsaw, at the speed of twenty-five kilometres per second, melting everything around, throwing the dust into the upper atmosphere and creating a crater that would set off a volcano!"'

He was so pleased with himself, he licked his lips like a cat who licks chocolate cream off a cream bun. Then he went on: 'And if Mr Mściszciszewski suggests to his Almighty that He produce the miracle gradually, well . . . Does he know that if God drops one silver dollar per second, it will take him 887 years 319 days 1 hour 46 minutes and 40 seconds to pay off our national debt, not counting the capitalist interest?'

'Ha!' Lady Cooper said and added another 'Ha!' not knowing exactly what she wanted to express by either.

'It isn't a laughing matter, my dear Jadwiga. I have just painted for you such a mathematical graphic picture of the situation to show you the scale of things our rulers are occupied with. Do you still think they would have time to bother about Miss Prentice and her handfuls of dust? No, dear friend. If I'm asking you to persuade her to keep quiet, it is not for their sake. It's for yours.'

'Mine?' Lady Cooper exclaimed. 'How absurd!'

'Not absurd at all. You see, I know you. Though I haven't seen you for such a long time. I know that you are not the kind of person to whom the News of the World would pay forty thousand pounds for a page of assorted revelations, what they call a scoop. No. On the contrary. You are a sucker who will be interviewed for nothing, you'll be interrogated, watched, kidnapped, assassinated, hanged under Blackfriars Bridge . . .'

'My dear Joseph,' she said, 'are you mad?'

His eyes looked straight into her. As if they wanted to modify the meaning of what he had just said. Not to erase, but to modify. Perhaps as the rhythm in a line of poetry modifies the meaning of the statement. And then, suddenly, they (his eyes) relaxed. They relaxed in a smile. 'Do you know when one tells stories?' he asked.

'When?'

'One tells stories,' he said, 'when one must tell a lie in order to convey the truth.'

'I see . . .' she said, not quite sure what it was that she saw. 'Go on . . .'

'Well,' he said, 'I'm not asking you to believe in my arguments. I'm asking you to be practical and accept them. OK?'

'OK.'

'Good,' he said. 'Now, tell me one thing about the girl. What sort of mystic rites and ceremonies does she want?'

'None whatever.'

'Not even some symbolic gestures? Like kissing the ground . . . ?'

'She isn't that kind of person. If she wanted to kiss the earth it wouldn't occur to her to kiss the tarmac of the airport, she would rather kiss the earth in a flowerpot.'

'I like that,' he said.

'So don't worry. She's very matter-of-fact. For her the ashes in the casket are physical ashes and all she wants is to return them physically to the – let me call it – ecology of General Pięść's motherland.'

He nodded his approval.

There was a brief silence.

And then, smiling at her confidently, he asked: 'Do you think she would like the idea of sprinkling the ashes on to the tops of the trees in some lovely part of a forest?'

'I'm sure she would.'

'With women, you never can tell.'

'I can ask her.'

'Do. Do ask her that, and ask her also if she will agree to keep away from the press. If she does *not* agree, ring me before midnight. If she does, no need to phone. If I don't hear from you, I'll take it that she does agree and I'll fetch you both from your hotel tomorrow. I don't know exactly when, I'll still have many things to do. You'd better be ready to start the minute I come.'

He rose.

And so did Lady Cooper.

They were now standing by the door leading to the hall.

'Joseph . . .'

'Yes?'

'You are made on a large scale, Joseph. How is it that you give so much of yourself to such ephemeral, trifling problems?'

He had already held out his enormous hand to kiss hers for goodbye. Now he retracted it and put it in his trouser pocket. To touch the piece of string he had been playing with?

'OK,' he said (he said it in English and pronounced it oh kah), 'I don't see why you shouldn't know my real motives, my – you can say – "philosophy".' He leaned against the door jamb and his head was now touching the doorhead. 'OK,' he repeated, 'listen. I'll tell you first about the sort of cases I don't take. If, let us say, a fireman comes to me complaining that he has burnt his thumb, I send him back, telling him, "Stop whining. You knew quite well what your job meant. You didn't join the fire brigade on condition that there would never be a fire, did you?" And I say the same to the poet who had the word "shit" cut out by the censor in the name of order, and to the militiaman who was hit by a brick in the name of freedom, and to the minister who doesn't enjoy being swiped at in a music hall, and to the dissident persecuted for his militancy. To the older ones I might add: "Were you not doing the same unto others when you were in power?" And to the younger ones: "Are you not hoping to do the same unto others as soon as you gain power?. . ."'

He stopped as if in the middle of a sentence.

'Would you agree,' he asked, 'that what we sometimes call "ethical behaviour" is a matter of good taste rather than of morals?'

'I certainly would.'

'Some people have that sort of good taste. Maybe most of us are born with it, but then it gets damped off by too much thinking and feeling.' He stopped again. 'Am I getting sententious?' he asked.

'Not at all. Go on. You have told me about the cases you don't take. What are the ones you do?'

He hesitated. As if he could not decide what sort of words were likely not to be misinterpreted by her.

'Extraordinary cases affecting some ordinary chaps,' he said. 'Ordinary chaps,' he repeated, 'chaps or girls who get themselves caught up by the cog wheels of the system for which they haven't fought or prayed or voted. Does that sound funny?'

The only thing that sounded funny – she thought – was to hear this enormous great elephant speaking so softly and timidly, as if he were afraid that one would laugh at him. He waited for an answer before continuing.

'Not at all. Please go on.'

'All right,' he said. 'Well, you see, all systems have three things built into them: the priest, the militiaman, and the paymaster. And when the system is perfectly perfect, then it may so happen that if a chap is OK not because the priest told him to be OK, or the militiaman told him to be OK, but because he is OK just because he is OK, then the paymaster may refuse to pay him, and the chap is caught by the machinery of the system.'

'And you are trying to rescue him . . .'

'Yes and no!' he protested hotly. 'It isn't so simple as that. What I'm doing is not philanthropy. It isn't charity. I'm not a Mother Teresa of Calcutta!' He was now aware that he had just revealed a quite different chemistry in his nature. Was he glad that it had so happened, or would he have preferred to conceal it? He took a deep breath, as if to cool something that was burning in him, and then he smiled, good-naturedly or ironically – it was impossible to say with certainty. 'You see,' he said very quietly, 'a perfect system can never be perfect. A system has to be imperfect to be perfect. A little corruption, a little bribery, a little hypocrisy, a little string-pulling, a little blackmail are good things. They provide perfect systems with those little imperfections, those little windows through which new mutations can fly in and inseminate our formal gardens. Without them, without those blessed little windows of imperfections, all perfectly planned systems are rigid. And everything rigid ends in chaos. One tiny little fact can topple a gigantic theory. The infinitesimal, misregarded by calculus, little imponderabilia, little pebbles which the priest, the militiaman, or the paymaster drops into the pond – making some insignificantly tiny little waves that disturb the heart of a tiny little man – can cause the whole system to vibrate with unplanned harmonics, increased perturbations, overlapping resonances, through which chaos sneaks in.'

'So that's why they let you do it!' Lady Cooper said.

'Who? Who lets me do what?'

'The authorities.'

'Do what?'

'Run to the rescue of the imponderabilia. They let you do it because, as you said, you are not Mother Teresa of Calcutta. They let you do it because you do it not for the sake of the little trapped man but for the sake of the system.'

'And so does she,' he said. 'For the sake of her system. Which fact doesn't reflect on the value of her charity.' He thought for a moment, and then said slowly, 'We are all trapped between the beautiful blueprints of the most perfect systems and the World that contradicts itself, the World that is "large and contains multitudes".'

They were now standing in that darkish hall-corridor, between its two old-fashionedly tapestried walls. The old frail woman and the old gentle giant.

'Joseph . . .' she said. 'It's such ancient history . . . So many years . . . I can't recall . . . Did we actually go to bed to make love, I mean really?'

He blushed.

She smiled and said, 'Don't worry. As you see I don't remember either,' and she added quickly, 'May I ask you another question?'

'Well . . . ?'

'How is it that you have so much power?'

'No power at all.' He spread his arms, palms open, as if to show that there was nothing in them.

'Well, then – so much influence on those who have power.'

He chuckled.

'I'll tell you,' he said. 'It's my bloody size that does it. Don't laugh. That's how it is. When I approach, the guard salutes me. When I march to the door of her boss, no secretary dares to stop me. When I appear in front of his desk, the VIP gets up and asks me to sit down so that he needn't look up at me. And he'll never say "Get out!" because he knows that if I refuse to budge, he will have to call a squadron of men to move me and make himself look ridiculous. Eh? Why are you giggling?'

'I noticed that your big body is equally effective when you speak, ever so softly, on the telephone.'

126

He roared with laughter. As if the laughter itself was sufficient answer. His left hand was already touching the doorknob. His right hand took hers. Cautiously. Her hand in his looked like a child's hand. He stooped and kissed it.

'If I don't hear from you before midnight, you'll see me sometime tomorrow,' he said.

'Yes.'

'Incidentally,' he said, opening the door for her. 'About Miss Prentice . . . is she good-looking?'

'She certainly is,' Lady Cooper said. 'Very.'

'Good!' he said. And then, as if he thought that some explanation was wanting, he added: 'Everything would be exactly the same if she were not. But some people feel better when they do something for a *pretty* damsel. Helicopter pilots, for instance. They prefer to play the role of a chivalrous romantic knight rather than that of a do-gooder. Even communist helicopter pilots.'

TWELVE

No Axioms are Immortal

That's how she found herself, the next day, high up in the air, some few hundred feet above the treetops, Miss Prentice on her left, Joseph – the 'Minister of Imponderabilia' – on her right, and the cedarwood casket (now empty) on her knees. It was so quiet, in spite of the atrocious noise made by the rotors which kept them stationary in the air.

'Well, mission accomplished, let's go back,' Joseph boomed out.

The pilot looked questioningly at Miss Prentice.

She nodded.

The green leafy heads of the forest trees rolled away like the waves of the sea. In this helicopter buzzing between heaven and earth, it was not difficult, it was quite easy to think about the Mad Hatter as a visitor from another planet who had made poor Mr McPherson's girlfriend pregnant and gone to Portugal to look at the proletariat packing sardines. But how could Joseph know about it? Lady Cooper wondered. Who has been sending all that silly gossip to his people? Somebody he did *not* mention? Whom did he not mention? Veronica, the French lady, Captain Casanova . . . ?

'Are you all right?' Joseph asked.

'Perfectly all right,' Lady Cooper said. 'Why?'

'Oh nothing,' he said. 'We're just landing.'

Decimating a swarm of honeybees which must have been migrating with their queen to establish a new colony, the helicopter landed softly on the wild green herbage of the glade, a dozen or so yards from the spot where Joseph's black saloon car was parked. As they stepped off the helicopter, Mr Mirek, the pilot, conjured up, as if from nothing, four already open tins of Coca-Cola.

'Thank you ever so much,' Miss Prentice said.

Was she thanking him for Coca-Cola? He didn't think so.

'It is I who thank you, madam,' he said, gallantly kissing her hand, 'for the great privilege of being able to be of some service to you. The memory of this memorable day will be remembered for ever, because it has alrady been engraved on the very bottom of my heart, madam.' He clicked his heels and saluted.

Lady Cooper took him on one side and told him that Miss Prentice would like to send him a present when she was back in England. Was there anything he would like to suggest? 'Oh, yes,' he answered at once, without hesitation. A book. Partridge's *Dictionary of Slang*. 'It isn't for me,' he explained. 'It's for my sister.' And then he corrected himself: 'Actually, to be honest, it is for my girlfriend. She's studying linguistics. At university. English linguistics. The seventeenth century.'

'Miss Prentice will do that,' Lady Cooper said. 'But it may take several weeks till the book arrives.'

'That's OK,' he said. He gulped down his Coca-Cola and whispered: 'I've never thought I'd be a funerary undertaker, because that's exactly what I've just been, isn't it? Well, anyway, she's a lovely lady, but, say, the ashes, were they really those of her son? She doesn't look like a mother who has lost her baby, does she? And . . . why all that secrecy? Were they not, by any chance, the ashes of some great *émigré* patriot perhaps? General Sikorski's? No? Anders'? No? or perhaps a writer's? Gombrowicz's? No? You say they really were those of her little boy? How old was he? Twelve? She doesn't look as if she could have had a son of that age. Lovely piece of nice. If you don't mind my saying so. Style. English. Long legs. Good bottom. If you don't mind me saying so. Pretty boobs. I say, is she Dr Kszak's lay? I wouldn't have thrown her out of my bed myself. If you don't mind my saying so. No offence. Well, back to base. Pleased to have met you, madam.' He kissed her hand and went back to his flying machine.

They were already sitting in the car, Joseph at the driving wheel (he hadn't taken his chauffeur for this expedition), Miss Prentice in the front seat beside him, Lady Cooper at the back, and were ready to start, when Mr Mirek, the pilot, came running towards them, carrying the cedarwood casket in his hands.

'You forgot your little coffin,' he said.

Lady Cooper put it on the seat beside her.

*

They drove along with the car windows wound down. The green sward and the trees, the birch and the beech and an occasional oak on both sides of the country lane looked the same as they must have looked a hundred years ago, and the air tasted as it must have tasted a hundred years ago. And then the trees gave way to a cornfield with poppies on one side and a hazel grove on the other, as they moved slowly, hesitantly, till the car joined the motor road and bowled along at an even pace towards the capital.

They were now driving on the same road as before, but everything looked different. What had been on their left was now on the right, what had been hidden and abandoned behind their backs was now coming towards them.

'I should like to invite you to dinner in my hotel restaurant,' Lady Cooper said.

'What did you say?' Joseph asked.

She repeated it more loudly.

'Let's,' Miss Prentice said.

Lady Cooper couldn't manage to see Joseph's face in his driving mirror, but the answer he grunted out seemed reluctant. It might have been that he didn't want to show himself eating a five-course dinner in that place which only some tourists, foreign delegates, free-enterprise businessmen, black marketeers and spivs could afford. The humming motion of the car and the wind behind the windows were lulling slleepilly . . . She must have dreamt some strange dreamy thoughts because now she shook herself out of her slumbery vision and shouted: 'I say, Joseph. I think that in the next century we'll have a dictatorship of the unemployed!'

He heard her voice but didn't hear the words. He slowed down and said: 'Let's go to my place. I'm not sure what we'll find there, but I always can cook some spaghetti or something.'

'Yes, let's,' said Miss Prentice.

*

130

As soon as they arrived, they went, all three, to the kitchen to see what there was they could eat. In the refrigerator they found a round box of caviar (25 grams), a small (100 grams) bottle of vodka, and absolutely nothing else. On the wall above the refrigerator, suspended from a nail, was hanging a twelve-inch-long sausage called *krakowska*. In a saucepan, on the stove, there was some boiled milk, covered with yellowish skin. In the cupboard, they saw half a loaf of brown bread, some salt, pepper, sugar, horseradish, a small tin of Russian tea, and a big tin on which was printed in Gothic characters KAFFE. It was empty. On the upper shelf, wrapped in a page of the newspaper *Zycie Warszawy*, were 3 (three) long rods of dry spaghetti. He was holding now those three long rods of spaghetti in his enormous hand and grinned, embarrassed: 'Shall I cook them?'

'Yes, please, do,' Miss Prentice said.

'Joseph,' Lady Cooper said, 'let me go down and fetch a bottle of wine and something . . .'

He didn't like it. The shops would be closed, and anyway there was nothing in them one could buy. But didn't he know that she had some English pounds sterling, and could go to one of those shops where you can get everything for foreign currency? No. He still didn't like it. 'But Joseph,' Lady Cooper said, 'this is a very special occasion, let me go.'

'Let her go,' Miss Prentice said.

Lady Cooper didn't like the way Miss Prentice said that. But Joseph had already half consented.

'Those shops are very far from here,' he warned her.

'May I borrow your car?' she asked, and immediately felt that the very suggestion was outrageous.

'I'll see if Mr Adamczyk is in,' he said as he walked out of the kitchen.

Mr Adamczyk was his chauffeur. Only now Lady Cooper realized that there, in the corridor, there was an intercom to the housekeeper's lodge.

*

Mr Adamczyk was waiting for her at the bottom of the stairs, by the lift. He already knew where to take her. The streets were dark. Not much traffic. The shops looked empty. Where does

Joseph feed his big frame? she wondered. Workers have their canteens, some better some worse; writers, architects, actors have their clubs where they may have their dinners, but where does Joseph eat? This simple, trivial question puzzled her. She spoke to the chauffeur, she said something vague, so worded that if he chose to answer, it would enlighten her. But his taciturnity was unruffled.

She was still more puzzled by herself. By her own feeling. The feeling of unease. She wasn't sure what it was, couldn't make out what it was, when – suddenly – she heard her own lips bringing out the word 'privileged'. With pound notes in her handbag she *was* privileged. And she didn't like it. Why was it so that in London she could go to Fortnum & Mason without having any qualms, though she had seen homeless people sleeping on the Embankment – she wondered – and here she was ashamed to enter the brightly-lit foreign-currency bloody shop? Was the state of being privileged OK in one kind of country and not OK in another? Dissatisfied with her own thoughts Lady Cooper shrugged her shoulders. It was funny that each time it happened that she shrugged her shoulders, she immediately thought about little Emma – little Emma sitting alone at the big table in the Majorca hotel restaurant, shrugging her little shoulders, and ordering an hors d'oeuvre for herself. OK, all right, OK, one day Atlas will shrug *his* shoulders and it will be the end of all our silliness. All right, all right, privileged or not, ashamed or not, she entered the shop, bought a bottle of champagne, two big packets of coffee, and a dozen tins and boxes bearing German, French, Italian labels, not at all sure what they contained, and paid in English pounds, which the lady behind the counter laboriously tried to convert into Almighty USA dollars. Back in the car, she sat in the front seat beside the chauffeur and, as they started off, she put one packet of coffee on his lap and said: 'Will that be of some use to you?'

Imagine an overcast sky with a big black cloud in the middle, and in the middle of this big black cloud a small, worn-away bit of it, much thinner but not yet a hole; and now, as you are looking at it, the sun moves and finds itself behind the thin bit, and the thin bit brightens up, and its brightness brightens the blackness that surrounds it, but only for a moment, because the sun moves westward and the cloud moves eastward and everything seems to be again as it was before, but the memory of the moment of brightness persists at the back of your eye. That was exactly what happened to his face. It brightened up. For a moment. Then it smiled. For a second. And Lady Cooper felt humiliated. By the fact that she had bought that smile. And the price was two pounds of coffee.

'That's very kind of you,' he said, but he didn't touch the packet. They drove for a whole minute in silence. Then he opened the glove compartment, put the packet in it, and said: 'I have decided to accept your *prezent.*' And then, suddenly, the black heavy cloud burst into a torrent of words. 'Who bloody whore do they think we are? Little children? And who do they think they are to teach us? We know more about life than they can ever learn from their rat-race consumer commercials. What do they think they've gained by their bloody sacramental sanctions? More TB for our kids? Do they hope that our hungry kids will pull down the government if they send them a lollipop in their sacramental Yuletide parcels? Has no bloody whore told them that by the time the fat man gets lean the lean man will croak? How do they expect us to pay our debts if they don't let us have spare parts for the machines we've bought from them? I know what I'm talking about. My brother lives in Włocławek. We've spent two hundred bloody million dollars to build a factory there, and they wouldn't let us have another ten-millions-worth of their bloody junk to get it going. Don't they see that makes us still more dependent on those we hate more than they do? But what do they care?! They would sell us all down the river for a few votes of some fat Poles singing patriotic songs in their Chicago. I'll tell you something, Lady Cooper, you *are* called Lady Cooper now, aren't you?, well, I wasn't born yesterday, I'll tell you how I see it. When Marshal Piłsudski put on his civilian clothes and went to Geneva, do you know what he said when he came back? He said: "What? The League of Nations? Words, words, words. Let them shut up and give me the command of an international militia and I'll make peace in Europe." He meant it as a joke, didn't he. A bleeding joke. But that's precisely the kind of a joke we've got now, isn't it? The bleeding NATO missiles targeted straight on us. The bleeding nuclear shit. And they bloody whore think their shit is clean, their shit doesn't stink, if you will excuse my language. They say it's thanks to it that we've had peace in Europe for nearly forty years now. Bloody lies. Do you know why we haven't had the Third World War yet? I'll tell you. It's because we've divided bloody Germany. And because the French have learned the lesson – have learned that no League of Nations yapping and no Maginot Line will ever stop the Germans fighting, the only thing they understand being Commerce. So they, the French, said, "Capitalists of the World, unite!" and they made the Common Market. That's why we haven't had the Third World War yet. Because of the Common Market. And the very thing they've done with the Germans they could have done with the Russkis: Commerce instead of missiles. But they wouldn't. Why would they not? I'll tell you. Because they're afraid. What are they afraid of? Of being attacked by the Russkis? Bullshit. The First World War wasn't started by the Tsar, it was started by the Kaiser. And the Second World War wasn't started by Stalin, it was started by Hitler. So what are the bloody whore's bastards afraid of? I'll tell you. They are afraid of beliefs. Because they're great believers, the Russkis. They believe that History is on their side. And, sure, they want to help History to be on their side. Because they too are frightened. They are frightened of having another Napoleon in Moscow, another Piłsudski in Kiev, another Hitler in Stalingrad. So now we have that fucking nuclear shit on both sides, on our left and on our right. As if one could fight with beliefs by dropping bombs! I know what I'm talking about, Lady Cooper. I was with the Russkis in Berlin, I saw Hitler's bunker. I was seventeen then. 'Twas something, I tell you. You couldn't beat it. And I was in their America too. Driving a limousine. With bullet-proof glass. I've seen the world. I saw the Statue of Liberty the French gave them a hundred years ago to enlighten the world. Sure, Lady Cooper, I was at the time naive enough to learn by heart the words engraved on the stone on which the freedom lady is standing:

"Keep, ancient lands, your storied pomp," cries she
With silent lips. "Give me your tired, your poor,
Your huddled masses yearning to breathe free."

'Scuse pronunciation. 'V'been in America for not very long. They chucked me out. And haven't heard much English since. Am not sure what the word "storied" means. *Your storied pomp.*

134

Does it mean many storeys like in their skyscrapers, or like social classes, upper classes, lower classes, or is it like a story meaning history?'

'I'm not sure,' Lady Cooper said.

'Well, anyway,' he went on. 'Things have changed, haven't they? Now their freedom woman is using napalm bombs and flame throwers on our huddled masses. Flame throwers and sanctions. She quite forgot that you conquer the beliefs of other people not by feeding their guns with ammunition but by lending them corn and sewing machines.'

He swerved to avoid a cat whose two green eyes were reflecting the lights of the headlamps. Was it paralysed with fear, or mesmerized by the strength of the beam of light, or afraid that it would drop the mouse it was holding between its teeth? They swerved, and, nevertheless, they hit it. Cats have nine lives and it wasn't the ninth of this one. Lady Cooper looked back and saw it limping towards the pavement. She didn't see the mouse.

*

She pressed a button, and it must have been the wrong button, because the lift took her to the wrong floor. A man was sitting there on a bentwood chair in the corner of the landing, by the door. Smoking a cigarette.

'What do you want?' he said.

'I want to go in,' Lady Cooper said.

'You can't,' he said.

'Why not?' she asked.

'Because I say so,' he said.

'Look here,' Lady Cooper said, 'I'm visiting Dr Kszak. He's waiting for me.'

'I think I've seen your face,' the man said.

'Possibly,' Lady Cooper said. 'I've been here before.'

'Doing what?'

'I told you: visiting Dr Kszak.'

'There's no Dr Kszak here,' he said.

On the floor, by the leg of the chair he was sitting on, stood what looked like a chamberpot. It was half filled with cigarette ends. Lady Cooper looked around. Only now she noticed that there was a different sculpture in the niche in the wall opposite the lift. It was Diana with a bow this time.

'I think I must be on the wrong floor,' she said.

'Christopher Columbus,' he said sarcastically.

'Could you tell me which floor it should be?' she asked.

'One below,' he said. And when she turned round, he added, 'Don't take the lift. Save electricity. One can bore ten holes in a steel plate with the electricity you'll use in the lift. Can't you walk?'

'All right,' she said.

'England?' he asked.

'Yes,' she said, turning round again to go down the steps.

'Not so fast,' he said. 'What do you have in that bag?'

'Food,' Lady Cooper said.

'Let's see,' he said.

He didn't move from his chair. He was authority. He was law and order. Lady Cooper wondered who the VIP was who lived behind the door he was guarding. She stepped towards him. He looked into the bag.

'Good grub,' he said. 'Enjoy it.'

He couldn't know that the grub was to be used to celebrate the successful scattering of a little boy's ashes over his father's motherland.

Yes, it was just one floor below, as he had said. The shepherdess with a crook stood there smiling in the niche (unless it was a young bishop with a pastoral staff) and on the door on the left there was a small copper plate with *Dr Józef Kszak* engraved in copperplate writing. She thought the door would be shut, but it was left unlatched. Hadn't she locked it properly, or had they left it unlatched for her? She stepped in. Some yellowish light from the staircase crept in with her. There was also a chink of white light under the door to the study, in front of her. The long, dark corridor with its old tapestried walls felt suddenly so familiar. She wanted to see that tapestry again. She knew where the switch was. The incongruously big crystal chandelier was hanging from the centre of the long and narrow ceiling. Only one small bulb lit, but the pieces of prismatic rainbow glass sparkled and the tapestry on the wall revealed a gondolier propelling his boat on a canal in Venice. There was no sound.

Lady Cooper hoisted her carrier bag triumphantly like a flag and opened the door, ready to shout: 'Look what I've got!' – but that was not to be. She tiptoed to the sofa, put her carrier bag gently on it, and sat down.

In front of her, by the opposite wall, stood a small chessboard table. Joseph and Miss Prentice were sitting at it, facing each other. But the chessmen were not on the table – must have been put back in the bright lacquered box, now standing on top of his desk, on the right of *War and Peace*. They were so engrossed in each other that they didn't seem to be aware that Lady Cooper had come back and was now sitting there on the sofa, watching. His two enormous hands, palms up, lay open on the chessboard. The tip of the thumb of her right hand was touching, lightly, the tip of the thumb of his left palm. The tip of the index finger of her left hand was pressing down the tip of the thumb of his right palm and the tip of the thumb of her left hand was pressing down the tip of the index finger of his right palm.

'. . . there is a trap in the words "free will", there is a catch in the word "destiny". Don't have them in your vocabulary . . .'

While she spoke, he was looking at her spellbound.

Lady Cooper had had enough of it. She felt as if she were eavesdropping. She took her carrier bag and tiptoed to the kitchen.

In the cupboard, she found three large plates, three small plates, three knives, three forks, three spoons, three small vodka glasses, three tumblers (they were actually empty washed-up mustard glasses), three coffee cups (no saucers), and she laid the table. No napkins. And only one chair. They'll have to bring their chairs with them. She opened the refrigerator, took out the bottle of vodka and the round carton of caviar and put them on the table. There was no ice in the refrigerator, so she said, *tant pis*, and put the bottle of champagne by the side of the vodka. Then she unpacked what else there was in her carrier bag. Coffee, lasagne verdi, pumpernickel, Gentleman's Relish, Camembert, and the rest of her haphazard purchases, biscuits, pickles, sardines, lemons, dates . . . After which, she looked into the study again to see if they had finished with each other. They definitely had not. Not yet. They seemed determined not to be hurried by her. Though they must have been as hungry as she was. She sat on the sofa.

137

Miss Prentice's forefinger was moving along the lines on his palm. Lady Cooper wondered whether it wasn't tickling him.

'. . . most amazing . . .' Miss Prentice was saying, '. . . your lines are exactly the same . . . carbon copies of his lines . . . Oh yes, I remember his hands so well, poor General. Have there been many similarities between your two lives? It cannot be just a matter of chance. One in a billion billions! Poor Jan. Poor General Pięść. General Pięść. He used to laugh when I tried to pronounce his name. Pięść. He liked me. I don't say that he loved me. And I liked him. I don't say that I loved him. Liking is more important. You don't hurt people you like. You always hurt people you love. And are hurt by them. Oh yes, he liked me and he liked talking to me. He said he liked talking to me because I received his words as they were said, without deforming them by my own thoughts, even when I didn't understand them, which – very often – I didn't, because they were coming from a world so different from mine. About himself . . . he liked to talk in the evening, when we were in bed; he would always shut his eyes and he would say: "Do you know, child . . ." He always used to start by saying "Do you know . . ."'

Lady Cooper looked at Joseph. She was afraid that he might say something cynical, something that would tell Miss Prentice not to make a fool of herself. She gave Miss Prentice a warning cough. But she didn't take any notice. Neither did he. She placed her right hand over his left palm. Her voice was quite different now. Lady Cooper wouldn't have recognized it if she had heard it on the telephone. It sounded as if she were singing. To herself. But from far away: 'When he was a little boy, he was told to be nice. He was told to be nice to women, to flowers, to animals, and to things and people he didn't like . . . There was no virtue – he was told – in being nice only to lollipops and to people one likes . . . One must also be nice to cod-liver oil and to spiders . . .

'When he was a bit older, he was told – if you like to eat flesh, you must know how to kill. A gentleman doesn't ask other people to do things he himself is not capable of doing. And he was given a sporting gun and taught how to shoot to kill. Outright. To use dogs for retrieving was all right. But to use a pack of trained hounds to kill a fox, instead of shooting it outright, was a most ungentlemanly thing to do.'

She wasn't looking at his hands now. No, she didn't pretend that she was reading the General's life from the lines on Joseph's hands. She seemed to be looking into herself now, retracing some paths in the mysterious grey matter of memory. Lady Cooper looked at her in silent wonder. She was so different. Even her vocabulary was different. Lady Cooper didn't remember having heard her laugh. And hardly ever had she seen her smile. And now a gentle smile appeared on her face, as she went on: 'And then he was taught good manners. To let ladies pass first, except when going up or down the stairs, to walk on her left so that your right hand could support her left elbow when helping her to jump over the puddle, to bow and kiss a married lady's hand – how did he know whether a woman was married, a Mrs (a *Pani*) or a Miss (a *Panna*) – I asked him, he said he didn't know how he knew but he was always right, it must have been intuition, he wouldn't kiss a peasant woman's hand, obviously, he said, but it wasn't prejudice, it was because a peasant woman would never hold out her hand to him unless to grasp his and kiss it. Peasants had their own good manners which had to be respected. And who was he, the little boy, to theorize on the subject. For him, his code of behaviour, his good manners, were like breathing, or eating, or riding. They were both natural and absolute. They were just there. They were the will of the world. They were facts of life . . .'

She took a deep breath.

'But then,' she went on with a sense of grievance, 'the religious instruction he had received disturbed him. Of the Three Persons of the Trinity, it was the Holy Spirit alone that he found congenial to him. It, the Holy Spirit, too, was like breathing, or eating, or riding. It was both natural and absolute; it too was the will of the world, the fact of life. And It was not really somewhere outside, It was *in* him, healthily, he didn't need to think about It, just as one doesn't need to think about one's heart, or liver, or bowels, so long as they are healthily in one. Yes, the Holy Spirit was OK, and he was at peace with It. The Holy Spirit had good manners. But the Other Two, the One of the Old Testament, and the One of the New, the Father and the Son, well . . . no, he had no feeling for Them at all. Perhaps because They had such bad manners. They wanted to be respected but They didn't respect him. They wanted to be under-

139

stood but They didn't bother to understand him. They wanted to be loved but he didn't believe that They loved him, no, not really. If They had really loved him, would They bully him without even asking what his problem is, what it is that's worrying him so much? Oh no, the Father was an autocrat who required things to be done according to His Rules, regardless . . . and the Son was His Steward, keeping people in suspense between heaven and hell, bribing them with the lollipop of the one, and frightening them with the brimstone of the other. A queer way of showing Their love . . .

'"You know, child," he said – he liked to call me child – "You know, child, when I was a little boy, of course I used to go through all the motions prescribed by the black-soutaned rooks. But I had no confidence in the Father and the Son. The Tsar of All the Universe and His Governor General of the Planet. Nobody even knew for sure – was He God pretending to be man or man pretending to be God. No, I didn't trust Them. I wouldn't lend Them my pony, I would be afraid They not only wouldn't give it back to me, but would find some fine excuse for not doing so and make *me* feel guilty. They would say the Son had suffered so much for my sake, and I grudge Him such a little four-legged thing which anyway was the Father's *gift* to Mankind. So I thought the Father and the Son were a sort of Jewish conspiracy, all right perhaps for the ancient Hebrews in Palestine, but not entirely *comme il faut* for a Polish gentleman. And when my heart was full of trouble, no, not to Them would I turn, but to Her, to Her who wasn't even a part of the Trinity, yes, to Her, the Holy Mother of God, the Virgin Mary."

'Her, he adored. In Her, he had full confidence. She, he knew, would defend him against the infallible self-righteousness of Her Son and His Father. That She was Virgin had no meaning to him. On the contrary, Her being Mother, Her full breasts, Her round belly, and Her calm face. were his harbour and his haven. By Her, he didn't need to be understood. She would protect him without asking any questions. She was much above such things as condemning or absolving. She was always on his side. "So you see, child," he said, "that was how I replaced the Trinity by my own trinity, my own private, secret, personal trinity. It consisted of the Holy Spirit, which was Life itself, and Mary, Mother of God, and the White Horse".'

She said clearly, 'the White Horse', and she burst out laughing. It was so unexpected that Lady Cooper jumped, and the sofa on which she was sitting gave a little squeak. They paid no attention. They were there, in the middle of their enchanted circle, and everything beyond it, including Lady Cooper and the sofa, was void.

'I must tell you why I laughed,' Miss Prentice said. 'I laughed at myself. I laughed at myself because I remembered that when he mentioned the White Horse for the first time, I thought he meant a bottle of whisky, White Horse whisky. That shows you how far away my world was from his world. It took me a long time, it took me twelve years, twelve years of sleep-walking, from the night of his death to the night of Ian's death, to understand him, and his White Horse, at last.'

Suddenly, Lady Cooper saw it. Suddenly, she saw what Miss Prentice was doing. She too was building a monument. A monument to General Pięść, her dead lover. *Exegi monumentum aere perennius.* A monument more lasting than Mr Mściszciszewski's brass. A monument made of words. Of thoughts. Of pictures in the mind. Of visions. Of noble lies. A magnificent myth. A legend. Here it comes along at an amble. Gracefully. The White Horse with its White Horse's burden: the General – astride, and the Virgin Mary – side-saddle. The Blessed Mary of Little Mercies, The Blessed Mary of Good Manners, The Blessed Mary of Imponderabilia. There they pace across Europe to the rescue of Joseph's unlisted *homo*, caught between the cogwheels of two perfect systems, one run by the Son according to the rules set by the Father, the other run by the Party according to the rules of History.

Was Lady Cooper awake, or was she asleep, dreaming? She looked at Miss Prentice, and couldn't believe her eyes. She listened to her, and couldn't believe her ears. It was fantastic. Under the chessboard table, the resonant sparking air-gap, the little Sistine Chapel space between the knees of Joseph and the knees of the palmist, was heavy as thunder. Lady Cooper got up and tiptoed back to the kitchen.

The table was beautifully laid for three. She removed one large plate and one small plate and put them back in the cupboard. She took one fork and knife and spoon and put them into the drawer. She took one vodka glass and one tumbler and

141

put them on the shelf. She bowed politely to the table and said goodbye. That was her exit. Her phantom exit. To make her physical exit from the kitchen she had to pass through the study again.

She opened the door.

No fumes there, except in Lady Cooper's eyes, no tripod, no chasm, but that was how Lady Cooper would imagine an entranced Pythian prophetess, her mind out of this world, though the voice Lady Cooper heard, the voice of Miss Prentice, the palmist, was strong and clear and contemptuous when, looking into Joseph's eyes, she said: *'Politicians are mortal, political ideas are mortal, poetry is mortal – good manners are immortal.'*

There was a long pause.

And then, suddenly, she was not a Delphian priestess any more. She bent over the chessboard table and buried her face in his immense hands.

It was sheer lunacy, but Lady Cooper had a lump in her throat as she tiptoed across the floor to the door. In the hall, the gondolier under the Bridge of Sighs – a palace and a prison on each hand – was still there on the wall, but during all that time his gondola hadn't moved an inch.

THIRTEEN
Occam's Razor

She closed the door noiselessly, not to alert the cigarette-smoking bodyguard on the floor above; she didn't take the clattery lift, not to wake up the chauffeur in the lodge on the ground floor; she walked down the stairs silently on the tips of her toes and glided out of the house.

Alone, at last! She liked to hear the sound of her own footfalls re-echoing in the empty street. Above her, the black sky, the beauty of its blackness, pinpointed by the Great Bear and the Little Bear and the countless stars of the Milky Way, was coming down sound and clear through the transparent, unpolluted air. She didn't know how far she was from the centre of the town. The street was rising slightly towards a dark open space – a garden? a park? – its trees mingling with the black sky above. Not long ago, this would have been the likeliest place to encounter a man with a brick for sale. You could buy it from him, or else he could give it to you as a present by hitting you on the head with it. You were free to choose. Poor, primitive brick! Small fry! In New York it would be a Colt .45, which their small thugs used to call a *peacemaker*, just as their big thugs call their MX missiles *peacekeepers*. She tried to keep in step with the rhythm of marching that had strayed into her memory, which was, of course, silly because she had forgotten her age. The other thing she had forgotten was her umbrella, which she used as a walking stick. Now, where did she leave it? In the hotel in the morning? No, she had had it in the car, hadn't she? Or had she? She didn't have it in the helicopter, she was sure, but in the car, yes, and in the shop. Did she leave it there? Or at Joseph's? Didn't she touch with it that enormous crystal crab, that monstrous chandelier hanging in the hall, to make the scales of light float across the waves under the gondola? Of

143

course she did. And then she put it in the corner, by the spittoon. Spittoon! Something she hadn't seen for ages. But was it there that she left her walking-stick? Oh God. Ha Ha! No. Such things can only happen to *other* people. Ha, ha! There it was. Her walking-stick umbrella. She was holding it in her left hand, upside down, on her left shoulder, like a rifle at the slope. Slope . . . arrrms! Order arms! As you were! Oh memory! Memory! How many times had she marched with a rifle at the slope? Or with a stick? Or with just nothing? 1939 – in Poland; 1940 – in Russia; 1941 – in the Middle East; 1942 – in England with the Women's Royal Army Corps, where she met Sir Lionel Cooper . . . Dear, dear Lionel. Public school, Oxford, poetry magazines, military intelligence, the George Cross, and then, after the war, they had only been married for six years when the news came – from Belgium, of all places! She had never learnt exactly how it happened, they hushed it up, they wrote to condole with her, but they didn't trust her. Oh Lionel! Lionel! You little know the sadness done!

She took her walking-stick umbrella in her right hand, and resumed her march. Now, when you walk with a walking-stick, there are three different kinds of rhythm you can produce: there is the LEFT right left right / ONE two three four / ONE two three four rhythm, when you stamp your walking stick on ONE and wave it gaily on three. Then there is the LEFT right LEFT right / ONE two THREE four / ONE two THREE four rhythm, when you are wise enough to stamp your walking stick on ONE and THREE. And finally, there is a short shrunk shank shin bone step ONE / TWO / ONE / TWO, when you put it down each time your left and right feet touch the ground. After that, there is only what the Bard called the Seventh Age, sans teeth, sans eyes, sans taste, sans walking stick.

Lady Cooper went on marching at the ONE two THREE four pace, and lost her way. She thought she must have taken a wrong turning, so she retraced her steps, and then lost her way for the second time. A solid ghost appeared on the other side of the dark street. The ghost was wearing jeans and had long hair and Lady Cooper could not decide whether it was a ghost of a man or a woman. Whichever it was, she wanted to ask it the shortest way to the hotel, and she started walking across, from her side to the ghost's side of the street. But the ghost must have

144

noticed her and did the opposite, so that at a certain moment they were both in the middle of the roadway though some distance apart. Lady Cooper did a smart about-turn, upon which the ghost also turned round, walked back to its side of the street, and started running away.

It took her a long while to realize that she had frightened the ghost. She, an old woman armed with a walking-stick umbrella. At first, she laughed. For a second. Then she felt sorry about it. And then again, she felt guilty. She felt ashamed of what had happened. She knew that her feeling of guilt and shame would start to grow uncontrollably, out of all proportion. It was one of those things. She thought she could understand all kinds of people, people who kill, steal, cheat, rape, torture, but she couldn't understand a man who likes frightening another man, or a child, or a chicken. She knew that her fear of frightening other people was quite irrational, hysterical, and she knew that it must have been caused by something, by some event, but she wasn't sure whether that event had happened in the past and been forgotten, or was only going to happen some time in the future. She turned round the corner, then stopped and leaned against the wall of a house.

The feeling of greater and greater emptiness was slowly changing into panic. It was not for the first time, and she knew that she wouldn't be able to stop it unless something happened, anything – a dog barking, a telephone ringing, a door slammed, it didn't matter what, but it had to come from the outside. She looked around for it, hopelessly, and then shut her eyes for what she thought was just a second, when she heard a voice:

'Good heavens, it's Lady Cooper! What on earth are you doing here?' A tall, hatless man was leaning over her. 'Do you remember . . . ? We met in Rome, at the Cardinal's, and then had tea at Princess Zuppa's . . .'

'Of course I do,' she said. 'Dr Gold . . .'

'. . . finger,' he helped her.

'Of course I do, Dr Goldfinger,' she repeated. 'Bless you, Dr Goldfinger. You are heaven sent, Dr Goldfinger. I've lost my way in this town which I used to know so well.'

She was still resting against the wall.

A car approached, slowed down – as if asking, 'Do you want a lift?' – and then accelerated again.

He took her gently by the wrist to feel her pulse.

'Oh, I'm perfectly all right, Doctor,' she said. 'A few minutes ago, yes, it occurred to me that perhaps I was going to die. But it was just a mood, rather. Nothing physical.' She straightened herself up and took a step forward. 'Thank you,' she said, as he supported her arm. 'Now, Doctor, I warn you, I'm going to tell you something that will make you laugh. But let's start walking. I'm feeling fine.'

They rounded the corner of the house and started down the street, retracing her steps.

'You see,' she went on, 'it so happens that I know something that nobody else knows. Nobody else in the whole world. And when I thought that I was going to die, it seemed to me so odd, such a pity, to take it with me . . . So I decided that I must tell somebody, quickly, at once, and there you came, Godsent . . .'

'Sometimes it's safer *not* to learn things,' Dr Goldfinger hesitated.

'Oh no, no. It's nothing political. Nothing of importance either, actually. I'm sure you'll laugh. And so will Princess Zuppa. You haven't brought her with you, Doctor, or have you?'

'No, she didn't want to come.'

'Well, I'm sure it will amuse her too. She has such a broad-minded sense of humour. And it is about somebody she knew. Something about the General. General Pięść.'

'Are you quite sure you want to tell me . . . ?' he asked.

'Of course I am. I'm sure you'll be laughing your head off. Listen, once upon a time, when our dear General was a boy of fifteen or sixteen, he crept – in the middle of the night – into the room of the governess, and into her bed. They called her a governess but she was just a pretty country girl of seventeen, employed to take care of some infant in the family. When the girl realized that she was pregnant, she told the boy's father. He was both very proud and very angry. Though she took some blame on herself by saying that it was she who went to the boy's bed. Anyway, the old squire proved to be quite a charac-ter. Can you guess what he did? He told the girl not to say anything to anybody about it. And, first of all, not to tell the boy. Ever. Till the end of her life. To swear by Almighty God. She did. By Almighty God and all that is holy. Then he married

146

her to a nice young man who was in love with her and he sent the couple to a far-away town where he arranged things for them, and when the child was born – a little girl whom they named Jadwiga – he, the squire, took care of her education. From afar. The girl didn't know about all that. She loved her mother and she loved the man whom she thought her father, and he loved her, and all she knew was that somewhere in the country there was a rich relative who was helping them financially.' Lady Cooper paused, and then said: 'I don't hear your laughter, and it is too dark to see your smile.'

He took her hand and kissed it.

'Please, go on, *Pani* Jadwigo,' he said.

'Dear Doctor! I'm so glad I met you. Life is so funny. So very funny indeed. Listen . . . It so happened yesterday that I had to visit a friend's bathroom. It was an ordinary bathroom. But I noticed something in it, something that, for me, had a very special meaning. It was my host's razor. An old-fashioned cut-throat razor. I remembered my father used to use one exactly like it. I always think about him as my real father. He *was* my real father. I liked to watch him when he was shaving. Oh dear, dear . . . I told you life is so funny. Very funny indeed. He also was in the 1920 war. When I was about five. You can't remember, Doctor. You were not born yet. Or just? Well, when the war was over, he wasn't allowed to go back home. First he had to pass through the camp in Jabłonna. Where they put those whom they suspected of having Bolshevik ideas. You see, he broke a little crown off the head of the tin eagle on his military cap. Many soldiers did. They thought Poland, just two years old at the time, was a republic, a *res publica*, not a monarchy, so why the crown? And so they had to pass through Jabłonna. Which wasn't so hard. But humiliating. For young soldiers who had just come back from the front. I think that was what turned him to communism. And made him join the party. He was a nationalist church-going party member. He wrote articles for radical weeklies. He thought that the *via moderna* started with William of Occam but it wasn't a straight road and we were on one of its tragic squiggles where the great words of generalities are thought to be more important than the *singularia* of particulars and so, in 1930, at the time of the Great Purges, he left the party and, for the sake of symmetry, I suppose, stopped going to

147

church, but still carried some beliefs, based on hope. "Remember"
– he told me – "there is a difference between two kinds of signs.
Natural signs, such as smoke that tells you there is a fire. And
artificial signs, such as the barber's bowl hanging outside the
shop, telling you there is a barber-surgeon inside. And people
go on quarrelling about the shape and colour of the barber's
bowl, and we can do nothing but hope that they will finally
notice the smoke too, and stop the fire spreading." That was the
hope his beliefs were based on. But ten years later, when Hitler
made a pact with Stalin and the war started, he lost his hope
and cut his throat. With his cut-throat razor. Which he used to
call his Occam's razor. I was with him at the time, and had to
leave his body unburied, and flee further eastward myself. Now
you see how it was that spotting a cut-throat razor in a man's
bathroom has brought all that back to my mind. Poor Father!'
    'And your mother . . . ?'
    'Oh, Mother . . . Yes, Mother . . . I brought her to England a
few years after the war. To live with me. And, in a way, she
didn't break her word, but you see, her mind was no longer in
the present, it was in her past; her past had become her present,
and so she used to talk about it, half to herself half to me, quite
unaware that she was revealing her secret. Brooding. Repeating
again and again. With more and more details. Mostly in the
present tense. As if the things had just been happening. That
was how I learned that my natural father was a boy of fifteen.'
She paused. Waiting. Had he laughed, she would have joined
him. But he didn't. So she went on: 'Once I had learned his
name, I asked some friends, "Ever heard of a Polish general
called Pięść?" It was just curiosity. But when they said "Oh yes,
he lives somewhere in London," I found his address, which was
not far from our London home, and I spied on him and discovered that he used to go to a pub on the corner where the two
streets met, his and mine, and I went there one evening and
saw him, I recognized him at once, he looked so different, such
an outsider, and then one day I asked Mother: "Mother, would
you like to see General Pięść?" She looked at me with suspicion,
as if she wondered who could have told me his name, and then
she said, "I don't mind if I do," just like that, so we went in the
evening and we saw him – he was sitting alone at a table,
drinking a pint of beer, and filling in a football-pools coupon. It

148

wasn't the one that won him that big fortune, you know, all this happened a long time before that. So he was sitting there, drinking his beer. Alone. For a moment he passed his eye over us, two old ladies, one some two or three years older, the other some sixteen years younger than he, but whether his mind registered anything at all, how can one know? Anyway, after that evening Mother stopped talking as if she lived in the past, actually she stopped talking altogether; it was as if she were reading a book, a big thick volume, and had come to the last full stop, after which there are only one or two blank pages and the back of the cover. Bang. A week later, a butcher's boy on a bicycle knocked her down on a zebra crossing; she wasn't badly hurt, but she didn't want to recover. Enough is enough, thank you. That's what she seemed to be thinking. And you know, my dear, my coming here this time, to our old country, must have been prompted by the same kind of feeling, a wish to find the last page with which to round off one's life. Such a luxury, if one compares it with so many of one's contemporaries whose life was cut off in the middle.' She struck the ground with her walking-stick umbrella. She looked into his eyes, searchingly. Then she shrugged, like little Emma used to do. And, mockingly, she said: 'Do you know, Doctor, what I did the very next morning after my arrival? I took a taxi, I showed the man a thick roll of dollar notes and asked him to take me some twenty or more miles out of town, to the little village where the General was born. We stopped when I noticed the word LIBRARY written above the door of a little cottage. I went in. There were a few shelves filled with books and a table covered with newspapers. I asked the woman there, who seemed to be the librarian, if she could tell me how to find the old manor house of the Pięściewicki family. You see, the General's family name was Pięściewicki, not Pięść. But it was the fashion then, among the high-rank military, to have a double-barrelled name: Dowbór-Muśnicki, Wieniawa-Długoszowski, Belina-Prażmowski, Sławoj-Skladkowski, Rydz-Śmigły, so our young Pięściewicki also called himself Pięść-Pięściewicki, which he later on shortened to: General Pięść. "Pięściewicki? Never heard the name," the woman in the library said and she sent me to the post office. The girl at the post office didn't know either and told me to go to the parish priest. He was a nice middle-aged fellow. I told

149

him at once I didn't expect any of the family would still be living there, but I should like to see the estate, the manor house, or whatever. When was it built? he asked. I said I didn't know exactly but it must have been some time before the war. Dear lady – he said – that's more than forty years ago. There isn't much as old as that here, and nobody old enough to remember. So I told him I meant the manor house itself must have been built before the *First* World War, and he looked at me as if I were in search of a dinosaur, and he led me to a collection plate. No, I didn't feel that the last page of my book was written there. Still, I asked my taxi to cruise around and we went through all the little lanes between the fields, and across the forest, and – believe it or not – it just so happened, whether it was so fated or just by chance, that it was the very same forest which I saw today, from above, from a helicopter, which reminds me, oh dear . . . let's go, do you think they'll still be serving dinner at the hotel at this hour? Because I'm starving, I haven't had a mouthful of food since breakfast, absolutely nothing, except a tin of Coca-Cola offered me by a helicopter pilot whose girlfriend studies linguistics, seventeenth-century English, and needs Partridge's *Dictionary of Slang* . . .'

*

'Fantastic . . .' Dr Goldfinger said aloud to himself once more. He had been repeating the word 'fantastic' frequently since he had said goodbye to Lady Cooper. Now, he took a sheet of paper and wrote:

Carissima,
> *It's nearly midnight. I'm sitting in my hotel room (small but quite comfortable) and . . .*

He stopped. He knew that Princess Zuppa would like to read a sober, matter-of-fact, and preferably funny description of how the medical staff in the hospital had received the gift of a thousand sterile single-use polypropylene syringes and kilograms of vitamins, antibiotics and analgesics which he had brought them, and that was what he wanted to write, including what had happened to his car, because of which he had had to walk back for miles and met . . . in a lonely street . . . out of the blue . . . well, that was precisely what was disturbing him and

150

made him repeat 'fantastic' to himself again. Would Princess Zuppa be amused by the story, would she like to learn that she was not the General's only daughter, would she too exclaim 'fantastic' at the news that Lady Cooper, of all people, was her half-sister? Dr Goldfinger put the pen down. Anyway, it made no sense to write a letter. He'd be back in Rome before the letter arrived. He swivelled round in his chair so that he was facing the door now. There was an armchair on his left. He had just kicked off his shoes and thought of moving to the armchair and stretching his legs, when he heard a knock at the door, and before he had time to say a word the door opened.

His first thought was that she must have made a mistake, but would she have knocked at the door of her own room? Her dark eyes were full of nice, friendly, humorous, giggling, chuckling mischief as she silently shut the door behind her, marched two steps to the armchair and sat down. She glanced round, casually, like somebody who is familiar with the topography of the room. Then she giggled again, and said lightheartedly:

'Two thousand zlotys. OK?'

She rose, went briskly to the bathroom, and shut the door.

Dr Goldfinger listened to the sound of running water and he focused his mind on the inventory of the bathroom: the bath with a shower, basin, bidet, loo. Then he struck a match and lit up. He had promised himself not to smoke, and it was already his second cigarette. He had lit the first in the afternoon when he had discovered that his car, which he had parked in front of the hospital, had no wheels. He had another puff and was putting the cigarette end into the ashtray when the door opened. She was wearing his dressing-gown.

'*Pan* is very funny,' she said, sitting down on the edge of the bed.

He raised his eyebrows.

'*Pan* is very funny,' she repeated, 'because *Pan* hasn't said a single word yet.' She giggled.

'Oh,' he said. 'That's because I've been told there are microphones in every room in this hotel. The very thought makes me self-conscious.'

'Silly . . .' she said. 'They can't listen to all the rooms all the time. And they can't make recordings because they don't have enough tape. The tape is imported. Costs dollars. So they listen

151

only to some Very Important Persons. Is *Pan* a Very Important Person?'

'I hope they don't think I am,' Dr Goldfinger said.

'And anyway, so what if they do? They are so poorly paid those miserable boys and girls, there in the listening post – let them have some acoustic satisfaction,' she giggled again.

Dr Goldfinger thought for a moment, then he moved his chair nearer to the bed, like doctors do, and with his good bedside manner, said: 'May I ask *Panią* a question?'

'Let *Pan* try,' she said.

'Is *Pani* a student?'

'Yes.'

'And what does *Pani* study?'

'Linguistics.'

The word 'linguistics' made him think again about Lady Cooper – what was she doing in a helicopter? What was that fantastic story about being served Coca-Cola by the helicopter pilot whose girlfriend was studying linguistics, English seventeenth century, and wanted Partridge's *Dictionary of Slang*?

'Is it seventeenth-century English that *Pani* is studying?' he asked with some apprehension.

'What? No,' she said, surprised. 'Why should it be?'

'Just a thought,' he said.

'Seventeenth-century English, indeed!' she mocked him. 'Certainly not. My linguistics is neither historical nor diachronical. It is synchronic. Structural. And French. It starts with Saussure and ends with Roland Barthes. Has *Pan* heard about him?'

'A little.'

'How much?'

'Down with Semantocracy!' Dr Goldfinger said.

'Down with Domination by Meaning!' the girl giggled.

'Long live signs!' said he.

'Let signs speak for themselves!' said the girl.

'No reading between the lines!' said he.

'Long live the Algebra of Literature!' said the girl.

'And what about Chomsky?' Dr Goldfinger asked.

'No. Definitely not. Chomsky is too much involved politically. For everybody here.'

'For everybody?'

'Yes. That's what I said. For everybody.'

She took off the dressing-gown and stretched out on the bed. Why, but it's Manet's *Olympia* – Dr Goldfinger told himself. Such deep tacit harmonics beneath the beautiful surface structure. How was it that she, Olympia, had produced such a scandal a hundred years ago? It couldn't have been her nakedness. Parents were dragging off their children to show them Canova's *Sleeping Nymph*, who was as naked as Olympia. Where was the difference? – he wrinkled up his forehead and pinched his retroussé nose – why of course, the smooth diaphanous marble of the Sleeping Nymph had no pubic hair. While Olympia . . . obviously . . . she must have had, mustn't she? But he wasn't quite sure, he didn't remember, he looked at the girl on his bed and, for a moment, he didn't trust his eyes. She was more like Canova than Manet. She had no pubic hair either.

'*Pani* has shaved, why?' he asked, disconcerted.

'Oh,' she said, chuckling, 'that's nothing. I didn't do it. They did it in hospital. I've just had an abortion.'

'Does *Pani* not use contraceptives?' he asked.

'Oh no,' she said. 'The Holy Father disapproves of contraceptives,' and then added gaily: '*Pan* will have to withdraw, OK?'

153

FOURTEEN
Euclid was an Ass

Back in London, Lady Cooper made a trunk call to the Revd
Paul Prentice to tell him that his sister had decided to stay in
Warsaw.
'For how long?' he asked.
'I don't know. Neither does she, I think.'
'But why?'
'She's got a job there.'
'What kind of a job?'
'Putting idiomatic touches on some English official trans-
lations.'
'How strange . . .'
'Well, not really . . .'
'Where is she staying? Could you give me her address?'
'I'm afraid I can't. I know it's c/o Dr Kszak. K–S–Z–A–K. But I
don't even know the name of the street.' Which was quite true.
But he, of course, wouldn't believe her.
'Well, I can't write c/o Dr Kszak, Warsaw. Can I? Unless he's
such a great man. Is he?'
'I can give you his telephone number.'
'You mean she's staying with him?'
'Yes.'
'What sort of person is he?'
'He's my age. I knew him when he was a young boy.'
That wasn't the right thing to say. He now assumed that it
was Lady Cooper who had introduced his sister to a Dr Kszak,
and the Revd Paul Prentice didn't sound pleased.
'It was a *coup de foudre*,' Lady Cooper said.
'Oh dear,' he said.

*

That night, she had a strange dream which she couldn't remember. She knew that it was very strange but she couldn't
recall a single picture. The only thing she remembered was the
dream's strangeness. But how can Strangeness, pure Strangeness be remembered? How can any abstract noun ending with
- ness be something that one can remember? She poured herself
a cup of strong black coffee and rang her solicitor. As it was
already more than thirty years since her husband's death, and
there was a thirty-year rule concerning the release of state
documents, she had already some time ago instructed her
solicitor to make enquiries.

'I'm afraid, Lady Cooper,' he now said, 'I've done everything
I could, but it seems that the relevant papers are under the fifty-
year rule.'

'Which means that I'll never learn the facts?'

'Well, perhaps . . . unless . . .' he started to stammer.

Lady Cooper understood that his 'perhaps' meant 'perhaps
it's better not to', and his 'unless' – 'unless you have some
friends or enemies who are in the picture and will tell you'.
Some of her husband's friends or enemies were also her friends
or enemies. But neither the former nor the latter would tell her
anything about the events in Belgium that had led to her
husband's death. It wasn't because she wasn't accepted, it
wasn't because she didn't belong, she *was* accepted, she *did*
belong, but, well, there was still one of those things – there was
still the fact that none of their wives or sisters had been at
school with her, and none of her brothers had been at school
with any of them. That little bit of her past biography belonged
to Joseph and his part of the world, and, for them, that little bit
was a blank never to be filled. She went down and started her
car.

She stopped on the corner by the pub where General Pięść
used to have his glass of beer. She went in. It was eleven a.m.,
the opening hour. There was nobody in, yet. She was the first.
She asked for a glass of gin. The barman turned round to fetch
the bottle, but he came back again:

'Did you say gin, madam?' he asked, to make sure.

'That's what I said, yes.'

She took a few sips and left. There was a parking ticket stuck
behind the windscreen-wiper. Ten pounds. She started off

155

again. From bookshop to bookshop in search of Partridge's *Dictionary of Slang*. She stopped for a quick lunch and got another parking ticket. When, at last, she found a copy of the book, she went home, made a parcel, PRINTED PAPERS REDUCED RATE, wrote the address of Mr Mirek, the helicopter pilot, which she copied from the visiting card he had given her, and went to the post office. It was already five-twenty p.m. She licked £2.82-worth of stamps. Back home, she switched the radio on. She heard the end of a sentence that contained the word Bukumla. She phoned a friend who should know.

'What was that news about Bukumla?'

'Wait a moment, let me make sure.' And, after a minute, 'It's about that little black Napoleon. They've got him, at last. The rebels. Dragged him into the bush. Literally. Presumably dead.'

'And his mother?'

'Mother? Nothing about the mother. Why?'

*

Before going to bed, Lady Cooper took out a small exercise book from her suitcase. Red cover:

NAME: *Ian Prentice*
SUBJECT: *Euclid was an ass*

Miss Prentice had given it to her. She had been to see her, at Lady Cooper's hotel room, and said, 'This is what Ian wrote and dedicated to that little girl, Emma, you remember? I feel now it belongs to her. Could you post it to her from London, or – better still – give it to her if you happen to be somewhere near?'

'Yes, of course,' Lady Cooper said. The request sounded somewhat familiar. Hadn't Princess Zuppa said something of the kind once upon a time? Well, anyway, now, in her London home, she tucked herself up in her fourposter bed, and started to read:

To my darling future wife Emma
Who doesn't know that when a lemma has solved the dilemma
We don't need any more the lemma.

The purpose of this paper is to prove that Euclid was an ass.
He was sure that what's good for a triangle the size of his
nose ⁃ , and for a circle the size of his bum , will be good
also for all triangles and all circles, never mind how enormous or
how tiny. He was so sure of that, that he didn't even bother to
write it down as one of his postulates.

And I, Ian Prentice (age $12^{3}/_{12} \pm ^{2}/_{365}$) challenge the ass.

My assumptions are as follows:

1. There is the very smallest bit of Space. I shall call it Emma.

2. There is the very smallest bit of Time. I shall call it Ian.

My definitions:

1. Emma is the smallest bit of Space. Emma is indivisible. Which
means that if somebody (like that ass Euclid) imagined that he
could divide Emma, her parts would have no characteristics of
Space. There would be no here and there, no left and right, no
bigger and smaller, in any of them.

2. Ian is the smallest bit of Time. Ian is indivisible. Which means
that if somebody (Euclid had nothing to do with this, the ass
thought he was timeless) imagined that he could divide Ian, the
part of Ian would have no characteristics of Time. There would
be no before and after, no quicker and slower, no shorter and
longer, in any of them.

Discussion:

My Emma has nothing to do with what that ass Euclid calls a
point.

My Emma has length and width and breadth; she has no shape,
of course, because to have a shape she would have to have parts,
and her parts (if any) are not of the world of Space.

157

She has no fixed position, because she exists only for one Ian, that's to say: one Ian after another, with nothing in between. Of which there will be more later, because it is something fundamental about the Universe.

My line has nothing to do with his line.

His line is made of his points which have no size, so it has no thickness, and yet, he says, it has length along which all his points can be numbered by integers or fractions. All except $\sqrt{2}$. So, silly ass, calls $\sqrt{2}$ an irrational number, while, in fact, it is not $\sqrt{2}$ but his silly line that is irrational (in the sense of being metaphysical).

There is no such nonsense about my line. My line is one Emma thick and some number of Emmas long. My line can be divided in half, but only if the number of Emmas is even. If the number of Emmas is odd, my line cannot be divided exactly in two halves. And that's that. Pythagoras would have liked it, I'm sure. And my circle is not like his bum. My circle doesn't need to have an arsehole in its centre. You can draw my circle step by step by walking step by step with one leg a bit shorter than the other. Because my circle is a polygon, each side of which is one Emma. So the smallest circle is a triangle made of 3 Emmas, and the next smallest circle is a square made of 4 Emmas, and so on, and the circle of the size of Euclid's bum is made of millions and millions and millions of Emmas. And so there is no silly nonsense about the decimals of π going on and on and on, whatever the size of the circle. In my circle when the decimal of π becomes as small as one Emma, it is silly nonsense to go any further.

So now you may ask: What is the size of an Emma?

My half-sister Princess Zuppa's boyfriend, Cardinal Pölätüo, calculated that the smallest possible distance is 10^{-32} of a centimetre. He found the figure by his theological methods, by assuming that the size of a Human Egg must be just in the middle between the size of the Universe and the size of the Smallest Bit of Space. As the Cardinal's distance doesn't differ much from Planck distance, which is 10^{-33} cm, I shall assume as my working hypothesis that there are 100000000000000000000000000000000 Emmas in one centimetre. Similarly, taking that Planck time is 10^{-44} sec, I shall assume that

there are
100000000000000000000000000000000C00000000000000 Ians in one
second.

We may say that the Tower of London is made of one million
bricks, but we do not define a brick as $\frac{1}{1000000}$ of the Tower of
London. Similarly, we may say that one centimetre is made of
10^{33} Emmas, but I do not define an Emma as 10^{-33} cm. On the
contrary, I define a centimetre in terms of Emmas and not the
other way round. Emma, and only Emma, is the basic bit of space
to start with.

We may say that Greater London is made of ten million people,
but we do not define a Londoner as being $\frac{1}{10000000}$ of London.
Similarly, we may say that one second is made of 10^{44} Ians, but I
do not define an Ian as 10^{-44} sec. Ian and Emma are fundamental
bits of Space and Time, and if we start all our calculations not
with the arbitrary macroscopic centimetre and second, but with
the natural microscopic Emma and Ian (as our basic fractals), we
shall see that we do not need any more any of those fancy
numbers like π or $\pm \sqrt{2}$, nor shall we need the calculus, integral
and differential.
Instead of vanishing in some fairy-tale smallness, my time in-
terval $\triangle t = t_2 - t_1$ is one Ian and similarly my space interval $\triangle x$
$= x_2 - x_1$ is one Emma and as for velocity limit, my $\triangle t$ does not
need to approach some fictional 0, because it is once and for ever
$\triangle x / \triangle t = $ Emma/Ian which is the velocity of light, and the only
velocity existing in the Universe. All other movements differ not
in velocities but in speeds. We get those various speeds by going
two Emmas forward and one Emma backward, or sideways,
clockwise or anticlockwise, and back again, and moving forward
only every 10th, or 100th, or 1000th or millionth or billionth Ian.
Even what that silly ass Euclid took for granted, as being some
sort of rigid, timeless, stiff immobility, is in fact one Emma
forward and one Emma backward, or sideways, because what we
call speed = 0 is in fact Emma/Ian, which is the basic vibration of
the Universe.

Conclusion:

When God created His Emmas, He thought He had created something perfect.

But then came that silly ass Euclid and said the only perfect things are his own, Euclid's, circles and squares.

So God, too, tried to make some perfect circles and squares of His Emmas, and He could not.

Because when He wanted to build a perfect square with sides equal to 100 Emmas, He found that its diagonal would have to be 100 $\sqrt{2}$, which is more than 141 and less than 142, and 141 Emmas is too short, and 142 Emmas is too long.

And when He tried to build a perfect square with its diagonal equal to 100 Emmas, He found that its sides would have to be 100$\sqrt{\frac{1}{2}}$ Emmas each, which is more than 70 Emmas and less than 71 Emmas, and whether He chooses one or the other, His square will be crooked.

And when He tried to build a perfect circle with the circumference equal to 100 Emmas, He found that its diameter would have to be $^{100}/\pi$, which is more than 31 Emmas and less than 32 Emmas, one being too short and the other too long.

And when He tried to build a perfect circle with the radius equal to 100 Emmas, He found that its circumference would have to be 200 π, which is more than 628 Emmas and less than 629 Emmas, so that His circle could not be perfect.

And all that is so because human mathematics is about counting fairy-tale things, such as Unicorns, or Numbers, or HRH Hamlets, while God's mathematics is about real things, such as tigers or Emmas.

Because with fairy-tale things it is so that a half of a Unicorn is still a Unicorn, and a half of a Number is still a Number, and a half of Prince Hamlet is still Prince Hamlet. But with God's real things it is different. Because half of a tiger is no longer a tiger. Because if each half of a tiger could still roar and be a tiger, then a tiger would be two tigers, and 1 = 2 is not how God made things. And what goes for such real things as tigers, goes also for such real things as Emmas. That's why Emma is not cuttable in two. And so God, stung to the quick by that silly ass Euclid, decided to make His own perfect squares and circles, and to do so He invented Time made of Ians, and He made His squares and circles vibrate so that the diagonals would be made of 141 Emmas during one Ian, and 142 during the next, and then 141 again, and so on; or that the sides of the squares would be 70 Emmas in one Ian and 71 in the next, and so on; and that the radius of His circles be 31 Emmas in one Ian and 32 in the next; or that their circumference be 628 Emmas during one Ian and 629 during the next, and then 628 again, and so on and on; and as He tried to make a great number of His squares and circles of various sizes, the whole Universe started to vibrate with those various oscillations, and the clusters of those oscillations are what we call MATTER.

And in 3 years from now, when I've been at Oxford for 2 years, and am given access to a big computer, I shall prove that all those hundreds of Leptons, Mesons, Baryons, which people call particles, are not particles but multivarious combinations of multivarious oscillations, all based on the fundamental frequency which is Emma/Ian.

So help me God.

FIFTEEN

As Old as Dust

... bumper to bumper, Volkswagens Fords Fiats, Hondas
Mazdas Ladas, Jaguars Simcas Bentleys, Skodas Datsuns Colts,
Talbots Daimlers Toyotas, Chryslers Citroëns Lancias, Mosk-
wiches Opels Reliants, Saabs Cadillacs Volvos, Mercedeses
Vauxhalls Peugeots, Rolls-Royces Rovers Audis, Alfa Romeos
BMWs Renaults, Deux-chevaux Porsches Austin sevens;
Highland-green Astral-silver Regal-red, Dark-blue Russet-
brown Primrose-yellow, Signal-red, Forest-green Lapis-blue,
Claret Georgian-silver Honey-gold, Viper-green Gentian-blue
Anthracite-grey, Walnut-bronze Peacock-blue Chrome-yellow,
Olive-green Tuscan-blue Jet-black, Havana-brown Lima-brown
Bronze-metallic, Thistle-green Lagoon-blue Classic-white,
Guards-red Racing-red Midnight-blue, Champagne-metallic
Light-Ocean-beige Athenian-blue, Baltic-blue Petrol-blue Blue-
chiaro, Ice-green Coronet-gold Sahara-dust, Metallic-copper
Regency-bronze Coffee-bean-brown, Royal-blue Minerva-blue
Pillar-box-red, Smoke-green Dark-olive Indigo-blue, Porcelain-
white Ascot-grey Manila-beige, Nutmeg Cashmere Gunmetal,
Orient-red Exeter-blue Silver-shadow, Madagascar-brown Kiln-
red Green-metallic, Onyx-metallic Chestnut-metallic Chestnut-
brown, Gleaming-black Moss-green Willow-gold, Squadron-
blue Creamy-white Manganese-brown, Caramel-metallic
Alabaster-yellow Mahogany-brown; limousines, saloons, family
saloons, sports saloons, sports coupés, convertibles, cabriolets,
two-door three-door four-door five-door family cars, estate cars,
taxis coaches minicabs minibuses double-deckers vans thirty-
ton trucks juggernauts caravans lorries trailers ice-cream vans
Rolls-Royce hearse jalopy hearse Black Maria panda ambulance
fire-engines motor-bikes motor-cycles, ten thousand exhaust
pipes, ductless glands on top of kidneys, stiff upper lip, bitten

lower lip, carbon monoxide, nitrogen dioxide, lead, honk! honk! adrenalin – it took her over one hour to get out of London, and another two hours on the motorway, westwards. A young couple thumbed a lift, but she didn't stop. She wanted to be alone with her thoughts. Though she didn't have any. She had just one more thing to be done and didn't want to be distracted. She had already phoned the Revd Paul Prentice, that was number one. She had posted the *Dictionary of Slang* to the helicopter pilot, that was number two. She had phoned her solicitors to learn that she would never learn, that was number three. She had stopped for a moment at General Pięść's pub and had a sip of gin, whispering softly to it *requiem aeternam dona eis domine*, that was number four. The only thing that remained now was to find the little girl Emma and give her the exercise book with *Euclid was an ass*. All that done, Lady Cooper would be free of her past and of her present. She'd be reborn . . . Except in the mirror, she was not too old for many a thing. But no, she was not going to muse about it now.

In front of her, high up, stretching across the motorway, was a bridge. The exit on her left led to it, and then, northward, to a country road on her right. If she were to take it, she would be in her country house in twenty minutes. The beautiful country house with all its . . . No, she was not going to think about *that* either. She didn't turn left to the exit. Anyway, she was in the wrong lane to do so. She went straight on.

She stopped at the next service station. To go for a pee and to have a meal. Smoked haddock, apple pie, and coffee. Back at the parking place, she couldn't find her car. It just wasn't there. A police patrol car was passing. She waved her walking-stick umbrella to stop it. They asked her to hop in. And they moved along at great speed. 'What sort of car?' they asked. 'Rover V8, bronze-metallic.' She said. 'Number?' She told them. 'Now, madam, that doesn't sound like a car number, does it?' She laughed. 'Of course not. I gave you my telephone number. How silly of me.' The man at the back took out his notebook. 'And your name, madam?' he asked. 'Cooper,' she said. 'Just Cooper?' he queried. 'Lady Cooper,' she said. He switched on his two-way radio. 'Slow down, please,' she exclaimed. 'There on the left . . . It looks like . . . Yes, I'm sure, there it is!' A bronze-metallic Rover V8 stood quietly in the lay-by. They stopped and got out. All three. Lady Cooper fumbled in her handbag for the car keys. 'Hm,' the policeman said. She looked at him. 'You are not Irish, madam. Or are you?' he asked. 'I'm not,' she said. And then, 'Why?' she asked. 'Something in how you sound, madam. If you don't mind,' he said. 'Oh, my accent. It isn't Irish at all. I was born in Poland,' she said. 'That's it. We've got lots of Poles in this country, haven't we? Since the war. The third generation already. All Catholics, like the Irish. And the Jews. But I must say, no terrorist we have had was a Pole,' he said. 'I bloody well hope not,' she said. They liked her saying 'bloody well' and they grinned. 'They are usually either Irish or Arabs.' And then, one of them said, 'Let *me* open the door, madam.' She handed him the keys. He peered through the passenger-door window at the inner side of the other door. Then he walked round, looked again and inserted the key. Gingerly. The door opened. He looked under the dashboard and under the seats. 'And as a matter of interest, madam, are there any terrorists there, in Poland?' he asked conversationally, opening the bonnet. 'Not really,' she said. 'Well, not exactly,' she added. 'I suppose that's because people have just one religion,' he said. 'You might be right,' she said. 'I can't figure out how commies can be so religious,' the other said. 'Well, it's one of those things,' Lady Cooper said. 'Yeah,' the first one said. And, after reflection, added, 'Maybe the young ones are commies and the old ones religious.' 'Or the other way round,' Lady Cooper said. 'Quite so,' they agreed. They had just looked into the boot of the car and found nothing. They took a big torch, knelt, and peered under the chassis. 'Just to be on the safe side,' they said, standing up. 'Must have been some youngster's prank.' 'But why leave it here, of all places?' 'Might have come with a girlfriend, stopped at the service station, quarrelled with her, pinched your car, but she followed him in hers, reconciliation, and now they'll be happy ever after. Things like that do happen.' He sat behind the steering wheel and switched on the ignition. The engine purred contentedly. He got out and kept the door open for her. 'If I were you, madam, I should check if anything is missing.'

'Oh dear,' she exclaimed with a sudden panic. She opened the glove compartment and took out the exercise book. 'This is all I care for,' she said.

Another exit, and the side road which she took led her straight to the centre of the little Town-on-Sea. She slowed down. On her left, a row of houses, a little post office, shops – butcher's, chemist's, grocery, stationer's, hairdresser's. On her right, a big empty square and then a garden, or a park, invaded by the trees that must have trespassed upon it from the forest beyond. And in front of her – the sea, half hidden behind a row of a few villas, and then a large grey building, further to the right, facing the garden.

Something caught her eye in the window of the stationer's. A poster: *Photocopying while you wait. A4. 8p*. She remembered how alarmed she was when the policeman asked her to check if anything had been stolen. Well, now, that's what she should have done before. Photocopy it. She stopped the car, took the exercise book from the glove compartment, and went into the shop.

*

The man behind the counter was on the phone. A boy in the corner of the shop was mending his bike. '. . . I know it's two months . . . Well . . . No . . . Yes . . . he, himself . . . he was using the letterheads all the time and only now spotted the mistake . . . yes, spelling mistake . . . the name of his residence is mis-spelled . . . of course it's our fault . . . Look, the admiral has been my customer for donkey's years, I promised to supply the new ones without charge . . . OK, I'll supply the paper and you'll repeat the printing . . . Good . . . No, the envelopes are all right . . . I'll send you a note with the correct spelling . . . Yep . . . That's the ticket. Roger.'

He put down the receiver and shouted at the boy mending the bicycle: 'I told you not to make that noise when I'm on the phone!'

'Yes, Mr Newman. Sorry, Mr Newman.'

Mr Newman turned to Lady Cooper: 'At your service, madam,' he said.

She stood there, holding her walking-stick umbrella in one hand and *Euclid was an ass* in the other, and . . . Oh no, it was all a mistake, the thought of making a photocopy must have come in a moment of aberration. A weakness. She does *not*, repeat

165

not, she does not want any photocopies. She does not want to drag any photocopies out of the past and into the future that is going to start tomorrow. She rolled the exercise book, put it in the pocket of her Burberry golf jacket, and instead of saying anything about photocopying, she asked Mr Newman if he could tell her how to get to the Chesterton-Browns' villa, if he happened to know.

'Do I know them?!' he exclaimed. 'Dear Mrs Chesterton-Brown, brave, beautiful, noble lady! And poor Mr Chesterton-Brown. Such a tragedy. Such a tragedy! We supply them with *The Times* and the *Guardian* every morning, *Radio Times* on Thursdays, *Higher Educational Supplement* on Fridays, and the *Sunday Times* and the *Observer* on Sundays. Their scholarly monthlies and quarterlies are sent them direct, by subscription. And poetry magazines for Mrs Chesterton-Brown. Nothing for Miss Emma now. She's just stopped reading comics. She's still a child of course but, well . . . Not really. Very pretty girl. Quite unusual prettiness, one must say, in a sort of way . . . But you ask how to get there, madam. It's very simple. Just a few miles. East. They live on the edge of the sea. The admiral, from his *Vasco da Gama*, G–A–M–A, residence could reach them in about a minute in his speedboat; by car it will take a bit longer, but you can't miss it, that's to say if you know how to go there, but if you are a stranger it's a bit more difficult because if you take the road going along the coast, which would seem reasonable, it will turn left and take you uphill away from the sea, and if you take the upper road, it will turn right too late and land you far too far, by the villa called Villanelle that belongs to some sort of ambassador, not very sociable, to say the least, he in his speedboat, could also reach the Chesterton-Browns in a minute, they are just in the middle between him and the admiral, and, whether you take the lower way or the upper way, you must know when to turn into the side road . . .' He stopped for a moment to get his breath, and then, pointing to the window, he asked, 'Is that your car, madam?'

'Yes,' she said.

He bowed with approval. Then, slowly, he turned to the boy who, standing by the back door, was polishing the bicycle.

'Bill!'

'Yes, Mr Newman,' the boy said.

166

'You will go with the lady in her car and you will show her the way.'

'I can't, Mr Newman, I haven't finished yet, I'm still working . . .'

'Bill!'

'Yes, Mr Newman.'

'No work must prevent a man from helping a lady.'

'Yes, Mr Newman, but . . .'

'Bill!'

'Yes, Mr Newman.'

'I do not accept any buts, Bill. You will wash your hands and do as I told you.'

'No, Mr Newman, please . . .'

'Yes, Bill. You'll go with the lady in her car and you'll come back by bus. The cost of the ticket will be reimbursed to you by me. Go!'

'No!'

'Yes!'

'No!'

'Yes!!'

'No!!!' the boy screamed, dropped the bicycle, and rushed out, slamming the door behind him.

'I apologize,' Mr Newman said. 'I hope this scene has not distressed you, madam. And, please, don't blame the boy. He was not being impolite, madam. He's a good boy. Yes, madam, he's a good boy but he's a psychological case, madam. Looking at him would you think, madam, that such a big, strong, muscular boy is a psychological case, madam? So sensitive? No, madam, he meant no disrespect to you, madam. It is a tragic story, madam. You see, madam, the boy's job was delivering papers to our customers' residences along the coast, the admiral, the Chesterton-Browns, the ambassador. On that horrid fateful day, he, as usual, delivered *The Times* and the *Guardian* to the Chesterton-Browns, then *The Times*, the *Guardian*, the *Daily Telegraph*, the *Financial Times*, the *Herald Tribune*, *Le Monde*, and the *Sun* to the ambassador, and then, coming back from his round, he again passed by the Chesterton-Browns' when it happened. He saw it all. He saw it all, madam. The black poodle, the explosion, the destruction. Blood. Death. Torn legs. Ambulances. Fire-engines. Police. It is since that day that he

167

refuses to do the along-the-coast delivery. I hoped just now, madam, that a ride with you in your Rover V8 would tempt him into going there, but no, as you have just seen, madam, no inducement is strong enough for him. That's psychology, madam. It's more than a year already, two years nearly, still, when Mrs Chesterton-Brown appears here, wheeling poor Mr Chesterton-Brown in his wheelchair, the boy blushes as red as a peony and turns away to hide his face. Which puts me to great inconvenience, madam, as I have to employ an extra pair of legs, a girl, to serve the customers along the coast, leaving the boy with the town, the school, and the castle.' He stopped abruptly, and exclaimed, 'The school!' He looked at his wristwatch, walked quickly from behind the counter, took Lady Cooper by the elbow and turned her round so that they were facing the door, looking through its glass panels. 'Do you see, madam, the grey building there, across the square, a little bit of it hidden behind the trees?'

'Yes, I do,' Lady Cooper said.

'Well, madam, that's the school,' he announced triumphantly. And, having consulted his watch again, he said, 'In five minutes, exactly, the girls will be coming out. You do know Miss Emma, of course . . .'

'Yes, actually it's her I want to see.'

'Excellent,' he said. 'You'll see her presently. The day Mrs Chesterton-Brown doesn't come down here to shop or to her hairdresser, and this is the day, otherwise I would have seen her, and I haven't, the little girl goes home by bus. You'll meet her at the bus stop, madam. Don't get confused by its being on the wrong side of the street. It is a one-way street. You may wonder why, as the street is so wide. Well, it's because it narrows considerably further up on its way to the castle. Anyway, there are no houses across the street, just the garden and grassland and the trees, and, as the bus stop is where it is, the girls don't need to cross the road, which is all for the . . .' He looked at his watch again. 'You have exactly four minutes now, madam,' he said, opening the door for her, 'my name is Mr Newman. Enchanted to have met you, Mrs . . .'

'Lady Cooper,' said Lady Cooper.

'Enchanted to have met you, Lady Cooper,' said Mr Newman.

168

The square was empty, the houses looked unlived-in, no wonder that no single customer had come to interrupt Mr Newman's monologue. He closed the door and returned to his place behind the counter. He glanced at the cash register. One pound thirty-seven pence were the day's takings. He leaned his left elbow on the counter and his left cheek on the left tightly-closed fist. Had he ever talked so much? Oh dear . . . Not for ages! Now he's left to himself again, and to his own thoughts, again, brooding over and over again and again . . . Where are they now? What are they doing? His wife and her lover. And the lover's glamorous daughter who, the other day, kissed him on the mouth, sang haha, and danced away.

'Ha, ha,' said Mr Newman, while his right hand was reaching for the handkerchief tucked in the sleeve of his left arm.

He blew his nose, straightened out, took from the drawer an empty record card, wrote on it: '. . . *the admiral doesn't hold it between his legs, it isn't viola da gamba, it is Vasco da Gama, G–A–M–A*', and put the card in an envelope which he addressed to his printer.

*

. . . shiny black shoes, white wool stockings reaching to the knee, scores and scores of them, standing, walking, running, dodging, turning, swerving, bending, kicking, jumping, stomping, dancing, trotting, rambling, wandering, sauntering, strolling, grey regulation skirts, grey regulation jackets, round grey hats with green hatband above young pink faces smiling, sulking, talking, swanking, jeering, laughing, frowning, pouting, sing-ing, filling the empty square with life. A few motherly cars appeared to collect some girls. Slowly, the square emptied. Then the school door opened again and two more girls appeared. They came out together but they were not holding hands, nor were they talking to each other. One of them was wearing a pair of long trousers, made of the same grey material as the other girls' skirts. Her face was brown. She pulled her hat well down over her eyes, turned right, and walked away. The other girl, swinging her satchel, walked up to the bus stop.

Lady Cooper had been sitting on a wooden bench at the edge of the garden. Now she got up and crossed the street.

'Hallo, Emma,' she said.

The girl looked her up and down and said nothing.

'You do recognize me, darling, don't you? We were in Majorca together. Last summer. Remember? I'm Lady Cooper.'

Emma shrugged her shoulders.

'Look, Emma dear,' Lady Cooper thought she must have started off on the wrong foot with the girl, 'do you see a car there, on the other side of the square, in front of the stationery shop? It's my car. Let's walk there, and I'll take you home.'

'I'm going by bus,' Emma said.

'Must you?'

'Yes.'

'Well, if you must, you must. But if you are home first, will you please tell your parents that I am coming to visit them?'

'No, you can't.'

'I beg your pardon?'

'I said, you can't.' She looked straight into Lady Cooper's eyes. 'You can't because there'll be nobody in.'

'Oh?'

'There'll be nobody in because Mummy is going to hospital.'

'Is she ill?'

'You may call it illness if you want to. She's going to have a bastard.'

'Emma!' Lady Cooper exclaimed.

Now she knew that the girl was lying. If Mrs Chesterton-Brown were nine months pregnant, Mr Newman wouldn't have said that she was wheeling her husband in his wheelchair. If she were really pregnant, Mr Newman would never omit to mention it. The girl was lying because she didn't want Lady Cooper to come. In fact, neither did Lady Cooper want to go, after all. Poor Ian. Poor half-brother. Poor *Euclid was an ass*. She extracted the exercise book from the pocket of her Burberry golf jacket. Why hadn't she sent it by post? Was her journey really necessary? The question reminded her of the wartime posters: *Is your journey really necessary?* Forty years, my God! Were all her journeys really necessary?

'Listen to me, Emma,' she said. 'You remember Miss Prentice, don't you? Of course, you do. Well, I saw her a few days ago. She's now far away, in a foreign country, and she asked me to come and see you. She sends her love. And she wants you to have this. It is something Ian wrote especially for you. That's why Miss Prentice wants you to have it. Ian dedicated it to you. Well, take it.'

The girl took it but didn't look at it.

'Goodbye,' Lady Cooper said.

The girl shrugged her shoulders.

A lonely seagull burst into the air space above them and quickly turned back to the sea.

Lady Cooper recrossed the street.

She was already at the edge of the garden when she heard a scream. Oh no, it couldn't be. She must have misheard.

She swerved round.

Emma was standing by the bus stop, as before, but now she stretched her arm, pointed her finger across the street at Lady Cooper, and shouted again: 'Dirty old woman!'

A moment later, the bus appeared. It was still far away, but Lady Cooper knew she would be too slow to cross the road before it arrived at the stop. And so she turned away, away, to escape from it all. Helping herself with her walking-stick umbrella, she passed through the garden and the grassland and into the wood. There she stopped. She felt quite safe among the trees. A squirrel climbed down one tree, and then up! to the top of another. Why did it do it? Was its journey really necessary? Or, are journeys the only important thing in the world? What a facile question to ask oneself; facile, stupid, and delightful, she told herself, indulgent of her own ease. It didn't last long. Suddenly, all that soft sweetness vanished.

'What did you do to the little girl?'

She hadn't heard him coming. All at once he was there.

Face to face.

'What did you do to the little girl, you dirty old bitch?' he repeated, his clenched fist in front of her nose. But it was the hatred, oozing out of every cell of his body, that stupefied her. It was as if all the fears she had managed to suppress during her long life had got unnailed now to get hold of her with a vengeance. She wanted him to strike, quickly, to stop the fear. And, as he didn't, she lifted her walking-stick umbrella and hit him first. He didn't move.

He took the umbrella from her and threw it away. When it was in the air, it half opened, frightening some birds.

171

And then he hit her and she fell down. And when his boot kicked her, she was just thankful that the fear was gone.

*

Slowly, she opened her eyes. Right above them was an undisturbed blue space. Bright blue. And nothing in it. She knew it was the sky. Slowly, her eyes shut. Time passed. She tilted her head to the right. Slightly. Her eyes opened again. She saw two feet. Close to her face, staring at her, were two round, gleaming buckles on high-heeled shoes. Her eyes moved up along the silk stockings towards the knees. Above, there was the hem of the skirt and a patch of shade. Her eyelids weighed down. A few blades of grass were again pressed by the back of her head as it turned a little to the left, to its previous position. Time passed. A dog barked. When she opened her eyes once more, they saw, as in a mirror, another pair of eyes, looking down at her. They were blue. Like the sky. And the face was pale. And the ends of the long blonde hair were falling loose, touching her face. 'Are you all right?' The words sounded tunefully, like a song. Her lips quivered. Voicelessly. And then there was nothing. Neither darkness nor light. Time lay in wait, supine, till the noise came, loud and shrill, and movement, up and forward, and time rushed full speed ahead, vibrating, and then there was peace. And when she opened her eyes again, she saw high above her a white rectangle. And she knew it was not the sky. She knew the white rectangle hanging above her was called ceiling, or *sufit*, or *plafond*, or *Zimmerdecke*, or *soffitto*, or *techo*, or *teto*, or *tak*, or *loft*, or . . .

*

'Sister,' she said, 'do promise . . .'
    'I'm not Sister. I'm Staff Nurse, duckie.'
    'Staff Nurse, be an angel and promise me that when I am dying you'll keep my eyes open, you will not let me shut them, Staff Nurse.'
    'You are not going to die, duckie. You've had a bit of a rough time, but you're doing well. Now, you don't need to move your head, but here is a police inspector who would like to ask you a few questions. All right?'

172

'All right.'

'Good morning to you, Lady Cooper,' the inspector said.

'Good morning . . .' she said.

'Just a few questions, Lady Cooper . . .'

'Yes . . .'

'Just now, Lady Cooper, I wondered why you told the nurse that you wanted to keep your eyes open?'

'Because when I have my eyes open I can see the ceiling. And the ceiling is white and beautiful. Beautiful white rectangle with no problems. When I see the ceiling, I'm at peace.'

'And when you shut your eyes?'

'When I shut my eyes, I see his face. And I don't want to have the picture of his face in my eyes. I don't want to take it with me, for ever, when I die.'

'That's exactly what we would like to know more about, Lady Cooper: what sort of face was it?'

'It was a face full of hatred.'

'What kind of hatred, Lady Cooper?'

'A sanctimonious hatred.'

'Can you say something more about that face, Lady Cooper?'

'There was a drop of spittle in the corner of its mouth.'

'But what else was there, Lady Cooper? A moustache? A beard? Was it blond? Or dark?'

'It was a face of many colours, Inspector.'

'All the same, try to describe it, Lady Cooper. Was it young? Or old?'

'It was as old as dust, Inspector.'

SIXTEEN

All the rivers run into the sea;
yet the sea is not full . . .

What Lady Cooper called her country house was a modernized eighteenth-century lodge by a stream at the edge of a park, and also, some five hundred steps uphill, standing in the middle of the park, a large mansion house (which the locals called the castle), now turned into a luxury health farm *vulgo* health clinic, run by Lady Cooper's son, Perceval W. Cooper, Esq. (W standing for Witold, pronounced Vitold).

Lady Cooper used to avoid the clinic, with its low calorie salads, water therapy, steam cabinets, sauna, irrigation, baths, chiropody, yoga, hairdressers and beauticians. When coming back from wherever she went to – London, Italy, France, Poland – she would go straight to her beautiful white lodge by the other bank of the stream ('There is excellent trout fishing on the estate. Please enquire at reception for details'), well screened from the rest of the park by tall trees and a belt of green bushes. It was to that lodge that the hired black Rolls-Royce hearse had brought her discreetly, silently – and for the last time.

There had been no inquest. The hospital doctors certified that she died of natural causes, not resulting from the injuries from which she had completely recovered. She had already been discharged, and was dressing to leave the ward, when she asked the nurse for a glass of water, and lay down on the bed, 'just for a moment' – as she told the nurse – 'to gather her thoughts.' She died quietly, with her eyes wide open. The eyes kept on opening, when they tried to shut them for her.

They buried her in the little cemetery by the village church. Her son, Perceval W. Cooper, and the gardener's wife, were the only mourners present. Though, when the coffin was already in the grave, a third person rushed in, panting heavily. A middle-aged man, unknown to Perceval W. Cooper. He was holding a bunch of flowers.

On their way back, as they were walking along the country lane towards the estate, the man said: 'Allow me to introduce myself, my name is Mr Newman.' From his wallet, he took out a visiting card – N.N. NEWMAN & CO STATIONERY PRINTING PHOTOCOPYING – and handed it to Perceval.

'How do you do?' said Perceval, dropping the card in his side pocket.

'I consider myself to have been a great friend of the deceased. Even though I saw the gracious lady once only, on the fateful day, the day of that tragic barbarous assault upon her. *O, tempora! O, mores!*'

'What?' P. W. Cooper said.

'I mean, what a world is this!'

'Quite,' said P. W. Cooper

'Lady Cooper visited me in my shop, and we had a very long conversation, a fascinating conversation' (he must have forgotten that it was mostly his own monologue) 'and the memory of it . . .'

'Yes, I understand,' said P. W. Cooper.

They were now standing at the entrance to the park.

'I won't ask you to lunch with me, Mr Newman, because I shan't eat at all, and I'm sure you wouldn't like what they can offer you at the clinic. The choice is a low-calorie salad or a high-calorie salad, and mineral water. But there is a nice pub in the village.'

'I wouldn't dream of imposing myself upon you, sir, and at such a time!' Mr Newman said, his eyes focused sharply on the beautiful young girl in a T-shirt and Bermuda shorts jogging purposefully in their direction.

'Now, that is what I call friendship!' the girl exclaimed. 'How exciting! But how did you find where I was? You crafty boy!' She took Mr Newman's head between her two hands, kissed him on the mouth, jumped back, and uttered: 'Ha, ha!'

'Actually . . .' Mr Newman started, embarrassed.

But P. W. Cooper forestalled him. The word 'funeral' mustn't be mentioned to the clinic's clients. 'We are lucky,' he said. 'Such fair, unclouded weather . . .'

'Quite so,' Mr Newman agreed. 'May I introduce my niece, sir, but, of course, you already know . . .'

'Your niece! My foot!' the girl laughed. 'My dad is the lover of Mr Newman's wife. That doesn't make me his niece, does it, or does it?' She stabbed Mr Newman's breast with the long manicured nail of her forefinger, and sang, 'What a splendid idea! How gorgeous of you to come all that way just to see me, but the timetable here is very strict and I must rush now-to have my aromatherapy massage – you may come with me and watch,' and, turning to Perceval, she said, 'It's all right to have a voyeur in the Treatment Room, isn't it? Or isn't it?'

*

The burden of wearing the name Perceval must have been imposed upon him by his father. Why, he couldn't guess. He hardly remembered him. He had his photographs, and an oil portrait representing Sir Lionel in his gala uniform, but it was not the same, not the same as remembering. And he didn't really know what had happened. Grown-up people were so damn vague about it. Was he killed? Or did he die a natural death? Or just disappear? Was he a hero? Or a traitor? Or a bit of both? And in Belgium, of all countries. Why in Belgium? A few years after the war, when Perceval was a little boy of three? or four? So many things he didn't know. Perhaps he didn't want to know? Perhaps he was afraid to learn? Well, anyway. His second Christian name, strange as it was, didn't worry him. Because he only used the initial. W was OK. You didn't need to tell people they should pronounce it V. V for Victory. Surely, it must have been his mother who made him have that foreign name Witold. He didn't mind being called W, but he hated his mother. He hated her with all his heart. Since he was seven, seven years of age, he had hated her as acutely, as ardently, as he had loved her before, as he had loved her for the first seven years of his life. When he was seven, he had been sent away to school, he had been sent away by her, Lady Cooper, his mother; he had been sent away to school where they made him drink two pints of squash, after which they put him into a wicker basket which they hoisted under the ceiling of the chapel, and let him hang there for hours, till he had to pee, the whole two pints, from high above down to the level of the ground, after which they made him mop the floor, with his own vest, shirt,

176

pants, and handkerchiefs, and tried to insert their little penises into his bum. The masters preferred not to know too much about it. After all, it was Plato's Republic, Spartan endurance, public school machismo, the Natural Selection of the empire builders that they aimed at being servants to, oblivious of the fact that 'the day of empires had passed away, the day of small nations had come'. That's how it grew to be that his stiff upper lip was adorned with two sardonic wrinkles whenever he had to listen about concentration camp atrocities. Well, of course it wasn't *exactly* the same sort of thing, but he knew some of it. And he survived. And he didn't whine. He hated. First of all, he hated that bloody snob, that bloody Polack woman, how could she do such a thing to him, she, his great sweet mother. That mute 'how-could-she?' stayed with him all his life. And now, as she was no more, it had to give way to a kind of puzzled, astonished, helpless emptiness and fear that there might be nothing to hate from now on.

As he looked through the window of his top-floor study, he saw the park, the lodge, the fields, the little village, the little church, and the cemetery from which he had just come back. He flicked the switch of the intercom: 'Anything? No? Good. I'm all right, thank you. Yes. OK. Look, I'll be going to London. A day or two, I can't tell you now. Of course you can manage. No, I'll phone you. All right, you can phone me at the St John's Wood number, *if* there is something *really* urgent. No, thank you, there's no need. Goodbye. Yes? Thanks. Bye.' He didn't like her calling him 'darling'. Though there was absolutely no significance in it. In the clinic, she addressed everybody as 'darling', but she pronounced the word exactly in the same way as she would if she was saying, 'Yes, sir' or 'Yes, madam'.

*

He parked his olive-green Bentley in front of the house. On the yellow line. So what? With a bunch of his mother's keys in his hand, he stood at the front door, wondering which one would fit the keyhole. The first he tried unlocked the door. He lifted his travelling bag and went up the stairs. At the entrance door to the flat, he stood and wondered which of the keys would open it. Again, the first he chose did.

177

The air in the rooms was still the same air she was taking into her lungs, taking it in and sending it out, and he felt now as if the breath of her life breathed into his nostrils. He put his bag on the chest of drawers, under the mirror, in the hall, when the telephone started to ring. He knew the flat, of course, he'd been there before, but he wasn't sure where the telephone was. When he found it, a male voice asked: 'Is that her ladyship's residence?'

'Yes.'

'This is the window cleaners. We have tried to ring three times, there was no answer. Will it be convenient if we come tomorrow at eleven a.m.?'

He looked at the windows. They were covered with a thin film of whatever it is that makes windows dirty. And there were some birds' droppings in the middle of a window-pane. 'All right,' he said. 'Tomorrow at eleven.'

He was now in the sitting room. He saw an old écritoire, a golden satinwood, Georgian, lady's writing-bureau with pigeon-holes and drawers. He rolled up the tambour. Her diary and her address book were lying on the blotter. He opened the diary. Monday Tuesday Wednesday Thursday . . . Was it Wednesday? He checked the date on his wrist-watch. It was. So, under Thursday, he wrote:

Window cleaners 11 a.m.

He turned the page to the previous week and, in the little box headed Friday, he drew a cross. He closed the diary, took the address book and gave it a flick-through. Good Lord! There must have been over two hundred addresses in it. And not a soul at her funeral. Except that chap Newman. Well, how could they know? Normally, one puts an announcement in *The Times* or the *Telegraph*. But *The Times* and the *Telegraph* were read by the patients of the clinic and the patients of the clinic mustn't be disturbed by thoughts of death. He felt in his side pocket for Mr Newman's card. STATIONERY PRINTING PHOTOCOPYING. He would ask him to print the notice and send it to all the names in the address book.

He opened the diary once more and, under

Window cleaners 11 a.m.

he wrote:

Obituary for Mr N.

Suddenly, he discovered that he was hungry. He had eaten a good English breakfast first thing in the morning (orange juice, bacon and eggs, kippers, toast, marmalade, coffee, not the health clinic weak tea and yoghurt), but nothing since, no lunch. He stepped into the kitchen. The bread had transubstantiated itself into stone, the carton of milk in the Frigidaire had become transmogrified into a mouldy copy of cottage cheese. But there were some eggs, and cheddar, and packets of crisp rye biscuits, and two shelves packed with tins and jars and a variety of gastronomical titbits and *tutti frutti*. He put on Lady Cooper's apron and concocted a *smørgasbord* meal, which he served himself from the kitchen table.

Back in the sitting room, he hesitated between gin and tonic and Pernod. The bottle of Pernod in the drinks cupboard surprised him. He had seen his mother drinking gin and tonic, he had never seen her drinking a Pernod. Somehow . . . that little, insignificant discovery seemed to him to be of great importance. What else was there that he didn't know? That vague thought made him feel hostile again. Oh God, he didn't need to, he didn't have to know everything, did he? He sighed. Well, anyway. What was he going to drink now? Pernod or gin and tonic? Eeeny, meeny, miney, mo – how was it that this counting-out rhyme, which he hadn't heard since he was less than seven, had somehow managed to survive among the memory hiccups of his brain? He poured water into the glass of Pernod and watched how the drink changed colour. He put the glass on the coffee table, in front of the big roomy armchair. He liked its shape and its softness. He took a cigar from the leather *étui* that used to belong to Sir Lionel, his father. Leaning limply back in his seat, cushioned against his own thoughts, he relaxed. There was nothing to disturb him now. No enemies, no obligations, no past, no future, no present, nothing. He lit his postprandial cigar. 'A woman is only a woman, but a good cigar is a smoke.' He knew it sounded like Sam Goldwyn or Groucho

Marx. Actually it was Rudyard Kipling. Which made a lot of difference. Or did it? He took a sip of Pernod. Where had she learnt to drink it? In France? What was she doing in France? Didn't it taste like cough medicine? for kids? Aniseed. No wormwood in it any more. The French forbade it in 1915. The First World War. He had another sip and another puff. The smoke made his eyes smart. Which was odd. He used to smoke the same brand of *corona* twice a day, after lunch and dinner, they never affected his eyes. And now, yes, definitely. His eyes felt hot. Itching. He shut them and kept them shut, tightly, for a whole minute. It didn't help. He rubbed them. That didn't help either. He wanted to have a look at them. It occurred to him that it was against common sense that his eyes could see his toes and his belly and his hands, and even the tip of his nose, yet they couldn't see themselves, anyway, not without a mirror. He got up and went to the bathroom where a mirror was hanging on the wall. He looked. Indeed. His eyelids were heavy and red. And moist. His eyes blinked. And when they blinked they didn't see themselves. And during the moments they didn't see themselves, the eyelids squeezed out some of the moisture down his cheeks. How awful. Somebody who didn't know him might think that he was crying. Ridiculous! He never cried. He had never cried since he was seven, never, not once. It might be allergy to London air, but you never know . . . Moorfields Eye Hospital is the best eye hospital in the world. He must phone them and find out who their top consultant is. Ophthalmitis is not a joke. A drop ran down his cheek to the corner of his mouth. He tasted it with the tip of his tongue. It tasted a bit like salt water. He went back to the sitting room, opened Lady Cooper's diary, and under

> *Window cleaners 11 a.m.*
> *Obituary for Mr N.*

he wrote

> *Moorfields Hospital.*

He balanced the smoking cigar on the edge of the ashtray and returned to the bathroom to look for some tissue paper to wipe his eyes. The medicine cabinet was hanging in the corner, by the loo. He opened it and exclaimed 'Oh, no . . .' On the shelf, in the cabinet, there was a packet of suppositories. So the Old Lady had piles. He also had piles. He always used to think that

180

his piles were the consequence of his experiences at boarding school. Now it seemed rather likely that he had inherited them from his mother, and he frowned. He was all ready to accuse her of giving him piles. And yet, at the same time, his heart went out to her. He knew how uncomfortable it was to have swollen veins in one's anus. And for the first time ever, anyway, for the first time since he was seven, he felt the warm feeling of tenderness towards her, even if still spiced with the latent dregs of grudge.

A laundry basket was standing under the medicine cabinet. He glanced at it but didn't look under the lid. He marched straight to the bedroom. It was already getting dark. He switched the light on. All three doors of the enormous built-in wardrobe were wide open. 'Good Lord,' he said. Loudly. What he saw was like a historical exhibition. On the top shelf, starting from the left, her old wartime WRAC stylish hat. Next to it, a fire-watcher's tin helmet. Then, the frivolous colourful toque and pillbox hat which she must have worn before he was born, and a cloche with feathers, and a beret, and a Panama with a scarf, and silk hats and felt hats and knitted hats and mink hats, their colours changing from all the colours of the rainbow on the left of the shelf to beige and brown and grey and white and black on its right. And the same with the fichus and shawls and gloves on the same shelf, pink and blue and green and yellow on the left, and white and grey and black on the right. 'She must have been buying and buying . . .' he thought. And then he reflected, 'If she bought just one hat for each of the four seasons, that would make, for these forty years or so since the war, some hundred and sixty hats . . . and there are . . . on the shelf . . . what? twenty?' No, it was too silly. He was not going to count her hats. Nor was he going to count her dresses. They were hanging on coathangers under the shelf, and they too seemed to have been arranged in chronological order, frocks, gowns, tailor-made suits, jackets, skirts, blouses, slacks, pull-overs, jumpers; silk, wool, worsted, tweed, flannel, velvet, corduroy, nylon; pleated, knitted, quilted, embroidered; step-in, pull-on, zip-up; classic, tailored, ready-made; bright and flowery on the left, and pale and colourless or dark on the right. And the shoes on the wardrobe floor, when did she wear those high-heels and boots and sandals, what did she collect them for, for whom? the Victoria and Albert Museum? The shelves in the

181

partition on the left were filled with lingerie, vests, chemises, girdles, panties, slips, brassières, stockings, tights, suspender belts, nightdresses, bedsocks, bedjackets, and the smell of lavender, oh no, he couldn't possibly know how to get rid of all that, what he needed was a woman, he needed a woman to help him, only a woman would know what to do. But who? The answer came at once. Sally.

He went back to his armchair in the sitting room, and to his glass of Pernod and the one third of the cigar in the ashtray. The cigar looked cold and dead, but when he puffed at it it revived. Sally. Of course. He could phone Sally now, and Sally would come at once, Sally would know what to do with all that stuff and she would go to the kitchen and cook a perfect dinner, and she would go to bed with him, and she would domesticate the whole place, and that was precisely what he was afraid of, because he knew that she wanted him to marry her. And he would, if he wanted to be married at all. But he didn't. No. A hundred times no. Thank you. Thank you very much. He was perfectly all right in his rooms at the top of the health clinic where he was the boss, had all the service he needed, a cook cooking specially for him, and a variety of sex without strings attached. It would have been different if he wanted to have children. But he didn't. The world was already covered thickly enough with human vermin, no need to add another individual to it to be squashed, or – who knows? – to become a squasher. No, marriage was neither here nor there. Even if she was such a nice girl. Sally. Had been a girlfriend of that young man who made her pregnant and got himself killed before the child was born. Silly boy. BA. Wanted to know the colour of some famous writer's eyes, went to another literary man to ask, and there was a bomb there, and the bomb exploded and blew him to smithereens. Poor Sally. He, Perceval, had met her when she was already the mother of a little baby girl. The little baby was a few months old when Sally gave it to Mrs McPherson, the baby's grandmother. And Sally said that she did it because Mrs McPherson begged her on her (Mrs McPherson's) knees to give her her (Mrs McPherson's) son's child, but he (Perceval) knew that Sally did it because she (Sally) thought that with no child to care for, it would be easier for him to marry her. Which he didn't. So she was now without the boyfriend, without the

182

baby, and without a husband. Still, she had her MP. She was a secretary to an MP. Whether she slept with him or not, he (Perceval) did not know and didn't care. The MP was until recently a Labour MP but then he switched to the SDP, and she called him 'my traitor'. Now, wasn't that 'traitor' some sort of cousin of his? Of course, he was. On his (Perceval's) father's side. As Dame Victoria was Sir Lionel's half-sister, wasn't she? And though he (Perceval) had never seen him he too could call him a 'traitor' as he had cut Lady Cooper completely since Sir Lionel's unexplained death. He (the MP) must have been un-lucky with his family anyway – didn't he have a niece who was involved in some hushed-up affair? That's what Sally had tried to talk about but he (Perceval) hadn't listened. He didn't like to hear about that sort of thing. Never did. Never really wanted to know what happened to his father, Sir Lionel, in Belgium, didn't really want to hear how that young man McPherson, Sally's boyfriend, was blown to pieces, and, actually, he was rather glad that the police had only informed him about his mother, Lady Cooper, when she was already dead. To feel hostile was one thing. Quite another thing was to rush there and see her beaten up, in the hospital bed, and listen to all the details of her being mugged. Though there hadn't been many details. They still didn't know who the mugger was. And they still weren't sure why the mugger didn't rob her of her money. Perhaps he didn't because she defended herself. That's what they suggested. They knew that she was defending herself because they found her broken umbrella. But, anyway, he (Perceval) didn't want to visualize all that. He wasn't a *News of the World* reader. Didn't Sally tell him on some occasion to get out of his health clinic sanctuary and grow up? Well, she did. But why should he? He didn't particularly like all those grown-up people who knew everything better and mugged other people in one way or another. The detective said that Lady Cooper either didn't remember or was reluctant to say what her mugger was like. He had 'sanctimonious hatred' on his face, he (the detective) said was all she (Lady Cooper) had said. 'Sancti-monious hatred', curious grown-up expression. An oxymoron, actually. Like 'clever foolishness'. Or 'childish grown-upness'. Well, wasn't all that sweet-and-sour world of ours rather oxy-moronical, actually? Rather. With its *si vis pacem para bellum*, that's an oxymoron, isn't it? And its food surplus and world famine, that too is an oxy . . . Good God! Well, yes, that's what he'd do. He put down his glass of Pernod. No, he was not going to phone Sally. He'd ask the Oxfam people to come and take Lady Cooper's wardrobe away, they would know what to do with it. Good God, why hadn't he thought about them at once? Had he just said, 'Good God'? But isn't 'good God' just another oxymoron? Is there anybody in the whole universe less good than God is? Hadn't He built its organic chemistry on the very principle of cruelty and injustice? And then put all the blame on us . . . He got up, walked several times all round the room, then sat down on the straight-back Georgian chair in front of the éscritoire, opened the diary on the same page as before, and under

> Window cleaners 11 a.m.
> Obituary for Mr N.
> Moorfield Hospital

he wrote   ring Oxfam.

Lady Cooper's diary was not a diarist's diary, it was a calendar with blank spaces, about one inch by two inches, for each day's memoranda, seven days of the week in the opening of two pages. Shyly, he turned back two pages, a fortnight back. There were only four entries, all in one day.

> phone Revd P. Prentice
> "   solicitors (30 year rule)
> Partridge's Dictionary of Slang
> Euclid was an ass

As those were the last entries, written – presumably – the day before she left, he wondered whether he shouldn't show them to the detectives. Would they be as mystified as he was? *Euclid was an ass!* Indeed! He turned another page backwards, to the past. There was the time of the departure of the plane from Heathrow to Okęcie (Warsaw) written in pen, and then, obviously added later on, in pencil:

> Met Miss Prentice on the plane
> Trouble with casket at customs
Next day: Taxi from Warsaw to village (20km)
> Nobody remembered Pięść (iewicki)

184

Two days later:	*Seen Joseph. Imponderabilia.*
	been grilled by him. Nicely.
Next day entry:	*8.30 a.m. Miss P.*
(overflowing	*Joseph. Helicopter. Back to Joseph.*
on to the follow-	*Shop. Driver. Statue of Liberty.*
ing space?)	*P.& J. tête à tête. Ha ha.*
	Miss P: 'politicians are mortal, politics
	is mortal, poetry is mortal, good
	manners are immortal.'
	Met Dr Goldfinger. Told him my biological
	father a boy of 15. To tell Zuppa am her
	½ sister. He now only person alive to know
	Gen. Pięść my father.
Two days later:	*Back to London* [hour of departure].

He thumbed through the remaining pages of the diary. Nothing of interest. Occasional memoranda, engagements, *hairdresser 2.30, dentist 11 a.m.*, etc. He thought he might find some diaries for the past years. He vaguely hoped there might be one some thirty years old, the time his father, Sir Lionel, died/disappeared in Belgium. There weren't any. Maybe she had destroyed them. Or kept them in the lodge. Anyway. What he found in the éscritoire was of no interest. Bills to be paid. Receipts. Some letters he decided not to read. Not now, anyway. Well, anyway. He was already standing up when he noticed, flat on the bottom of a drawer, a yellow paper folder. He took it out, went to the bedroom, and put it on the bedside table. It had been a long day and he was tired out. He took off his jacket, kicked off his shoes, pulled off his socks. Lady Cooper's soft pink mules were standing by the bed. He tried them. They were all right. He fetched his travelling bag from the hall. Took out his pyjamas and the toilet set. Folded up and put away the bedspread. The bed had been slept in. Naturally. Should he change the sheets? Oh, no. He couldn't possibly. What nonsense! He undressed. His pyjamas were on the dressing stool. Now, he noticed, under the pillow, Lady Cooper's pair of pyjamas. Pyjama jacket and pyjama trousers. He held them in his hands. They were pure silk. Winston Churchill always wore silk underclothing. Even under his wartime siren suit. Silk next to the skin. How does it feel?

185

Silk and lavender. He looked round, as if to make sure that nobody was watching him. Then, gingerly, he stepped into the silk pyjama trousers, they were an inch too short but not too tight; he put on the silk pyjama jacket, buttoned it easily, and he lay down on the bed, under the quilted duvet. After a moment, he stretched out his hand to seize the yellow paper folder on the bedside table, but he had already come to the borders of sleep and his weak and weary hand fell down before touching it.

A dark black borderless river started running through his dream. There was a bridge over the river but it looked rather like the bridge of a ship, only so out of Time and out of Space that you couldn't see its ends. And a solitary tall slim man, his head held high, was standing on the bridge smoking a pipe. And there was no sky above him, only a deep black limitless body of air. And the deep blackness of the river flowed under it and it was terrifying. And, further down, the river divided into two rivers, leaving some mud, sand and soil in the space between them, and each of the two rivers divided into three rivers, and each of the three rivers divided into four rivers, and each of the four rivers divided into five rivers, and there were hundreds and thousands of rivers streamlets rivulets, running oozing meandering, and they all were alive and each had the name of somebody he knew or knew of but he couldn't remember their names, their names were there, on the tip of his tongue, but he couldn't remember them, and then a loud, ecclesiastic voice said: 'All the rivers run into the sea; yet the sea is not full.' And he heard the voice, and he came awake all at once, and he exclaimed: 'Who's there?'

There was nobody there. The bedside lamp was still on. There was no traffic noise. Not a sound. Nothing. And yet . . . 'Goodness me,' he said to himself. He had just noticed that he had wetted his bed, that he had ejaculated in his dreamless sleep, he was quite certain he hadn't dreamed. 'Goodness me!' he repeated, 'At my age!' Nocturnal emissions were quite all right, quite normal, for adolescents, but he was in his thirties, wasn't he? and his sex life was no problem, no problem at all, was it? What then? Was he oversexed, were his testes producing too many hormones, were his seminal vesicles overgorged with secretions, was his prostate producing too great a pressure, or else was he a bloody neurotic, well, anyway, wasn't he going to see an oculist about his eyes, perhaps he'd ask him, why not? An oculist is a medical man. He got out of bed, stripped off the silk pyjamas and put on his own. He hung Lady Cooper's wet pyjama trousers over the cane chair by the dressing-table, and went to the kitchen to brew himself some strong black coffee with plenty of sugar. As the kettle started to sing, it occurred to him that perhaps he *did* dream, after all. But what the dream was about – how could he force himself to remember? He couldn't. Instead of recalling the dream, his memory retrieved from the past the long forgotten lines he had learned by heart when he was no more than seven:

> From too much love of living,
> From hope and fear set free,
> We thank with brief thanksgiving
> Whatever gods may be
> That no man lives forever,
> That dead men rise up never;
> That even the weariest river
> Winds somewhere safe to sea.

Now, yes, there was something like a river in his dream but was it a weary river, no, a weary river would be Lady Cooper, but there certainly was no Lady Cooper in his dream, definitely not, it was *not* about any particular person, it was overcrowded with people, millions and millions . . . alluvial . . . ecclesiastical . . . slimy . . . well, anyway . . . He yawned. He took a cup of black coffee to the bedroom and put it on the bedside table, by the telephone, on top of the yellow paper folder. He glanced at the silk pyjama trousers hanging on the cane chair. No need to wash them. When the wet patch dried, he'd crumble it to dust, millions of reproductive cells, enough to fuse with all the ova of the world. He took a sip of coffee. He sat down on the edge of the bed and took another sip of coffee. He kicked off Lady Cooper's soft pink mules which he'd been wearing. He stretched out on the bed. He thought that he liked that bed better than the one in the health clinic. And he liked the quilted duvet. The bedside lamp was on. The grey dawn was breaking behind the pearl-grey window. He smiled. Somewhere, a half-awakened bird piped up thinly. He took the yellow paper folder from under the coffee cup when, suddenly, the telephone started ringing.

He didn't answer. But it kept ringing. Persistently.

He took the receiver off the cradle and laid it aside.

It stopped ringing, but its earpiece said and kept on saying, *Hallo Hallo Hallo* . . .

He grasped the receiver, screamed, 'Fuck off, please. Will you!' and slammed the receiver down. He didn't know why he had done that. Who could it have been? Another skeleton in the cupboard? he murmured. He took the yellow paper folder again. Looked at it for a moment. Then opened it. It was empty. There was nothing in it.

He laughed.

Then he drew the telephone towards him and dialled Sally's telephone number.

CODA
Not a Single Sardine for his Footnote

The early-morning sun was already climbing up the roofs of the houses along the rue de Médicis and from there hitting the tops of the trees when the man at the iron gate looked with astonishment at the man who was going out of the garden. 'Comment?' said he, 'I have just opened the gate, how can you be going out if you had no time to go in?' After which he added: 'Don't tell me you slept there all night, à la belle étoile?'

The man in the brown suit didn't bother to answer. At that early hour, the undisturbed dust of the streets of Paris began to stir under the running feet of the harassed human beings hurrying in all directions. The man in the brown suit walked slowly, turning left here and right there, as if it didn't matter in the least where he'd find himself, or when. It was half-past ten when he stopped by the Café des Trois Univers and, without hesitating, went in.

He looked at the sixty-three bottles displayed in front of him at the far end of the café. He just knew, without having to count them, that there were sixty-three. They, people, *they*, at a glance, they can see that there are two, or three, or four bottles, or (if the bottles are arranged in some sort of symmetrical pattern) perhaps even eight or twelve – but to know how many bottles there are, if there are more than a dozen, they have to count them. He didn't have to. He was not a computer. He just saw there were seventeen on the top shelf, twenty-two on the middle shelf, nineteen on the bottom shelf, four on the counter, and one in the hand of the barman. But what really puzzled him was not their number but their colours. So many colours and so few words to name them. What a poor language, really! To say, as *they* do, that both *Chartreuse verte* and *Diabolo menthe* are green, or that *Chartreuse jaune* and *Eier-Kognak* are both

189

yellow, is just silly. And what about wine? There are hundreds of different colours of wine and they, people, have only three words for them: red or rosé or white, which is still funnier because no white wine is the colour of the snow, no rosé is the colour of a rose, and no red wine is the colour of the Flanders poppy.

He looked at the multicoloured drinks in the café and reflected that none of them was blue. No, he hadn't seen any of these people drinking anything blue. Or eating anything blue. Except, perhaps, some tiny little veins in Gorgonzola cheese. But then, again, to call this blue-veined cheese 'blue' and to call the sky 'blue' – what a crude vocabulary! *He*, he could distinguish hundreds and hundreds of colours, and yet they had only seven genuine names for them all. Just seven plus black and white and grey and brown and gold and silver (which are not strictly speaking colours). It was, of course, still worse with smells. He could distinguish thousands. Yet none, not a single one, had its own proper name. How ridiculous! He drew a sample of air into his nostrils. There was the smell of the pale yellowish(?) – greenish(?) Pernod emanating from the tall glass in front of him. And the smell of paper and printing ink of the *New York Herald Tribune* being read by the man who was sitting at a little table on his left, puffing out molecules of malt and hops each time he put down his glass of blond(?) beer. And smells of pastry, and of cream, and of chocolate, and of one black(?) and one white(?) coffee from the little table on the right, at which two women sat sending out in all directions their sex pheromones. Their sex pheromones, deep in his nasal cavity, made him turn his head towards them more often than he wished. Other men in the café did the same, yet – not able to smell the pheromones (which all the same triggered off their reflexes) – they thought it was the women's looks that attracted their attention.

He called the *garçon* and asked for *de quoi écrire*. Once upon a time one could ask, *Donnez moi de quoi écrire, s'il vous plaît* in a Paris café. But he didn't look old enough to remember those days. How did he know? 'We don't have any,' the waiter said. 'But you can buy some at the *bureau de tabac* by the entrance door.'

He bought some envelopes, notepaper, postage stamps, and a ball-pen. Back at his little table, he noticed that the man reading

190

the *New York Herald Tribune* was observing him closely. But he didn't mind. He took a piece of note paper and put pen to it:

Dear Mama,
My body understands their bodies perfectly well. I make the same movements, feel the same hunger, become tired or sleepy, and react positively to all those sex pheromones these females exude around me. It is their logic that I don't quite understand. Which puzzles me. Because, if my brain is an exact Madame Tussaud copy of theirs, then it should be working in the same way, shouldn't it? Well, perhaps Teacher will explain why it doesn't.
Now, dear Mama, even with their kind of brain, one can easily fall into a trap. A man I met not long ago was boasting about some things he had done in the war. 'Which war?' I asked. 'What does it matter, you can't remember either,' said he. 'But I do,' said I. 'Don't be silly. How old are you?' asked he. 'Thirty-four,' said I. 'Well, you see, you weren't in this world at the time,' said he. 'But I was. I've been here for seventy-four years now,' said I. "I thought you said you were thirty-four,' said he. 'Yes,' said I, 'I am thirty-four. I have been thirty-four for all these seventy-four years,' which, as you know, is quite true, but he looked at me as if I had said something wrong, and called me, for some reason, the Mad Hatter.

Your aff. son,
The Mad Hatter

P.S. Thanks for my pocket money.

He struck a match and, holding the letter in his left hand, lit the left upper corner. The flame started to travel to the right and down. Everybody's eyes turned towards it. The waiter came running: 'Monsieur, you can't do here that sort of . . .' he stopped. He shut his eyes and opened them again. There was no flame, no ash, no smell. The gentleman was sitting at his table, sipping his drink, and reading a perfectly ordinary letter. The waiter turned round and retreated. The café now sounded as if a hundred budgerigars had flown in through the open windows. The man with the *New York Herald Tribune* pushed his chair sideways, and said:

'Excuse me, but may I speak to you for a moment?'

'What is it?'

'Well, let me introduce myself first. My name is Krupa. It's a Polish name, but I'm an American. How do you do, sir?'

'How do you do.'

'I presume you must be an illusionist, if you don't mind my saying so,' Mr Krupa said.

'A what?'

'A magician.'

'Why?'

'Well, burning that letter . . . To your fiancée, I presume?'

'No, it was a letter to my mother.'

'Well, well, burning a letter to your mother, and then – hey presto! – holding it intact in your hands . . .'

'But this one here is not the same letter. This one is her reply.'

'Ha ha ha,' said Mr Krupa with a mixture of enthusiasm and jeering. 'This is Paris! This is Europe! Well, you know, if you can perform that sort of trick on the stage, you could make a lot of money in the States. I know some people who are in the profession, they could help you.'

'But I don't need any money.'

'Nonsense, one always needs money. You need money to post your letter.'

'Oh, no. I told you, I don't need the post to correspond with my mother.'

Mr Krupa was very thoughtful.

'You mean you wrote a letter to your mum, you burnt it, and at once had in your hands her answer?'

'That's right.'

'And what does she say in her letter, if I may ask?'

'She tells me to come back home.'

'And are you going to?'

'Yes,' said he, and vanished.

*

'Where is that monsieur? He hasn't paid his bill. Was he with you?' the waiter asked.

On the marble top of the little table, by the half-empty glass of Pernod, was a letter. Mr Krupa moved nearer and put his hand on it. 'That's all right,' he pacified the waiter. 'I'll pay.' And when the waiter had gone, he took his reading glasses out of his pocket and put them on:

192

My dear son,
(or do you wish me to call you the Mad Hatter now?) The news is not
very good but please do not take it too much to (your present,
provisional, distorted) heart.

I spoke to Teacher and we both agreed that your prolonged (and
costly) consorting with those people tends to impoverish your brain
(by 'brain' I mean, of course, your mind proper and not that piece of
anatomy you are being temporarily burdened with at present). Well,
in short, Teacher is dissatisfied with you. He has already finished
writing a monograph on the our-true-Earth image as it exists in the
distorting mirror into which he sent you to do some research and bring
him material for just one single footnote, and he is still waiting for it.
All he asked you to do was to go to a place called Portimao and visit
the factory where they pack sardines in oil in hermetically sealed tins,
and write him a report on both the people who pack the sardines and
the sardines which are packed. Now, it is already seventy-four years
since you were sent on that mission of inquiry, and it seems that you
have not yet managed to find a single sardine for his footnote.

No wonder Teacher is disappointed. And annoyed. Especially
when, instead of telling him about sardines etc, you send him some
odes, ballads, hymns, songs, elegies, epigrams, sonnets, and plenty of
irregular descriptive stanzas of blank verse. True, in one of them you
did mention something of interest to Teacher: something about a lady
poetess who hadn't actually written any poems but claimed to have
seen the True Earth orbiting around the sun. Teacher was furious
with you that you didn't bother to ask her immediately what were the
coordinates of what she saw: azimuth, altitude, the exact time; right
ascension, declination, and hour angle; celestial and galactic longitude
and latitude – so that he could check whether she really saw us, or
was just giving rein to her frustrated poetic imagination.

Now, to cut this long letter short, Teacher asks you to return. He'll
publish the monograph without the footnote about the sardines. But
don't let it upset you too much. The real reason is that the aberrations,
pincushion-distortions, barrel-distortions, etc, of that mirror-image-
Earth of theirs have become too dangerous. The crinkled mirror made
them so stupid as not to know that one mustn't be too clever. That's
why, though there are few right roads they wouldn't have been on,
there are few they wouldn't have abandoned by taking wrong turn-
ings. In theology, in politics, in art, and now – alas – in science.
Teacher tried to warn them. He told them that no axioms are

193

immortal, that the only immortal things are good manners. 'Politicians are mortal, politics is mortal, poetry is mortal — good manners are immortal,' he said. And his message got through. It was received by a little palmist girl. But it was too simple for them. They wouldn't listen to oracles that have no hidden meanings. And so their world will go puff! and we shall never know how they packed their sardines.

Well, then, come back, come home. Wherever you are, stop being there and start being here, instantly.

Your loving,
Mother

About the Author

Stefan Themerson (1910 -1988) was born in Poland, moved to Russia during the Revolution, studied physics and architecture in Warsaw, and lived in Paris before settling in London. Aside from his writings—which include novels such as *Hobson's Island* and *Tom Harris*, children's stories, philosophical essays, and poems—Themerson also composed music and made a number of films with his wife Franciszka.

SELECTED DALKEY ARCHIVE PAPERBACKS

PETROS ABATZOGLOU, *What Does Mrs. Freeman Want?*
PIERRE ALBERT-BIROT, *Grabinoulor.*
YUZ ALESHKOVSKY, *Kangaroo.*
FELIPE ALFAU, *Chromos.*
    Locos.
IVAN ÂNGELO, *The Celebration.*
    The Tower of Glass.
DAVID ANTIN, *Talking.*
DJUNA BARNES, *Ladies Almanack.*
    Ryder.
JOHN BARTH, *LETTERS.*
    Sabbatical.
DONALD BARTHELME, *The King.*
    Paradise.
SVETISLAV BASARA, *Chinese Letter.*
MARK BINELLI, *Sacco and Vanzetti Must Die!*
ANDREI BITOV, *Pushkin House.*
LOUIS PAUL BOON, *Chapel Road.*
    Summer in Termuren.
ROGER BOYLAN, *Killoyle.*
IGNÁCIO DE LOYOLA BRANDÃO, *Teeth under the Sun.*
    Zero.
CHRISTINE BROOKE-ROSE, *Amalgamemnon.*
BRIGID BROPHY, *In Transit.*
MEREDITH BROSNAN, *Mr. Dynamite.*
GERALD L. BRUNS,
    Modern Poetry and the Idea of Language.
GABRIELLE BURTON, *Heartbreak Hotel.*
MICHEL BUTOR, *Degrees.*
    Mobile.
    Portrait of the Artist as a Young Ape.
G. CABRERA INFANTE, *Infante's Inferno.*
    Three Trapped Tigers.
JULIETA CAMPOS, *The Fear of Losing Eurydice.*
ANNE CARSON, *Eros the Bittersweet.*
CAMILO JOSÉ CELA, *The Family of Pascual Duarte.*
    The Hive.
LOUIS-FERDINAND CÉLINE, *Castle to Castle.*
    Conversations with Professor Y.
    London Bridge.
    North.
    Rigadoon.
HUGO CHARTERIS, *The Tide Is Right.*
JEROME CHARYN, *The Tar Baby.*
MARC CHOLODENKO, *Mordechai Schamz.*
EMILY HOLMES COLEMAN, *The Shutter of Snow.*
ROBERT COOVER, *A Night at the Movies.*
STANLEY CRAWFORD, *Some Instructions to My Wife.*
ROBERT CREELEY, *Collected Prose.*
RENÉ CREVEL, *Putting My Foot in It.*
RALPH CUSACK, *Cadenza.*
SUSAN DAITCH, *L.C.*
    Storytown.
NIGEL DENNIS, *Cards of Identity.*
PETER DIMOCK,
    A Short Rhetoric for Leaving the Family.
ARIEL DORFMAN, *Konfidenz.*
COLEMAN DOWELL, *The Houses of Children.*
    Island People.
    Too Much Flesh and Jabez.
RIKKI DUCORNET, *The Complete Butcher's Tales.*
    The Fountains of Neptune.
    The Jade Cabinet.
    Phosphor in Dreamland.
    The Stain.
    The Word "Desire."
WILLIAM EASTLAKE, *The Bamboo Bed.*
    Castle Keep.
    Lyric of the Circle Heart.
JEAN ECHENOZ, *Chopin's Move.*
STANLEY ELKIN, *A Bad Man.*
    Boswell: A Modern Comedy.
    Criers and Kibitzers, Kibitzers and Criers.
    The Dick Gibson Show.
    The Franchiser.
    George Mills.
    The Living End.
    The MacGuffin.
    The Magic Kingdom.
    Mrs. Ted Bliss.
    The Rabbi of Lud.

    Van Gogh's Room at Arles.
ANNIE ERNAUX, *Cleaned Out.*
LAUREN FAIRBANKS, *Muzzle Thyself.*
    Sister Carrie.
LESLIE A. FIEDLER,
    Love and Death in the American Novel.
GUSTAVE FLAUBERT, *Bouvard and Pécuchet.*
FORD MADOX FORD, *The March of Literature.*
JON FOSSE, *Melancholy.*
MAX FRISCH, *I'm Not Stiller.*
CARLOS FUENTES, *Christopher Unborn.*
    Distant Relations.
    Terra Nostra.
    Where the Air Is Clear.
JANICE GALLOWAY, *Foreign Parts.*
    The Trick Is to Keep Breathing.
WILLIAM H. GASS, *The Tunnel.*
    Willie Masters' Lonesome Wife.
ETIENNE GILSON, *The Arts of the Beautiful.*
    Forms and Substances in the Arts.
C. S. GISCOMBE, *Giscome Road.*
    Here.
DOUGLAS GLOVER, *Bad News of the Heart.*
    The Enamoured Knight.
KAREN ELIZABETH GORDON, *The Red Shoes.*
GEORGI GOSPODINOV, *Natural Novel.*
JUAN GOYTISOLO, *Marks of Identity.*
PATRICK GRAINVILLE, *The Cave of Heaven.*
HENRY GREEN, *Blindness.*
    Concluding.
    Doting.
    Nothing.
JIŘÍ GRUŠA, *The Questionnaire.*
JOHN HAWKES, *Whistlejacket.*
AIDAN HIGGINS, *A Bestiary.*
    Bornholm Night-Ferry.
    Flotsam and Jetsam.
    Langrishe, Go Down.
    Scenes from a Receding Past.
    Windy Arbours.
ALDOUS HUXLEY, *Antic Hay.*
    Crome Yellow.
    Point Counter Point.
    Those Barren Leaves.
    Time Must Have a Stop.
MIKHAIL IOSSEL AND JEFF PARKER, EDS., *Amerika:*
    Contemporary Russians View
    the United States.
GERT JONKE, *Geometric Regional Novel.*
JACQUES JOUET, *Mountain R.*
HUGH KENNER, *The Counterfeiters.*
    Flaubert, Joyce and Beckett:
    The Stoic Comedians.
    Joyce's Voices.
DANILO KIŠ, *Garden, Ashes.*
    A Tomb for Boris Davidovich.
ANITA KONKKA, *A Fool's Paradise.*
TADEUSZ KONWICKI, *A Minor Apocalypse.*
    The Polish Complex.
MENIS KOUMANDAREAS, *Koula.*
ELAINE KRAF, *The Princess of 72nd Street.*
JIM KRUSOE, *Iceland.*
EWA KURYLUK, *Century 21.*
VIOLETTE LEDUC, *La Bâtarde.*
DEBORAH LEVY, *Billy and Girl.*
    Pillow Talk in Europe and Other Places.
JOSÉ LEZAMA LIMA, *Paradiso.*
ROSA LIKSOM, *Dark Paradise.*
OSMAN LINS, *Avalovara.*
    The Queen of the Prisons of Greece.
ALF MAC LOCHLAINN, *The Corpus in the Library.*
    Out of Focus.
RON LOEWINSOHN, *Magnetic Field(s).*
D. KEITH MANO, *Take Five.*
BEN MARCUS, *The Age of Wire and String.*
WALLACE MARKFIELD, *Teitlebaum's Window.*
    To an Early Grave.
DAVID MARKSON, *Reader's Block.*
    Springer's Progress.
    Wittgenstein's Mistress.

FOR A FULL LIST OF PUBLICATIONS, VISIT:
www.dalkeyarchive.com

SELECTED DALKEY ARCHIVE PAPERBACKS

CAROLE MASO, *AVA.*
LADISLAV MATEJKA AND KRYSTYNA POMORSKA, EDS.,
    Readings in Russian Poetics: Formalist and
    Structuralist Views.
HARRY MATHEWS,
    The Case of the Persevering Maltese: Collected Essays.
    Cigarettes.
    The Conversions.
    The Human Country: New and Collected Stories.
    The Journalist.
    My Life in CIA.
    Singular Pleasures.
    The Sinking of the Odradek Stadium.
    Tlooth.
    20 Lines a Day.
ROBERT L. MCLAUGHLIN, ED.,
    Innovations: An Anthology of Modern &
    Contemporary Fiction.
HERMAN MELVILLE, *The Confidence-Man.*
STEVEN MILLHAUSER, *The Barnum Museum.*
    In the Penny Arcade.
RALPH J. MILLS, JR., *Essays on Poetry.*
OLIVE MOORE, *Spleen.*
NICHOLAS MOSLEY, *Accident.*
    Assassins
    Catastrophe Practice.
    Children of Darkness and Light.
    Experience and Religion.
    The Hesperides Tree.
    Hopeful Monsters.
    Imago Bird.
    Impossible Object.
    Inventing God.
    Judith.
    Look at the Dark.
    Natalie Natalia.
    Serpent.
    Time at War.
    The Uses of Slime Mould: Essays of Four Decades.
WARREN F. MOTTE, JR.,
    Fables of the Novel: French Fiction since 1990.
    Oulipo: A Primer of Potential Literature.
YVES NAVARRE, *Our Share of Time.*
    Sweet Tooth.
DOROTHY NELSON, *In Night's City.*
    Tar and Feathers.
WILFRIDO D. NOLLEDO, *But for the Lovers.*
FLANN O'BRIEN, *At Swim-Two-Birds.*
    At War.
    The Best of Myles.
    The Dalkey Archive.
    Further Cuttings.
    The Hard Life.
    The Poor Mouth.
    The Third Policeman.
CLAUDE OLLIER, *The Mise-en-Scène.*
PATRIK OUŘEDNÍK, *Europeana.*
FERNANDO DEL PASO, *Palinuro of Mexico.*
ROBERT PINGET, *The Inquisitory.*
    Mahu or The Material.
    Trio.
RAYMOND QUENEAU, *The Last Days.*
    Odile.
    Pierrot Mon Ami.
    Saint Glinglin.
ANN QUIN, *Berg.*
    Passages.
    Three.
    Tripticks.
ISHMAEL REED, *The Free-Lance Pallbearers.*
    The Last Days of Louisiana Red.
    Reckless Eyeballing.
    The Terrible Threes.
    The Terrible Twos.
    Yellow Back Radio Broke-Down.
JULIÁN RÍOS, *Larva: A Midsummer Night's Babel.*
    Poundemonium.
AUGUSTO ROA BASTOS, *I the Supreme.*
JACQUES ROUBAUD, *The Great Fire of London.*
    Hortense in Exile.

    Hortense Is Abducted.
    The Plurality of Worlds of Lewis.
    The Princess Hoppy.
    The Form of a City Changes Faster, Alas,
    Than the Human Heart.
    Some Thing Black.
LEON S. ROUDIEZ, *French Fiction Revisited.*
VEDRANA RUDAN, *Night.*
LYDIE SALVAYRE, *The Company of Ghosts.*
    Everyday Life.
    The Lecture.
LUIS RAFAEL SÁNCHEZ, *Macho Camacho's Beat.*
SEVERO SARDUY, *Cobra & Maitreya.*
NATHALIE SARRAUTE, *Do You Hear Them?*
    Martereau.
    The Planetarium.
ARNO SCHMIDT, *Collected Stories.*
    Nobodaddy's Children.
CHRISTINE SCHUTT, *Nightwork.*
GAIL SCOTT, *My Paris.*
JUNE AKERS SEESE,
    Is This What Other Women Feel Too?
    What Waiting Really Means.
AURELIE SHEEHAN, *Jack Kerouac Is Pregnant.*
VIKTOR SHKLOVSKY, *Knight's Move.*
    A Sentimental Journey: Memoirs 1917-1922.
    Theory of Prose.
    Third Factory.
    Zoo, or Letters Not about Love.
JOSEF ŠKVORECKÝ,
    The Engineer of Human Souls.
CLAUDE SIMON, *The Invitation.*
GILBERT SORRENTINO, *Aberration of Starlight.*
    Blue Pastoral.
    Crystal Vision.
    Imaginative Qualities of Actual Things.
    Mulligan Stew.
    Pack of Lies.
    Red the Fiend.
    The Sky Changes.
    Something Said.
    Splendide-Hôtel.
    Steelwork.
    Under the Shadow.
W. M. SPACKMAN, *The Complete Fiction.*
GERTRUDE STEIN, *Lucy Church Amiably.*
    The Making of Americans.
    A Novel of Thank You.
PIOTR SZEWC, *Annihilation.*
STEFAN THEMERSON, *Hobson's Island.*
    The Mystery of the Sardine.
    Tom Harris.
JEAN-PHILIPPE TOUSSAINT, *Television.*
DUMITRU TSEPENEAG, *Vain Art of the Fugue.*
ESTHER TUSQUETS, *Stranded.*
DUBRAVKA UGRESIC, *Lend Me Your Character.*
    Thank You for Not Reading.
MATI UNT, *Things in the Night.*
ELOY URROZ, *The Obstacles.*
LUISA VALENZUELA, *He Who Searches.*
BORIS VIAN, *Heartsnatcher.*
PAUL WEST, *Words for a Deaf Daughter & Gala.*
CURTIS WHITE, *America's Magic Mountain.*
    The Idea of Home.
    Memories of My Father Watching TV.
    Monstrous Possibility: An Invitation to
    Literary Politics.
    Requiem.
DIANE WILLIAMS, *Excitability: Selected Stories.*
    Romancer Erector.
DOUGLAS WOOLF, *Wall to Wall.*
    Ya! & John-Juan.
PHILIP WYLIE, *Generation of Vipers.*
MARGUERITE YOUNG, *Angel in the Forest.*
    Miss MacIntosh, My Darling.
REYOUNG, *Unbabbling.*
ZORAN ŽIVKOVIĆ, *Hidden Camera.*
LOUIS ZUKOFSKY, *Collected Fiction.*
SCOTT ZWIREN, *God Head.*

FOR A FULL LIST OF PUBLICATIONS, VISIT:

www.dalkeyarchive.com